The Wedding Gift

Bart Baker

Big Muddy Books

Dedication

To my family, Joe Elvis, Isaiah, and Emmanuel for their love and support. To the Born Bad/Married Bads, my extended family, and friends, you bring me joy, make me laugh, and are the most colorful, hilarious, and interesting people I know. What a gift to call you family and friends.

To my readers, viewers, and all who support my writing. I love what I do, and am blessed to have your support. Thank you so much.

To my fellow authors and screenwriters, who keep me on task, teach me, and share the trenches. Especially to The Authors Conference and Writers On The Storm. I have learned more about the business of prose listening in these groups than anywhere else. Thank you for the knowledge and the wisdom I've gained.

I wrote The Wedding Gift because the story moved me deeply. I was busy with other projects but I couldn't shake this story. It compelled me to write. These characters lived in my head and my heart. Writing about characters who love deeply, sacrificing everything for a friend, filled me with gratitude and happiness. It taught me again that love is the most powerful tool in our lives. I hope you are as moved by experiencing reading this story as I was writing it.

Blessings - Bart Baker

ONE

I t was perfect.

Donna's eyes combed the room carefully, seeking anything out of place, any flaw, even those unnoticeable by anyone other than a professional. But it is exactly what Donna had in her head when she imagined it. Coordinating destination weddings were always a challenge, especially in a foreign country. But they are Donna's stock in trade. And this wedding allowed her to spend two weeks in Puerto Rico, pulling everything together after six months of planning with a meticulous, verging on neurotic, bride, turned out exquisite. A gorgeous banquet room at the Condado Vanderbilt with its gasp-inducing view of the beach where the ceremony was held just an hour earlier, a fabulous buffet which the bride insisted on over a sit-down meal, and, of course, an open bar—much to the delight of each and every groomsman.

Content that it was as beautiful as she hoped and loving what she did, Donna stood near the entrance, taking it in, her eyes moving from buffet line to bar, to dance floor, to tables making sure everything was running on time. The toasts were next, right after dinner.

Catching sight of herself in the mirror over the bar, Donna noted that the heels she was wearing, while not the most comfortable, helped her posture, which after being on her feet for the last couple of days needed a lift. The pale-yellow Annie Klein knock-off fit her curves well without drawing unnecessary attention, and dropping to the perfect length, just above the knee. After all, she's the wedding coordinator, not a lonely cousin of the bride looking for a little company from a drunk groomsman.

Donna will work until the last guest is out of the banquet hall, and she will be up early in the morning, making sure the bridal party is on the planned boat excursion and the others are grabbing shuttles to the airport for their flights back to the States.

But more than anything, Donna was relieved that she had time to straighten her hair prior to arriving the necessary three hours early to make sure the wedding day is perfect for the bride and groom. Island humidity, not unlike the summer humidity in St. Louis, sends her hair frizzing out like a cartoon character sticking their finger in a light socket, so she's pulled it back neatly in a small, tight braid, giving off a vibe of don't-mess-with-me efficiency; the desired effect on the day of any wedding she puts together.

Moving past the buffet line, making sure the entrée and side trays were filled, Donna nodded positively at Miguel, the buffet manager, before thanking him in Spanish for the wonderful meal and his top-notch serving team. She hoped she wasn't saying something sexual or ridiculous in her fractured, rudimentary Spanish which she learned online. Either way, he thanked her in English and told her he hoped they would do business again in the future.

Feeling her phone buzzing in her hand, she flipped it over. The screen read 'DAVID TENNBROOK', which instantly made Donna smile but then just as quickly brought a furrow to her brow. *Why would he be calling? He knows I'm working.* They don't usually talk until after she's back in her hotel room. She didn't have time for boyfriend drama, not in the middle of a wedding reception. But then again, if it wasn't important why would David be calling? He knew the rules.

"David..." Donna's voice filled with concern and just an edge of annoyance as she strode into a tiled hallway between the banquet room and the kitchen.

"Hey, yeah...how are you?"

"Working."

"Yeah," David repeated, "I figured. But this couldn't wait."

His voice echoed slightly, causing Donna to question where he was.

"Don't tell me you're on a plane down to Puerto Rico," she responded, secretly hoping this clean-cut, young man with the look of a quirky Republican Senatorial aide—who she'd been dating for a little less than a year—actually was.

"No. No...I'm not," he answered, almost in a whisper. "I'm...I'm in a bathroom. In this girl's apartment."

"What?"

"I'm going to have sex with her. I really like her, she's hot, and I'm going to sleep with her."

Donna's mouth opened but nothing poured out. Seldom caught off-guard and even rarer with nothing to say, Donna's eyes glanced across the beautiful room as tears quickly rim her bottom eyelids.

"I'm sorry. But, you know, we don't see each other that much. You're always working somewhere. I...I need something a little more," continued David, his voice whipping together guilt and need, as if it was something Donna was going to be forced to drink.

"I can't do this now," Donna said.

"I have to. For me. I just wanted you to know. I'll collect the things you have at my place and leave them at the door to your apartment. Take care of yourself," he yammered, though Donna had stopped listening.

Donna's trembling thumb found the disconnect button. She took a sharp breath; a searing pain ripped down her right side, not allowing her to take a deep one. Donna's body was responding to the conversation even before David's words had a chance to connect to her mind. Spinning, she put a smile on her lips and marched back into the banquet room, dabbing both eyes as discreetly, before giving the bride a positive signal.

She then hastily slipped into the hotel lobby, and dashed across the Spanish-influenced lobby, heels clacking off the tiles. She pushed into the bathroom furthest from the banquet room, slipped into a stall, and allowed herself a few minutes of intense sobbing, leaning over the toilet to let the tears drip from her eyes into the bowl without ruining her makeup, which she didn't have time to fix.

Fuck him! she thought. She wanted to call her best friend, Cameron but didn't have time for this conversation. It would have to wait until she returned to her hotel room later that night.

She would wake him up and sob again. Cameron would vow to hunt David down and beat the shit out of him. And then Donna would make him promise not to do something so stupid, though secretly she wished he would.

Or better, that *she* could.

The rest of the reception progressed smoothly, except for a drunk bridesmaid that Donna had to whisk up to the girl's hotel room and put to bed after she ripped her dress and then threw up off the terrace, thankfully out of sight of the other wedding guests.

Throughout the rest of the night, as she battled to keep her emotions in check, Donna handed out a dozen cards to prospective clients, including to a few mothers who were planning for their daughter's future weddings, and even a couple of guys. Dubious about what the guys actually did with her business card, Donna points out that the number on her card is her business number, not her personal number. She pushed back the advances of one of the groomsmen, Tommy, with his Irish face and wrestler's body, who Donna guessed made a bet with the other groomsmen that he could score with the wedding planner.

Not that she didn't toy with the idea after the phone call from David. Comforting herself with revenge sex certainly crossed her mind. But Donna had a hard and fast rule that had served her well over the last seven years in the wedding planning business: never sleep with anyone at a wedding.

Most especially an alcohol-lubricated groomsman.

Kicking off her heels and tossing them near the desk in the spacious hotel room, Donna's body immediately slumped. It was quarter after one a.m., East Coast time, which made it an hour earlier in St. Louis. As Donna pressed Cameron's number on her phone, her emotions tackled her and she fell back on the bed, letting tears dribble onto the duvet.

"Donna?" Cam rasped, eyeing the glowing red of 12:14 a.m. on his bedside clock. "Everything okay?"

Barely able to get the words out through her tears, Donna muttered, "He dumped me."

"David?" Cam asked.

"Tonight. In the middle of the reception. Called to tell me he was about to sleep with another girl. I guess his guilty conscience wouldn't let him get it up without telling me first." She wept, catapulting herself off the bed and towards the balcony door, sliding it open to take in a breath of the ocean air.

Laying amid a pile of sheets and pillows, Cameron held the phone to his ear as he pulled his hand through his curly mane and then rubbed his eyes. "That piece of shit," he responded. Half-asleep, Cameron's azure eyes shimmered as he flipped on the bedside lamp. "I'm going to find that prick and beat the shit out of him!"

"No. You're not." Donna smiled, needing to hear that, before adding with a sniffle, "There goes a year of my life. He blamed me for being gone all the time."

Cameron remained silent, knowing better than to take that bait.

"I know I am," Donna sniffled again, "but it's my job. Sorry I have a damn business that takes me away sometimes."

"Never liked that shady ass," Cameron responded, rolling over on his back.

"Now you tell me," Donna chuckled as her face scrunched up, ready for an ugly cry. "I'm going to die alone," she bawled, each word disconnecting from the previous.

Cameron laughed. "You're not going to die alone. Jeez. You're twenty-eight. You'll meet someone. Screw David. He's a dope. He isn't half as funny as he thinks he is, his stories are boring and he's not as smart as you. I mean, come on, the guy manages a Game Stop. Grow up, already, douche. My friend, Matt, he's funny as hell, makes bank trading tech stock. I'm going to fix you up."

"No! Stop. I don't want to think about another guy. I want to hate David for a while," Donna moaned.

"He's not the end of the world. General rule, no guy that works in a mall is the world," Cameron avowed, before adding, "Call me when you get back in The Lou. While you're there, pick up some Rico Suave and let him samba your world."

Donna laughed. And hearing her laughter, Cameron smiled.

"Thank you," Donna answered.

"If you need me, you know I'm here," Cameron reassured his best friend.

"Okay," Donna answered. "I love you."

"I love you too. Talk to you soon."

As Cameron hung up, he slipped his iPhone back onto the nightstand and turned off the light, snuggling against Andie, the beautiful blonde sharing his bed. She was propped up on one elbow, concern locked in her eyes.

"Rico Suave?"

Cameron winced. "I know. As soon as I said it, I thought 'creepy', right?

"Her boyfriend broke up with her?"

"While she's out of town, working."

"What a dick!" Andie snapped. "But you're not beating the shit out of him. Not that he doesn't deserve it, but you're not," she added, eyeing the clock which now reads 12:23 a.m. before asking, "Why didn't you tell her I was here with you?"

"I didn't want to rub it in," Cameron answered.

Recognizing the validity of that, Andie rolled herself over on top of Cameron, gazing down at him, her hand moving to his mop of dark, curly hair, which she pulled back off his forehead. Andie smiled with unabashed delight. *God, this man is beautiful,* she thought, never connecting the word "beauty" with a man until she met Cameron. She swore his blue eyes almost glowed in the dark.

Cam's full lips parted in a smile of their own. He wondered what this gorgeous woman, whose blonde hair fell around her striking face, touched by an elusive hint of the Asian heritage from her father's side, was pondering, wondering what her smile meant. Cameron couldn't remember another woman who drew him in as immediately as Andie did. Not quite all-American, not quite exotic, Andie's look was so unique and arresting, it dared people not to stare at her.

She kissed Cameron, letting the kiss linger. The heat between them rose quickly as Cameron slid his arm across her back and his other hand around her waist, holding her fully on top of him, their lips never parting.

This relationship still felt new to both of them. It has been a few months, most of them in the shadows—with reason—but what started for both as an undeniable physical attraction, flourished as they steadily learned about each other, transcending their physical connection into a tremendous, passionate connection. Cameron had no words for it but he intrepidly accepted that he was falling in love. And while Andie would never admit that what they have was that profound, she had never come close to these feelings with any other man.

It scared the hell out of her, and she wasn't about to let it go.

The only piece of Cameron's life Andie really hadn't uncovered was Donna. Cameron's "best friend", the woman he spoke with only slightly less than he spoke with her. While she'd concealed any uneasiness, Andie had never met a man whose best friend was a woman. In Andie's estimation, it was hard enough to meet a guy she felt actually liked women. But here was Cameron, the man she had these intense feelings for, and he openly spoke about his best friend, a woman he'd known since kindergarten.

There were big questions. The most obvious being what if she and Donna didn't like each other? Andie knew that was Cameron's greatest fear, but for Andie, what if something in how Donna and Cameron behaved together made her jealous? Would she tell him? She wasn't the type to forbid him to see her, and she knew that Cameron wasn't the type to respond to that threat. But what if Donna was actually in love with Cameron and Andie found herself in some sort of psycho-competition? Andie had seen enough Lifetime movies to know people made a lot of money writing about such things, so it had to exist. She never had to fight for a guy, and though Cameron would be worth it, would she do it? Andie hated herself for mentally preparing for such silliness. But how could she not? She was a lawyer. She didn't go into any situation ill-prepared.

Cameron swiveled her body beneath his, his lips discovering her neck, and Andie forgot all about competition. She intended to stay in the now. Because the now was awesome.

TWO

Dragging her suitcases into the hallway, Donna took a deep breath. Coming home from a destination wedding was always hard. While she loved her Dogtown apartment, she loved hotels more. Loved that the bed was made daily, that there were always fresh towels and a restaurant downstairs. And because she was usually staying at the hotel where either the wedding or the reception took place, she was treated inordinately well. A perk of her business.

Making her way down the narrow hallway to her apartment, Donna could see David had been true to his word. An old Amazon box sat perched against her door filled with items she recognized. Unlocking her apartment, she kicked the box inside near her bicycle, yanking her suitcases behind her. Donna braced herself for an apology note buried inside. Maybe a change of heart after the lousy sex she hoped he had with the girl whose bathroom he called from. She smiled at the thought, but her smile vanished as she found the note. It was only one sentence: *I think this is everything.*

"Asshole," she muttered with enough vitriol to shield herself from turning into a puddle again.

There were a few DVDs she'd left at his place, one being a Redbox DVD which Donna probably owed more in late fees than it was worth. Some Jason Stratham action movie she rented to make David happy. And while she found Stratham's balding, weary, tough-guy persona very sexy, she would only keep the DVD if he took his shirt off, and she couldn't remember if he did in this movie. Besides, now it would just remind her of David.

Thanks for ruining that too, she rued silently.

At the bottom of the box were a few items she'd bought David over the past year, including a Hamilton t-shirt she bought him after they saw it at the Fox. Donna couldn't stop herself from smelling it, to see if it had his scent. The shirt still held the aroma of newness. He never wore it.

Stuffing it all back in the box, she sadly mused *I don't want this crap.* She pushed the box off the bed and laid down, staring at the brick wall across the room. Usually, she loved the exposed brick in her apartment, but at this moment it seemed like a prison wall. She wasn't feeling great; she was tired, which was to be expected after this job, and needed some R&R. Right now, those R's seemed to stand for "reflection" and "regret".

For a woman who made other women's wedding days as perfect as possible, Donna surmised, sadly, that she might never see her own; a day she'd been fantasizing about since she was a little girl. She had everything about that day planned, each nuance locked in her head to create the most perfect wedding ever designed, short of something royal, down to the napkins.

All that was missing was the guy.

But that dream paved the way into her career; a life filled with itineraries and planner books, brochures of wonderful foreign locales, as well as local hidden gems that are exceptional for some bride's wedding day.

And while meeting someone else's new squeeze, even her best friend's, wasn't on the top of Donna's to-do list, now that she was home, maybe, before she threw herself back into the dating pool, or singles' pool, or whatever pathetic pool it might be, filled with minnows and sharks, leeches and bottom feeders, with lots of algae floating on the top and piles of trash crowding the bottom, the distraction might be welcomed.

Waking up to her cell phone ringing and in the same clothes she wore on the plane ride back to St. Louis, Donna had no idea whether it was day or night.

"Oh shit..." she muttered, digging around next to her until her hand found her phone.

Cameron.

"I fell asleep. What time is it?" she asked, looking at her phone again. "Tell me that it's 2:39 in the afternoon and not 2:39 in the morning."

"It's the afternoon. Boy, you must be out of it."

"Traveling. Not as much fun as it was even a few years ago. I have to start making the people I work for spring for at least business class. Flying coach, especially from another country, is brutal."

"You know, those are good problems to have," Cameron relayed, before announcing he's at work to keep the call short. "Can you grab coffee tomorrow? Andie is dying to meet you, so we are both taking a personal day," Cameron stated.

Hesitant, but without an avenue out, Donna shrugged. "Sure. Gives me the rest of the day today to get my life together."

"I'll text you the time and place. Can't wait to see you. And I can't wait for you to meet Andie. You're going to love her."

"Cam..." Donna huffed, a hint of agitation minted in her voice. "Do you know how many times you've said that about a girl you were infatuated with that I never met at all?"

"You're going to meet her," Cameron tossed out like he was throwing candy to a child.

"Point, Cameron," Donna snorted back. "I hope she's everything you say she is."

Donna could literally hear Cam smile through the phone.

"She is."

THREE

A ndie wished she was going anywhere else. A day off, a middle-of-the-week oasis, where they could go to Forest Park and jog around the lake, taking in the turning of the leaves, go to the museum and view the new 1970s abstract exhibit - which would bore the hell out of Cameron but Andie would love - then head over to Ted Drewes for the best frozen custard anywhere, or maybe have lunch down on the Hill or at one of the new, trendier U-City bistros. There were so many ways to spend a beautiful fall day, but Cameron had already planned morning coffee so Andie could meet his best friend.

It's not like Andie didn't want to meet Donna. She did. But she resented Cameron doing everything short of tying messages to balloons and sending them skyward to God in hopes that she and Donna would instantly bond, making his life enormously easier. If Cameron's best friend was a man, he wouldn't be sweating this comingling. But because she and Donna were two women, Cameron was doing his level best to squish them together into a heart-shaped photo on his internal vision board. Andie couldn't imagine any reason not to like Donna except for Cameron's insistence that he "just knew" they would be besties, carpet bombing any chance for something organic to occur between them.

Betty Blue, the blue 1973 Camaro convertible, which Cameron bought for four hundred dollars as a teen and restored himself, turned onto Maryland Avenue, in the Central West End, one of the older, trendy areas of St. Louis, with its hot restaurant scene, stately turn-of-the-century homes, and pre-war buildings. Andie glanced at Cameron as he sang along with the radio. Sorry Pink, sorry Sia, sorry Adam Levin. Singing was Cameron's nervous tell, which he believed made him look like he didn't have a care in the world.

But Andie knew better.

Trying to tune him out, her mind drifted to when she and the off-key crooner in the driver's seat, whose hand she held as he drove, actually became a couple. But she couldn't pinpoint the moment. She wasn't even sure that Cameron viewed their relationship the same way she did. They've never discussed being a couple. She hadn't even told her parents how deeply she felt about Cameron. She hadn't mentioned Cameron to anyone really; Andie didn't have any close girlfriends to confide in. And now, here they were over six months in. Whatever this was, with all its jumbled, heady feelings, lacked an actual definition. Which was just fine. Actually perfect, as far as she was concerned. A non-rushed, unnamed pool of happiness where she could paddle around in effortlessly bliss. For the first time in her life, Andie was co-piloting with a man who filled her with joy.

Checking her mascara in the car mirror, Andie unconsciously practiced her smile, hoping that when she had to use it, Donna wouldn't catch on. But Andie knew that while the insincere smile would be enough to appease Cameron, Donna would be astute enough to catch her putting on appearances. They were women. It wouldn't be the first or last time they did something they didn't want to do for a man they loved.

In this case, a man they *both* loved.

FOUR

It was as painful as Donna feared. Agonizingly banal conversation overloaded with polite laughter and vapid bobble-like nodding. Sitting on the patio of the Kingside Diner, one of few tables occupied on this brisk morning, Donna traded excruciating pleasantries, as bland as Cream of Wheat, with Andie. Having to smile this much had already caused her face to go to war with her mind. She had to sit on her hands to keep from gesturing too much, a trademark of Donna's so that this beautiful woman in the Blues stocking cap across the table from her didn't think she was off her medication.

Donna detected that Andie was also tolerating this morning's coffee meeting only because of Cameron and, while she would love to connect with Andie for real, Donna had a bigger fish she felt needed to be filleted, breaded, and fried; to make sure Andie was comfortable with her presence in Cameron's world. To understand that her friendship with Cameron was not in any way a threat. She wasn't judging, she wasn't looking for flaws, she wasn't trying to make waves. Donna didn't know if this relationship had legs and she didn't want to put any pressure on it. She was more judgmental about innocuous pablum babbling from her lips than she was about Andie.

Equally on guard, Andie was trying twice as hard as Donna to be what she assumed was the version of herself she thought Donna would enjoy. It was apparent Donna was "a gabber" as Andie liked to call anyone who could hold a conversation without actually saying anything. Not having many female friends, Andie was unrehearsed at small talk. That was a gift her father possessed but not her. Luckily for

Andie, Cameron could talk to anyone and make them his friend, and he was capably filling in the silences at the table. Part of what attracted Andie to Cameron was his ability to seem at ease in most situations. And as far as Andie was concerned, this fit as Donna continued to smile while filling her in on all things Cameron.

Even with the weather being crisp and sunny, Andie shivered like she was standing in a cold rain. She couldn't keep this up much longer and wondered how hard it would hurt if she flung herself over the railing separating the patio from the sidewalk and dashed out into traffic. A trip to the emergency room had to be better than this.

As both women suffered through what passed as conversation, they silently hated on the man between them who sat and smiled like a cartoon puppet. *What the hell?* they both thought almost simultaneously, unbeknownst to the other.

But Cameron wasn't about to let the smile disappear from his face, not about to let either of them know he was sweating profusely under the Mizzou sweatshirt he had on. The two people he thought would have a million things to talk about, things that mattered to both of them, were jawing about things he knew were empty mental calories, or worse, talking about him in vacant superlatives, joking softly about his quirks. Which would be fine if he felt it was truly something they were bonding over. But he envisioned a future where the two most important women in his life endured each other in a puddle-deep relationship, spending any moment together play-acting a friendship until the other was gone. His life was going to be hell. And compartmentalized.

This day was sucking the bottom of the tank, he thought, as he gripped his coffee mug like he was going to smash it against his forehead just to break the tension.

And then it took a turn for the worst. Both women stopped speaking. The quiet between them built, their eyes darting around, their mouths slightly ajar, wishing for something to pour out to resuscitate the conversation, their minds racing for some toxic-free topic to keep the chatter from dying face down in a pool of its own silence. But it grew. Cavernous. Frozen. The silence sliced into them like shrapnel from a homemade bomb. But while their minds wrestled with mutual blankness, their looks begged the other to say something.

Donna cackled. Hard. Laughing herself into tears, her hands waving in the air as if waving a white flag. Andie's eyes widened as she watched Donna, then she broke up laughing just as deeply until she snorted. Seeing this beautiful woman snort always tickled Cameron into howls of heaving laughter. The three of them bellowed in unison, enough to drown out the traffic on Maryland Avenue, each realizing that the other two felt exactly as they did; that this meeting had been an epic disaster, no one willing to admit they were sinking and unable to come up for air.

"Oh my God!" Donna huffed out, trying to catch her breath. "That was the most painful hour of my life!"

"I know, right?!" Andie responded, still chortling nervously. "I was jumping out of my skin. I can't believe I just did that. And I'm not talking about the snorting. Thank you for laughing at that," she added, swatting Cameron's shoulder. "I'm talking about...everything else. I'm not that boring, I promise. That was horrendous!"

"I'm sorry. I suck. I can't believe I held a conversation about nothing, literally nothing, for over an hour. With you sitting here," Donna exclaimed, hands waving at Andie. "I was having old lady hot flashes I was so nervous."

"You?!?" Cameron stood up, pulling up his Mizzou sweatshirt, revealing that the white t-shirt underneath was almost soaked through with sweat, "Holy shit, whatever was going on here, it nearly killed me!"

"This is your fault!" Donna answered him, swatting his other shoulder.

"Me?!" Cameron exclaimed. "You two were like what I would imagine two blow-up dolls would say if they could talk."

"Oh, that's a perfect comparison. Two blow-up dolls?! Thanks for that," Andie responded, sarcasm dripping. "Donna's one-hundred percent accurate. If you hadn't drilled into me, and I'm sure Donna, how important it is to you that she and I like each other and how you were sure we'd be BFFs forever...hell, I've never felt this much pressure to be nice to anyone in my life. Not from my parents. Not from my job. I'm not good at pretending to be nice."

"You are nice!" Cameron fired back.

"Being phony is not nice! It's awful. I'm not a person who likes talking about the color of my office walls. Or rugs. We talked about rugs, for God's sake. We made the Blues' season sounds dull, and agreed about pizza, even though I got the sense you don't like Chicago-style pizza," Andie sighed.

"I don't. I prefer St. Louis-style," Donna stated.

"Me too! But I eat Chicago-style because Cam could live on it," Andie huffed, before looking at Donna squarely. "I want you to like me! The me I am. Not whoever that person was who was just sitting in this chair."

"I thought you two were just messing with my head," Cameron added, taking a drink from his coffee. "Shit. I was scared. Having you two hate each other is my biggest fear."

"We know!" Andie and Donna answered at the same time, causing them both to laugh loud enough for people even inside the restaurant to turn and give a side-eyed look.

"You made us afraid..." Andie started.

"...to be ourselves," Donna finished.

"Can we start over?" Andie asked Donna with sweet candor.

"If I can get some Irish Cream in this coffee, we can," Donna responded with a laugh, although she was deadly serious.

"Now you're talking!" Andie responded.

Relaxing with new drinks, Donna now gesticulated with her hands as she spoke. Andie dragged over a chair from another table to put her feet up. They laughed at their idiocy. Embarrassed, but relieved, each felt like they had kicked off the sweaty blankets after a fever broke, and were now bonded in their shared embarrassment and mutual relief.

"I do have something I want to know. How did you two actually meet?" Andie responded. "Cam's mentioned kindergarten and something about a swing, but that's all I know."

Donna's eyes lit up as if she just hit ten million on a pinball machine as Cameron popped up in his seat. "I'm telling this story!" he announced quickly. But Donna was on her feet just as fast, her mittened hand going over his mouth.

"My story. You are almost criminally incapable of remembering it, or telling it with as much panache! You sit there, look pretty, and let me tell it instead of hijacking my memories!" Donna demanded.

Cameron wrestled free, trying to shout out his side of the story but Donna was having none of it. Wrapping her arm around his neck, she put both hands over his mouth to shut him up as he started laughing. She was determined to tell the story. And when Donna—all five-foot-five of her—was determined, as Cam knew, she was a force of nature and whatever she wanted was pretty much going to happen.

Which was part of the reason she was so great at her job. And not always great in love.

Now it's on, Andie thought with a smile as she lounged back to get more comfortable on the two chairs she was occupying. She pulled off her Blues stocking cap and ran her hand through her hair as she giggled, watching Cameron and Donna wrestle with each other, each wanting to give their side to this tale as if somehow it would be two very different answers. Not having a sister or a brother, or even a lifelong friend, this sort of easy playfulness was foreign to Andie. Since Cameron and Donna had been friends since childhood, Andie surmised these antics had been going on for years. And strangely, it wasn't intimidating. Other women might be uncomfortable with it, wanting it for themselves, but Andie far preferred this filial one-upmanship between Cameron and Donna to the dirge of polite conversation they had all just slogged through.

Besides, this slap-dash interaction between Cameron and Donna carried no sexual undertone, nothing threatening, which allowed Andie to easily surrender to the frivolity. This facet of Donna, brash and loud, hands flying as if her wrists were boneless, was something Andie was more attracted to in a friend than Cameron would ever be in a woman in which he had a romantic interest. But most of all, Andie wasn't the jealous type. She never learned how to be. Her mother, Caroline, never seemed to worry about Andie's father, Henry, straying. And Andie surmised that having an affair would be far too much work for her mother, who preferred her life placid to the point of immobility. Until Cameron, Andie had never been in a relationship worth the effort jealousy required. If there was anything that bothered Andie at all as she watched Cameron with Donna, it was the prickly feeling that she was an interloper in a moment that had played out many times in the lives of the two other people at the table.

"I am sure I had on something pink. I always wore pink when I was that age," Donna continued, slowly pulling her hand back from Cameron's mouth, waving it in the air as if conducting the words as she spoke, a playful glare in her eyes warning him not to interrupt her again.

"Always," Cam popped in with enough emphasis to be derogatory.

"To be honest, I still love pink but I'm now more of a pale lavender type of gal, sophisticated bitch that I am," Donna opined with a throaty laugh, brushing off Cam's disparaging interjection with a pinch to his arm, which made the off-balance Andie smile again.

"And while I was very different than most of the oblivious kindergarteners, a little too self-aware and too much of a smarty-pants for my own good, I wore pink to school every day like some savage girly-girls. Anyway, I had fallen off the swing. Clumsy. That has never gone away. You should see me walk in heels, I'm a disaster. But I had torn my tights and bloodied my knee, tears were streaming down my cheeks, snot bubbling from my nose. I know, very attractive.

And while some of the other kids laughed, Cam ran over and picked me up, scowling at them. I remember looking up through my tears, his face was blurry but his eyes were so blue, almost the color of the sky behind him. Cameron asked if I was okay and I blubbered something through the snot and tears. He walked me over to the teacher who was monitoring the playground and told her I fell off the swing and I needed a Band-Aid on my knee right away or to be taken to the hospital.

That's Cam. It's either a Band-Aid or an MRI. There's nothing in between. I didn't really know Cameron, other than he was in Mrs. Gordon's kindergarten class with me and sat two people over in art and somewhere behind me the rest of the day. As I wiped my nose on the sleeve of my wool coat—which my mother loved and I hated with every fiber of my five-year-old being—I thanked him. And somehow I knew at that moment that this boy with the bluest eyes in the whole world would be in my life forever."

Chuckling, Andie announced, "That's epic," as she brushed back her blond hair and repositioned the stocking cap over her head. The gray sky hovered low, a canopy that didn't allow the river city's chill to escape. "A very auspicious first meeting."

Speaking casually, her arm over Cameron's, her hand moving to his, their fingers automatically interlocked. Andie smiled across the table at Donna, the two women Cameron had mythicized each to the other just enough to make this initial gathering intimidating, both realized something almost simultaneously. This meeting, as disastrously horrible as it was, would be something they would talk about for years.

FIVE

"I know it had to be hard coming into this. Meeting your boyfriend's best friend is always odd because you don't know what's been shared between them. And in this case, the best friend is not a frat brother, an army buddy, or some goofy, high school chum; it's a woman he's known since he was five years old," Donna said, hugging her down jacket around her. She loved that in St. Louis she could wear a jacket three seasons a year.

"One short of perfect," she would add when the topic came up.

Relieved she was witnessing the real Donna, all pretense discarded, Andie was able to let down her guard. But with the warmth and history between Donna and Cameron on full display, Andie questioned herself. Had she ever had any real friends, female or male, who she could count on in a crisis? She had a list of people who claimed to have her back, but she realized as she watched Cameron and Donna interact, that it wasn't until she and Cameron began dating that Andie felt she could relax her need for self-reliance. Snuggling against Cameron's shoulder, Andie appreciated that she had found someone who would take care of her through anything.

As Donna continued talking, she mused silently about how her best friend's casual confidence—and Cameron had confidence in abundance—meshed seamlessly with Andie's almost serene sense of self. Donna wished she had even a sliver of the self-confidence either one of them possessed. *Do gorgeous people always have built-in security?* she wondered.

Donna was not raised to possess confidence. As she used to say, "Our people just don't have that gift." And when she finally realized that, she worked hard at compensating for it. Couple that with her lack of any sort of casualness, and even less sense of serenity, what resulted was that everything about Donna became outsized, much bordering on epic. It was a burden Donna had grown up with and never quite grew comfortable owning. But she did come to an agreement with it and she found an outlet for it in her work.

Love her or hate her—and she knew a lot of people at minimum disliked her—Donna was who she was. She realized that, while she and Cameron were a classic case of opposites attract, Cameron and this gorgeous creature he was now in love with were ideally "a couple." Even in the short time they were finally being themselves, Donna recognized that Cameron would never be happy with anyone else. Equally yoked didn't begin to describe it.

While Cameron was laughing about something at work, Donna, caught up in her thoughts, muttered aloud, "My God, could you two be any prettier and more perfect together?"

Andie sat up, eyes darting to Donna. "Please tell me you didn't just say that," Cam sighed self-consciously.

Caught, Donna froze, realizing a piece of her never-ending inner monologue popped out of her mouth. "Oh, shut up. Not like I'm the only one thinking it. I'm sure everybody who has driven past us and spotted you two making googly-eyes at each other thought the same thing! You know, you two would make some damn pretty babies." Donna laughed, directing her words at Cam before turning to Andie, adding, "Sorry, sometimes what's in my head jumps out of my mouth before I can stop it. But please, don't either of you respond with false modesty, that will really make me crazy. You're both pretty on your own but together..."

Donna didn't finish the sentence, she just waved her hands in the air, signaling that she'd made the definitive remark and the discussion, if there were to be one, was already finished.

Andie didn't know why, but more than anything else, Donna's blurting out her unfiltered thoughts sparked Andie's deep affection for Donna. Not because of the compliment but because this woman saw her and Cameron together. And it was the first time Andie had to look inward and agree that this thing was already more profound and more loving than any relationship she ever had in her life.

And to Andie's surprise, she wasn't scared.

As they smiled at each other, another revelation smacked Donna hard: *My God, they're in love!* This one she made sure didn't fall out of her mouth. Sorta-joking about them procreating was one thing, but using the "L-word" was a chasm Donna didn't want to have to talk her way out of. No need to scare them with more of her emotive blatherings, not at the first official meeting. They almost crashed into the rocks right out of the marina; now that they were at sea, Donna wanted to keep sailing.

Donna truly wanted to become Andie's friend. Yes, part of it was because Andie was so taken with her lifelong best friend, and Donna felt in her bones that, unlike the other women Cameron had fallen for, this girl was going to stick around. Donna hoped to forge some sort of relationship that didn't include Cameron, something exclusively theirs since both women recognized they would be seeing a lot of each other. But there was another reason, one that neither would suspect about the other.

Neither of them had a true female friend.

By its nature, Donna's job lent itself to intense but short-term relationships with the bride-to-be *du jour*. But these were relationships with an expiration date. Even prior to her business, Donna was never much of a girl's-girl, more comfortable with her guy friends than girlfriends.

Donna couldn't imagine that Andie suffered from the same loneliness. And being as outgoing and gregarious as Donna was, not in her wildest dreams could Andie believe she didn't have a list of friends calling her every time Donna was back in town, wanting to hang out, get drunk, and laugh together.

Andie was a loner by nature. Even in high school, though she played field hockey and basketball, performed in three plays, and sang in the choir, she preferred time by herself.

Andie worked overtime not to get caught up in the drama that inevitably soaked every hallway of her high school.

A lot of girls felt Andie was the pretty bitch; distant, aloof, thought she was better than them, even though their families had more money or prestige in the city. Andie didn't care who liked her. Getting people to like her, even *wanting* people to like her, was way too much effort for what would inevitably be far too little return. If people thought she was an off-putting ass, good. They would stay away. Even at college, she stayed as busy as she could with her studies, blowing through her undergrad in three years, with the help of a heavy workload and advanced college credit courses she took in high school.

She thought she would take a year off to travel but it sounded so cliché every time she mentioned it to anyone. So, she applied to every law school she thought her 3.8 GPA would get her into and when Washington University accepted her, Andie felt she could live at home and save some money while going to law school and pick up a part-time job; which she did, working at Neiman's in Frontenac.

The money wasn't much but selling blouses to wealthy women was enormously mindless, and she always kept notecards on her phone so she could review her law school work when she had a moment. And since most of the women who worked there were a decade or so older than her, Andie floated through her shifts without much camaraderie. She did her job, smiled at the customers, studied on her breaks, and went home to study some more.

Finishing her coffee and Bailey's, Andie felt a simmering, mellow buzz. "You know, prior to Cameron, I've never met a guy who had a woman as a best friend," she admitted, which didn't surprise Cameron or Donna.

How could it? It was rare. Or odd, depending on your take. A wide swath of humanity doesn't believe men and women can ever be just friends. Not Cameron and Donna-type friends. Yet, here they were, the living, breathing exceptions to the rule. Cameron had told Donna that when he discussed their twenty-plus-year friendship with Andie, she didn't believe him at first. Thought he was making it—and Donna—up just to get a reaction.

"You told me that it was strange," Cameron reminded Andie.

"I also told you that if it was true, it said something positive about your character," Andie piped up in her defense as Cameron stood up, pulling out his wallet.

"I'm going to go pay. You two talk about me while I'm gone," he joked.

"What the hell else do you think we're going to talk about? We already covered sports, weather, and every other idiotic topic. You're all that's left," Donna replied, almost before he finished his sentence.

As he shook his head in defeat, walking into the building, Andie smiled. "You know, one of the things I like most about Cameron most is that he actually enjoys the friendship of women," she said.

"He does. Despite what his dating record might indicate, he really does," Donna assured her, before adding, "You're lucky."

"I'm beginning to understand that," Andie answered, knowing that besides being physically attracted to Cameron the moment she saw him, she found his self-confidence and openness truly sexy. He was the whole package.

Being with Cameron, Andie witnessed how women were drawn to him. Innately, they knew there was something solid about him, substantial, they felt safe with him, which added another layer of allure to him. Even though they had only been dating a relatively short time, Andie had grown comfortable with the fact that the handsome man she was falling in love with had what best could be described as magnetism. Cameron turned as many heads as she did. Sometimes more. "You're the girl!" she howled at him once in CBGB's, a South City bar, when a table of both men and women turned and eyed Cameron as he strolled past.

For most of Andie's life, she had endured the kind of attention that came to Cameron as he matured. Andie's beauty induced stares from men and women alike. Unlike Cameron, it was Andie's normal and something she gave little heed to. Even as a little girl, there were far more important things in life than someone telling her how pretty she was. She would pop off a "thank you" before twirling off to find something fun to do.

"I know how ridiculous this sounds, but I get the sense that most women want to be with him and most men want to *be* him," Andie confided in Donna as Cameron approached the table, people turning ever so slightly in their seats to get a glance at him.

"Or be with him," Donna added with a laugh.

"I've seen that look too," Andie agreed.

Donna didn't gravitate toward handsome men. "Too much competition with no way to actually compete," she avowed. In her line of work, Donna had met her share of good-looking men but most did nothing for her. She liked men idiosyncratic. If there was something slightly off about them, something she couldn't put her finger on immediately that gave them an odd appeal, she was drawn to them. That peculiarity made them weirdly sexy. David had it. So had the last four guys that Donna had slept with. Quirk over classic, as she described it.

"Just so you know how much he values your opinion," Andie said softly to Donna so that Cameron wouldn't overhear, "he was less nervous about me meeting his mother than you."

That wasn't a surprise to Donna. Their friendship spanned decades. It had become the bedrock in each of their lives. Donna openly admitted her friendship with Cam was the most important relationship in her life, even more than with her mother. But Donna always added the words "so far" whenever she spoke about it. She was absolutely sure that one day she too would find an exceptional man who would love her for who she was and Cameron would be pushed into second place.

As Andie watched Cameron return to the table, his shoulders wagging while he sauntered casually, she suddenly realized she had tipped from falling in love with Cameron to *being* in love with him. She certainly wasn't ready to say it to Cameron, though she was toying with telling Donna, knowing that through Donna she could probably get a read on precisely what Cameron was feeling.

The whole concept of being in love with anybody gave Andie the shakes. Love? Really? How did this happen to her?

Yes, she was from St. Louis, the tiny suburb of Ladue in fact, and yes, falling in love is an expected event in the lifecycle of a privileged, young woman from the sheltered suburbs. There was an unwritten rule in this city that moneyed, young women between twenty-three and thirty-three must find a mate, desirable not only to her but to her parents and accepted by their friends, marry him, and propagate the lineage. While she knew a litany of young women from high school and college were gushing over finding the guy and getting engaged, Andie was creeped out by the whole expectancy of it all, like humidity in summer only twice as oppressive.

Andie seldom followed expectations. Most especially upper-class, suburban expectations. Love was something she figured would happen down the road. And while she wasn't actively avoiding it, love was a tar pit that Andie wanted to postpone as long as possible. Same with marriage. Same with kids. The last thing she needed was to get stuck in any quagmire that would lock her down until she felt she was where she needed to be in life.

Yet she couldn't imagine her life without him. Andie was reminded of the phrase Grandma Hune used to utter whenever something surprising happened. "See!" Grandma Hune would exclaim. "Never say never or life will make you a fool."

As much as she hated being wrong, in this case, being wrong made Andie's heart sing.

SIX

C ameron grew up on the poor side of Rock Hill, a suburb of St. Louis best known back in the day because it had a quarry, which had since become a landfill. People in the neighborhood quietly referred to it as "the dump."

Only a sliver of Rock Hill was a place you would refer to as "prosperous". Especially when Cameron was young. But that changed as he became a teen and the more well-to-do suburbs that surrounded it – Brentwood, Webster Groves, Glendale, and Ladue – bled in and people who couldn't afford the often-lofty prices in those burbs could afford something in Rock Hill. It became the beacon for middle-class mobility, safe and convenient, as it pushed and shoved its way towards a new identity, other than being considered the poor neighbor.

Rock Hill was a mixed bag. Much of it was small, boxy two and three-bedroom, one-story brick homes. This was prior to the days when they retitled them "ranch homes", with unfinished or paneled basements and yards big enough to kick a ball. Very working class.

Both of Cameron's parents worked; his dad, Paul Ostroski, was a non-union laborer, and his mother, Lola, was a cashier at a cafeteria. She worked odd hours, for barely-over minimum wage, to put food on the table and give Cameron the education they demanded to excel past their station in life.

Donna's upbringing wasn't much better but living on the border of Webster Groves, she could at least pretend she resided in Webster, which in most people's minds, was the area around the University and stone churches on Lockwood. It was dotted by well-kept, turn-of-the-century, two-story homes with manicured yards filled with large trees and detached garages. Donna's home was a tiny two-bedroom bungalow but she never corrected people who thought she was living the high life. Why bother? She liked people thinking she was more than she was.

In St. Louis, your social status can often be summed up by where you went to high school. Some consider it a conversation ice-breaker, allowing people to make an initial and immediate connection since St. Louis is a place where if you don't know someone, you know someone who knows someone. And once you establish a high school, you can flip through your mental Rolodex and remember a name or two to toss into a conversation to establish a groundwork for continuing any interaction.

St. Louis is truly the smallest major city in the world.

Since Donna grew up Methodist, she didn't attend any of the posh all-girls Catholic High Schools, nor could her family afford any of the other elite private high schools the name families of the city attended. Including Andie, a product of Whitfield.

Instead, Donna spent four years at Webster Groves High School, usually sitting alongside Cam, which landed both of them somewhere in the middle of the high school social strata of St. Louis. Not that Cam cared. When people asked him where he went to high school, he took a slug from whatever he was drinking and snarled, "Got my GED in prison."

Never having much, Cameron's parents swore—like so many of the parents living around them in tiny, brick ranch homes—that their children would never be them; struggling paycheck to paycheck, always one calamity away from a week of pasta and beans. Or worse, an eviction or repossession notice. Aware of their sacrifices, Cameron's gratitude pushed him to work harder than everyone else. Donna always said Cameron was the hardest-working person she had ever met. His parents drilled into him a sense of personal responsibility that pushed him to want more, to strive for better. The shove his parents gave him meant he would never rest until he got what he wanted or where he wanted to go. And he was determined to make them proud.

The sacrifice his parents made was a weight he would always bear, something he knew he would proudly carry into every aspect of his life and instill in his own children. Cameron had made it about something larger, bonding it to the idea of family and what family sacrifices for each other; this was the depth of commitment that he usurped from his parents.

Just another reason to love him, as far as Donna was concerned.

It sated Donna that throughout Cameron's life she had been the person who kept him grounded, the shoulder he leaned on, the ear always there to listen. With Andie now at his side, that responsibility would transfer, but Donna was proud she and Cameron had each other's backs.

His parents' physical absence, left by their work schedules, created a void. And Cameron saw that their sacrifice, their struggle, took years off their lives—causing them to appear much older than they actually were. And unlike young parents today, they didn't overly concern themselves with trivial things such as appearances. Cam's parents were salt-of-the-earth people who worked their asses off, week in and week out, looking forward to their Sundays off so they could go to church and thank God for what little they did have, then come home and barbecue hotdogs, or if they could afford it, hamburgers and chicken thighs, while swilling Budweiser or Busch beer that they stocked up on when it went on sale. They went to their kids' weekend soccer and baseball games and his dad always made sure he got off early enough on Fridays to catch his son's football game.

For Cameron's dad, as well as many other folks in the city, his son's high school football games were better than having season tickets to the Rams, a team many St. Louisans cannot mention without feeling their upper lip curl into a sneer and the overwhelming desire to knock the shit out of Stan Kroenke if they were to ever meet.

Cameron relied on Donna to fill the emptiness his parents left. He knew, no matter what, she would always be there if he needed her. Equally, Cameron was her rock, her shoulder, her sounding board, an undiluted advice-giver no matter how wrong-headed she felt his advice might be, especially when it came to men.

Of course, there were whispers about Cameron and Donna's relationship. Even their parents thought they hung around each other too much for something not to be going on. And while Donna admitted she was aware of Cameron's good looks and would joke about the benefits of being with the most handsome guy in the room, their friendship was infinitely more important than any other aspect of themselves or their relationship.

There existed a line neither was willing to cross. The sacrifice would be too vast.

Cam being Cam and Donna being Donna, they would laughingly discuss what a horrendous couple they would make. Some people simply make better friends.

For one thing, when Cam and Donna argued—which he was reluctant to do with her—he accepted that she would never let him be right.

"Why would I acquiesce to your opinion? Even when I'm wrong, I'm usually more right than you are," Donna once told Cameron. He didn't understand her peppered word salad but he completely grasped the gist. For Cameron, arguing was almost always pointless. Most especially with Donna. Cam used to joke with other friends that his friendship with Donna was a never-ending rehearsal for being married. In the last few months, he replaced Donna's name with Andie's. She had easily usurped that mantle.

Donna accepted that her relationship with Cameron was partially to blame for her not having found a lasting relationship of her own. She couldn't help comparing all potential mates to Cameron. He'd been her male bellwether for as long as she could remember. And on far too many levels and far too many dates, the guys she went out with just didn't measure up.

And it wasn't the looks. "Something odd, sketchy, or edgy never hurt a man's appeal as far as I'm concerned," she would remark. It was that Cameron was a straight shooter, a solid man, and what Donna discovered, more often than not, was that the guys she was attracted to weren't men at all. They were "over-ripened boys, under-ripened men," as she put it. Donna was actually surprised that she and

David lasted as long as they did. Looking back, she couldn't believe it took David nearly a year to realize he wasn't cut out to be in a relationship with a woman who wasn't always there to hold his hand, and that infidelity was only a few beers away.

"Most guys," Donna surmised at a fitting for one of a bride-to-be and her bridesmaids, "have three weeks before they are out of game. At that point, any charm they possessed dissolves like sugar candy on a hot sidewalk leaving nothing but a sticky mess that attracts flies." Noting that the young bride and her bridesmaids were all nodding, Donna added, "Unfortunately, three weeks is just enough time for us girls to believe there's hope that's there's more, and we drop our panties."

Even though they all agreed with her, Donna wished she hadn't said it.

Both Cameron and Donna accepted that their relationship was unconventional to most and overly ripe for scuttlebutt. But they had been living with the slings and arrows long enough to be impervious to any damage. Being secure in their relationship meant being secure in themselves. Donna never minded being talked about. It amused her when someone let slip something someone else said about her, good or bad. And while Cameron soured when it was mentioned, more so now that he'd fallen for Andie, he let it roll.

He knew one thing was fact. Andie had his heart, Donna had his back.

SEVEN

Taking advantage of the day off from work, Cameron and Andie decided to spend the rest of it at the zoo. Fall was the perfect time. You weren't drowning in your own summer sweat, and it still wasn't too cold. In either extreme of the St. Louis thermostat, the animals wouldn't bother coming out of their dens.

As he drove the few miles over, Cam's mind wondered to when he first told Donna about Andie. He remembered raving to her about this "great girl" he met but Donna brushed off his gushing exuberance. She'd been on this subway ride to nowhere with him more than a few too many times for this new girl to even make a blip on her mental radar. Even Cameron had to admit that every relationship he found himself in started off with the avid enthusiasm of the crowd watching the Fourth of July fireworks display over the Mississippi River, but never amounted to anything more than a backyard bottle rocket that fizzed into the air with a barely audible "pop", leaving the kid who lit it feeling ripped off from the lack of bang.

"You know I keep a list of your girlfriend's names taped to my wall," Donna had chided him. "I don't even try and keep track. I do remember a Cindi with an 'I', there was a Shannon, there was a Claire, there was, there was, there was. The list is yellowing and I cross each name off after you dump them."

"Why do you bother then?" answered Cameron.

Donna had laughed. "So, you think I care. But I don't because I know the name on the bottom of the list will have a line through it soon, swept away on a wave of your indifference, and there will be another name underneath.

But meticulous as I am, at least when we talk I can say 'How's so-and-so' and you think I actually care about these girls you say are so 'perfect' for you...until you find out they're not."

Cameron knew she was right. Until Andie Hune.

Donna told Cam that what tipped her off was that this girl might be someone special in Cameron's life and not just another name crossed off a yellowing list and buried in an unmarked dating-grave, was that it was the first time Cam ever fretted over the relationship.

"I don't fret," Cam had scoffed.

"Yeah, you do," Donna corrected him. "You're worried about what this girl feels about you. I want to call her and ask what she did with the Cameron I know. She's the first of these girls I actually want to meet. I want to shake her hand."

Cameron had gotten quiet for a moment, a smile involuntarily crossing his lips. "I want you to meet her too."

As Chris Stapleton blasted from the speakers in Betty Blue, Cameron drove through the zoo parking lot while Andie was also musing about their relationship. She knew she had plenty of time. Cameron wouldn't park Betty Blue just anywhere. He had to find a spot where he felt assured no one would hit it with a door, no one would pull into it, no kid would run by with ice cream and splotch it against the paint job. It was his most flagrant peccadillo, as far as Andie was concerned. And it usually meant they parked a hike away from wherever they were going.

For Andie, the complexities of a relationship that had traction were just as foreign as they were for Cameron. Guided by her father, Henry, Andie aimed for success in every aspect of her life. But because of who she was, there was an unspoken requirement that it also appears to never break her. Guys were no different. She attracted boys like bees find lilac. And maybe because she was hit on from an early age, by the time she was a sophomore at Whitfield High School, she was adept at shutting down guys without breaking their hearts. Like her father, Andie preferred to be direct. If she wasn't interested, she wasn't interested. She refused to be coy for attention or ego. There wasn't any way her "no" could be misconstrued as a "maybe."

Barely seeming to have time for what she wanted, Andie wasn't about to spend time on what she didn't. Her internal clock ticked a little faster than most and she felt there was someplace she should be going even when there wasn't. Sometimes it created anxiety as if she knew an answer to a very important question but just couldn't put her finger on it. She was striving to be the best at anything, but she always felt there was something else waiting for her out there. So, anything that didn't interest her, especially men, was left standing on the side of the road staring at the gray cloud of exhaust as she raced away.

Until Cameron.

While she loved her father, being employed at his firm was never part of Andie's plan. Working for family was something she viewed as limiting, almost stifling. After graduating from Washington U. Law School, her plan was to move out of St. Louis and find a law firm somewhere in the southwest that had mountains she could hike and where she wasn't looked at as some overly privileged girl whose father owned a well-respected, always-busy architecture/construction company, and whose mother's lineage was viewed with scornful jealousy. Andie wouldn't deny that she wanted to *be* somebody, but she wanted to be somebody on her own terms; not because she happened to be the offspring of successful, connected parents.

She had lived her entire life in St. Louis and if there was ever a time for her to discover who she was outside of this city, it was right after law school when various firms were wooing her, and possibilities elsewhere were within her grasp.

Reluctantly and not without some cajoling, Andie agreed to do some contract work for her father after his in-house counsel gave birth and was taking a few months off. Obligation kept Andie anchored. After all, her parents had paid for seven years of undergrad and law school. Whitfield as well, which was as expensive as many universities. She loved her dad so much, that it wouldn't be a burden, but she made him promise he wouldn't try and hook her into working full-time.

"I'm not spending the rest of my life here," she avowed to her father, seeing in Henry's eyes that he was concocting some scenario where he could woo her into becoming his permanent in-house counsel for his firm. Henry couldn't comprehend why Andie, who had a foot-up at his firm, wouldn't want that. But Andie's motor was running full throttle. She desired something greater, feeling in her bones that whatever the end-game was for her, it wasn't here. It wasn't in St. Louis.

"If it were here, I would have found it by now," she declared to Henry in one of their many discussions about moving away.

Andie was right about her father, he had other ideas for her future and every one of them kept her tethered to the city. Henry was nothing if not crafty at getting what he wanted; it was part and parcel of how he operated. And his determination to make sure his only child stayed in St. Louis was fervent. So, while he laid the tracks to keep his daughter close, what Henry didn't know-yet-was his ace was already in his office building.

Cameron Ostroski.

On her first day in the small office three doors past her father's, Cameron walked by and did a double-take. All Cameron knew about her was that she was new, she was beautiful, and while her office wasn't big enough to swing a cat, it was still pretty sweet—with a floor-to-ceiling window that overlooked downtown Clayton. So she must have some pull in the company.

Asking officiously so as not to draw any suspicion, Andie found out Cameron was her father's newest architect. She'd seen his work on Henry's desk, and while Andie recognized his renderings weren't groundbreaking, they were sturdy, deliberate, and timeless. Qualities in his work that she found very attractive.

She found so much modern architecture to be about the artist overthinking ways to be edgy; she liked that Cameron's work was solid and unobtrusive as if it knew exactly what it was supposed to be. That percolated her desire to know more about this handsome guy who preferred black jeans and solid shirts that clung to the body of an athlete, who said nothing to her but nodded hello as they passed in the hallway and always threw her a smile he knew worked for him when he strolled by her office, which

Andie sensed was becoming more often with each passing week.

She wasn't stupid. Andie knew without being told that Cameron had been warned away. It wasn't something new to her, though she didn't think her father would have done it, not at work; more likely by someone else in the office doing her father's unspoken bidding.

Cameron and Andie ended up in a meeting in her father's office, sitting side by side. There were problems with the City of Clayton on an office building her father was constructing. Cameron had his hand in the design; a geometric steel and glass structure with a lobby that was pure Cameron—wood, used brick and stone, to give the building an earthier physicality as you entered than one would expect from the sleek yet surprising design on the outside. Cameron had to fight Henry for the lobby concept. Henry imagined it to compliment the outside with granite, quartz, and metal when Cameron suggested the interior should be more surprising, and ultimately more welcoming.

"How many new buildings in this city do you walk in and notice nothing? They're exactly as you would expect them to be. This structure should be different. It's being built for a unique client, can't we at least offer them a unique vision?" he cajoled Henry. Henry enjoyed debating concept and design with Cameron, this whip-smart upstart with the disarming smile and a passion that was part youth and part uniquely Cameron. Henry loved that Cameron didn't back down from what he felt was best. Andie was immediately attracted to that. Too many guys were intimidated by her father; Cameron didn't seem to be one of them. He stood his ground. That was about as hot a thing as any man could do to get her attention.

And what else made her tingle is that Cameron loved his job. He loved architecture. Loved design. Loved St. Louis. His eye was immediately drawn to the physical heritage of this city, with its old cobblestone streets, brick homes, stonework, and greenery. He didn't treat the city as if it weren't hip enough or sophisticated enough and he was riding in on a white horse to save it. He was from here and this was a damn great place to be. Cameron knew how to put just enough of a cool twist on a basic idea to make it not only fit in but stand out with his unassuming signature.

As she got out of the car and took Cameron's hand, they headed towards the zoo entrance. She smiled, correlating how his designs actually sealed the deal for her that she wanted to truly get to know this handsome guy; he had something special she had never found with any other man. Cameron Ostroski was who he was. No bullshit. No pretense. He made being himself look easy.

Andie's reaction to Cameron was missed by everyone at the meeting other than her father, his eyes bouncing back and forth between his daughter and the young, overly attentive architect with the bright blue eyes he'd hired seven months earlier. What Henry realized was that Cameron might be the secret weapon in the battle to keep his daughter in St. Louis. And as much as he felt there wasn't a guy good enough for his daughter if Cameron was the best chance at getting what he wanted, Henry was all in. Andie remembered when her father told her this.

"You know, if I'd known that, I wouldn't have dated Cameron on principle," Andie reacted.

Henry just smiled which pissed Andie off more. But secretly, she was grateful.

EIGHT

G od, my feet hurt, Donna thought after having been
up since five, phone to ear, in front of her
computer, tackling the litany of unfinished business for
the Dumont-Mackenzie wedding taking place on the
two-hundred-and-sixty-acre farm Patricia Mackenzie's
parents owned near Branson. Patricia was a nervous wreck,
as was her mother, Dr. Martha Mackenzie. More than
most, this wedding was the curtsy of new Missouri money,
the Mackenzies, to old Missouri money, the Dumonts.
Martha enjoyed the showy ostentatiousness that would
be her daughter's hard-earned debut into society. They
were never invited to the Veiled Prophet ball, or other
old-money events, so this wedding was Martha's shot over
the bow. Old money be damned. And Patricia was happy to
oblige her mother.

Donna bore the brunt of Patricia's insecurity. This
wedding was a done deal, that Donna knew. Usually, she
could calm the self-doubt and uncertainty in a bride, but
Patricia was crumbling. Donna recognized this marriage as
a mistake from the moment she was hired. Edward coyly
double-entendred way-too-many comments, fishing to see
if Donna would take the bait. This was his M.O., putting just
enough spin on a line so that if called out, he could mea
culpa his behavior with an "I was joking!" Donna wanted to
punch him in the face but Patricia would laugh and excuse
his boorishness with a shrug and a "he's always like this."

That's the problem! He's not going to change, Donna mused
silently, sliding on a bogus smile wishing she wasn't feeling
dread for this young, hopeful bride-to-be.

But now the wedding was eight hours away, and Donna had sat on the edge of Patricia's bed, watching this sobbing girl wonder whether she was making a monstrous mistake by being in love with a man she knew deep in her heart could never be faithful, with a mother who really didn't care as long as the day was remembered as an event.

Once she finally got Patricia to nod off for a few hours, Donna retreated to her hotel suite.

How do these girls get in this deep? she wondered, kicking off her shoes and wincing as she stretched her back. It hurt. Her body hurt. Her head hurt. And she knew the next twenty hours were going to be a grind.

But vows were exchanged, promises were made, kisses were traded.

The reception was exquisite. With nearly a blank check, Donna had transformed the farm into a wonderland of light, the reception extending from the large barn that had been converted into a dining room, to another large outbuilding where the band played. The toasts were made and the cake was cut. Donna had covered passageways erected in case of rain, which was always a possibility in Missouri. And she had to round up two of the groomsmen, who she learned had made a wager as to who could "nail" the most women over the long weekend. They kept escorting young—usually drunk—women away from the party and out into the dark pastures.

"I swear to all things good in the world, if I have to come look for you again, I'll tie a knot in that little dick of yours," Donna had snarled at one of the groomsmen, a frat brother of Edward's who was clearly cut from the same cloth, after she yanked him out of a tack house with some girl who apparently wasn't wearing any panties to the wedding, making situations like this a little easier for the groomsman.

Even that didn't stop the same groomsman from hitting on Donna later in the evening.

As Donna stood in the back of the gorgeously transformed outbuilding, watching the bride and groom have their first dance to John Legend's *All of Me*—not exactly the most original but they picked it—Donna's eyes continued to land on a very attractive middle-aged couple standing off to the side, engaged in a dark conversation filled with stiffness and quick sentences that rattled off the lips while they refused to look at each other.

He was in his late forties, tan, a head full of gray hair, and a trimmed gray beard that made him look like an aging cologne model. She was icy beautiful, and trim in a curve-fitting crème dress, clearly designer, her blonde hair pulled back tightly like a Hitchcock heroine. Though Donna didn't know why, she was fascinated with these two and found herself stepping around the perimeter of the dance floor to get closer, possibly to hear what they were bickering about.

She wore a ring. He didn't.

And they were definitely pissed off at each other.

Donna assigned them characters. He was in the banking business, twice married, three kids, all of whom were here somewhere in the crowd, maybe a groomsman or bridesmaid; they were close family friends. She was the woman who broke up his second marriage. She worked in high-end retail. Now in her late forties, she needed to dig her claws into someone because she was acutely aware, as beautiful women often are, that her looks—which had always been the ace up her sleeve—had an expiration date.

He had come into Barneys or Saks, where she assisted him in picking out a bag and scarf for his then-wife. He thanked her but stopped near the door, turned, and walked back to her, handing her his card with the line, "I normally don't do this..." which she knew was a lie but slid the card from his fingers with a smile.

Donna knew she'd never know how accurate she was, especially since it didn't seem like they would be attending too many more weddings together. But she couldn't deny they looked gorgeous together.

Finally arriving back at her hotel suite at two in the morning, Donna took two mini-bottles of tequila and emptied them into a glass. She thought about calling Cameron; she hadn't talked with him in a while, but he was probably with Andie. And Donna had two more destination weddings coming up in the next six weeks, so she needed to sleep. Business was business, and since she no longer had a personal life, burying herself in the minutia of someone's wedding sounded like a great place to hide. It beat burying herself in a quart of Ted Drewes frozen custard.

The molecules of Donna's business formed directly out of college. She knew so many girls getting married to their high school or college sweethearts that it was pretty much a no-brainer. It was no secret to anyone she ever met that she was obsessed with weddings, gaga over them ever since she was a little girl. It was the joy of the intimate spectacle. A relationship was a place for reality, a wedding was the place for fantasy.

From the time she was six, she'd spent hours perusing wedding magazines, aglow at the beauty of the brides in their white gowns, enthralled by the decorations, the locations, grooms in tuxedos and tailored suits, the bridesmaid's dresses, the formal dinners with their amazing centerpieces, and beautiful people all dressed up dancing to a full band. She believed it should be the greatest event in any woman's life and still did.

When Donna first started her business, she worked her ass off for very little money, dumping every dime she made back into the business. Year by year, she pulled together ridiculously showy weddings and then started specializing in unique destination weddings. Which meant a lot of travel, a lot of pulling off something wonderful in a foreign place that didn't particularly jibe with her regimented style of getting things done, and a few times in places where she didn't even speak the language. But each and every time she managed to make the day memorable for the bride and groom and impressive for their guests.

Usually on very little money and even less sleep.

People talked about her weddings. A couple of her early brides raved about them to friends, bragging she was tyrannical about the particulars so the bride wouldn't have to be. What could be better than actually enjoying your own wedding instead of worrying whether dinner would be on time, the limo would be where it was supposed to be, the driver would be drunk, having a great photographer who knew what to do even if the weather didn't cooperate, and how to dodge your new mother-in-law who you'd managed to put up with this far but didn't want to on this day? Donna handled all of that and more. Her Yelp page was a glowing testimonial from happy brides. Because a happy bride pretty much guaranteed a happy first year of marriage for the groom.

"After that," Donna joked with Roger, one half of Roger-and-Amy, who were married on the beach in Mexico, "my job is done, and you need to step up your game."

"I want someone to drive insane," Donna often said with a smirk. "But I know exactly what the entire event will look like, smell like, feel like, from start to finish. My wedding won't just be a wedding; it will be an experience," she announced to a prospective client over lunch at Sugarfire Smoke House.

Donna wanted her guests to always remember her wedding. From sounds to textures to colors to design, and every piece in between, she wanted that day to be a marvel. A wedding that everyone else would measure theirs by for years. Cameron always joked that the man she married better come from big money because the wedding she had in her head would cost a king's ransom.

"Considering what I do for a living, mine should be better, shouldn't it?" she responded with a smile. A smile that wavered ever so slightly, not sure that day would ever happen.

The next six weeks were insane, even by Donna's standards. Two weddings, three weeks apart. The first on a spectacular dude ranch in Wyoming at the base of the Tetons, the next on an even more spectacular beach in Maui. The Maui wedding turned into an explosive ordeal, with a groom who had gotten cold feet two weeks out, causing the jittery, pouty bride to morph into a raging Bridezilla.

By the time she actually wed on that breezeless August day, dripping with humidity and tension, she wasn't speaking to her own mother or her maid-of-honor. Donna hoped the make-up sex with her new husband was incredible because they could barely look at each other through the vows.

But the most interesting thing about the wedding was that the bride's "favorite uncle" was the same tan, handsome, well-tailored man with the mane of gray hair. And again, he was in attendance with the remote yet stunningly put-together late-forties blonde. *St. Louis,* Donna thought, *everybody knows everybody. And if you don't know them, you know somebody that knows them.* She also assumed the handsome man gave expensive gifts.

At this wedding, they didn't hold the same animosity for each other that bellowed in their body language at the last. Noting that he still didn't wear a wedding ring, which was not totally uncommon as some men never wore, Donna watched as they smiled at each other, talking closely, obviously not in the same snit as they were at the wedding a few months ago.

They still weren't particularly connected as some long-married couples were. The blonde holding a distance, not just with him but with everyone, a frosty glimmer in her eye warning others that she wasn't one for chit-chat. And the favorite uncle, with the enviable mane of gray hair, never actually looked right at her, talking with her from the side, as his eyes focused on the crowd. Donna wondered if they had reached a point in their marriage where the connective tissue of their relationship was wire-thin, a marriage running on fumes. Even when the woman smiled or laughed at something he whispered to her, her spirit seemed so fragile it seemed composed of butterfly wings and tissue paper.

Donna wondered if she dictated the relationship or actually needed a shoulder to cry on. She'd love to inch closer, to try and break through the barrier the woman created with just her eyes, but Donna had a day filled with obligations and duties. Weddings certainly didn't stop once the bride and groom said their vows.

Donna observed the woman all night. Even as the favorite uncle tried to make things better, holding her hand, sharing a few kisses, albeit on the cheek. The bride's sister had gotten engaged a few months prior and had cornered Donna to discuss planning her wedding. Donna wagered with herself that the distant blonde wouldn't appear on the arm of the handsome gray-haired man at the next family wedding.

Even though she was utterly exhausted, to the point it felt like her bones hurt, Donna smiled to herself as the reception was winding down. The last few days were pure hell but the wedding turned out spectacularly detailed. And she had a first-class seat for the flight home.

Arriving back in St. Louis, as fatigued as she had ever been and running a slight fever Donna was already making notes of the two new clients she booked on top of the two weddings she already had looming. Cameron had left her a message that he and Andie wanted to take her out.

"To lure her back to the land of eligible men," he told her.

"Thank you for making dating sound that much creepier," she answered.

Getting serious with Andie, Cameron felt some weird compunction to have his best friend's life sync up with his own, which meant finding Donna a suitable mate. Even Donna recognized that, as Cam and Andie were teetering into a serious relationship, it would get infinitely more difficult for her to tag along as the third wheel. Not that Andie seemed to mind. In fact, she was the reason behind Cameron inviting Donna along when they went out to certain places. Not only was Andie growing more comfortable with Donna's company, enjoying having a woman friend she could really laugh with, but Andie also wanted Donna to find a guy. But more to the point, Andie wanted to keep Cameron from fixing Donna up with a guy he thought would be *perfect* for her, because Andie felt Cameron had no idea the kind of guy Donna would respond to. "You know everything about her but who's right for her," Andie chided Cam. But there was a deeper reason, Andie enjoyed Donna's presence and Donna knew Cameron better than anyone. Who better to glean insights about the man she was falling in love with?

Walking through McGurk's, a popular bar in the Soulard section of the city, Cameron spotted Andie waiting at a table on the patio, with Donna. *Good God, how could I not fall in love with her,* he thought as he continued to the table. Cameron always believed men fell in love with what they saw, while women fell in love with who they got to know. Smiling, Cameron accepted that not only had he fallen in love with what he saw, but he was also falling deeply in love with the woman he had gotten to know.

When they were together, Cameron's and Andie's eyes locked in a waltz every time they gazed at one another. Everyone and everything around them disappeared. That was the thing about them that gave Donna the greatest pangs of jealousy. Donna knew that even if she met a guy and fell madly in love, she didn't believe she would ever have that. She's only observed it a few times in couples getting married, which made Donna appreciate just how extraordinary it was.

"*Recherché*," Donna muttered unconsciously.

"What are you mumbling about now?" Cameron asked, his head tilting slightly as it did when he already knew the answer to questions.

"Sorry, sorry, I gotta stop doing that," Donna chortled, quickly slamming a gulp of her beer before reaching across the table and touching Andie's arms.

"I was listening. I promise. But I've known Cameron a long time and though he'll hate me for saying this, he's dated a lot of girls and you are the first one where I've said to myself, *"she belongs with him."*

Andie didn't know what to say. Her eyes locked on Donna for a moment then moved to Cameron and then back to Donna. A smile finally crossed her lips.

"I think you're starting to crush on me like I'm crushing on you," Andie said with an artful grin.

Donna howled. "Are we laying our cards on the table? I didn't know at first. I mean, Cameron made you out to be too good to be true. And you can imagine how much I hate that in people."

Andie laughed, raising her hand for Donna to high five as Donna added, "But now...I want us to be friends because I am crushing on you too."

Cameron took both of them in, a disgruntled smirk on his face. "Are you two going to kiss now?"

Andie laughed, waving Cameron off. "You can leave now," she said, causing Donna to almost fall out of her chair.

"We're going to be great friends," Donna stated assuredly.

Strolling through Soulard, with its eclectic bars, eateries, and brick storefronts, they kept a leisurely pace, Andie between Cameron and Donna.

"I know this isn't the first time you were asked, and Cam insists nothing has ever happened between you," Andie stated with a big smile. "But I want your side. Why didn't you two ever hook up?"

"He told you we didn't?" Donna asked, smirking.

"That's because we never have," Cameron punched into the conversation.

"He swore nothing has ever happened between you two," Andie said, talking over him.

"Did he? Wow. I guess he forgot our first kiss," Donna said, raising a brow.

Cameron sighed hard, shaking his head causing Andie to fire him a look. Seeing his discomfort, she smiled.

"Do tell," Andie jumped in.

"We were twelve..."

"Not this pathetic tale again. And we were thirteen," Cameron corrected her.

"You were thirteen, I was twelve. Junior high school. Awful time. Don't think those straight, white teeth came natural - he wore braces."

Andie again glanced over at Cameron. "You wore braces?"

"It's the results that count," Cameron added.

"His head was bigger than the rest of his skinny body. Thankfully, his body grew because he looked like a balloon in the Macy's Thanksgiving Day parade."

Andie laughed. "Like *you* were some prize," Cameron clucked at Donna.

"I was going through an awkward girl stage," Donna deflected. "I wore glasses, really ugly glasses, that only my mother thought were cute. I had started getting zits, and I sucked at everything. I wasn't a very good student, I couldn't play a single sport, I was too shy to join the debate team or the school newspaper. Only thing I did was work the crew for every stage show in junior high. Guess that helped me become a wedding planner. I know how to get things done behind the scenes. But back in the day," she said like it was eons ago, "it was painful to be me."

Taking a few steps, Donna smiled at the memory. "It was one of those days, I was throwing a pity party for myself. We were walking home from school and I was whining about how no boys would ever love me because

I was so ugly and wasn't good at anything. I was totally
invisible to most of the class. Of course, my best friend
kept telling me it wasn't true. That guys notice me all the
time—though he isn't a very good liar, as I'm sure you
know by now—and working in the wedding business and
dealing with soon-to-be husbands and wives, be glad he
isn't. Anyway, when I pressed him on who found me so
alluring, he couldn't come up with a single name of any boy
who had asked about me. And while the other girls were
getting notes stuffed in their school bags, mine was always
empty. Anyway, I was practically crying by the time I got
home---"

"You weren't crying," Cameron slipped in with a beaming
smile, "you were sobbing. She was a blubbering hot mess."

"That may be how you remember it but Andie asked me,
this is *my* story," Donna crowed, pushing him away, "As I was
saying...so he walked me to my house and when we got to
the driveway as I turned to wave goodbye, he leaned over to
try and kiss me and it sort of freaked me out, and somehow
I got my hand up near his face and this little braided metal
ring I wore all the time got caught in his braces."

"What?!" Andie bellowed with laughter.

"And we couldn't unhook them. He's freaking out, drool
is pouring out of his mouth, and every time he tries to
say something he's biting my fingers. So, I sort of lead
him by the mouth into my house so we can sit down and
see if we can unhook ourselves from each other. We are
in the bathroom and I'm putting soap on the ring, trying
to get it off my finger but with his braces hooked into
it, I couldn't get my finger out. He's swallowing soap and
gagging, threatening to throw up. I start crying—"

"Harder," Cameron added.

"Harder," Donna concurred, "and we had to wait another
hour locked together until my dad, rest his soul, got home
and used some cutters to get the ring off my finger and then
unhook it from Cam's braces. Years later when I brought it
up, he told me the reason it happened was because he was
leaning in to kiss me because I was so pathetic."

"I didn't say pathetic."

"You didn't have to. I knew I was pathetic," Donna
responded before turning to Andie. "But it meant so much

that he would do that because I was feeling so crummy about myself. That's the kind of guy he is, and I can see really cares about you. You're lucky."

Andie's smile grew and under the lamplight it was apparent she was blushing, "I know," she said, without the need for another word.

NINE

After driving Donna to her car, she and Andie hugged as Andie got out of the back to return to the front seat. Cameron walked Donna across the busy street and opened her car door for her.

"I told Andie I loved her," he said with a big grin.

Donna's eyes lit up. "You did! That's huge for you! Congratulations! Now, the big question. Did she say it back?"

As if his smile wasn't big enough, it widened and he nodded. Donna made a cooing sound and threw her arms around him, hugging him tightly, swaying back and forth with happiness.

TEN

"Golf..." Andie remarked with a roll of her eyes as she and Donna walked around Forest Park, while Cam played golf with her father. "He hates it. But my father's addicted, so to stay in his good graces, Cameron goes. I keep telling him he doesn't have to but he says it's about business and not about what he wants."

"You're...getting serious," Donna declared more than asked, trying to suss out where Andie was now that she knew what Cameron's intentions were. She didn't want to pry but Donna was itching to make plans.

Andie weighed her next words before speaking.

"I'm guessing he'll officially propose soon."

"Officially?" Donna asked with a raised eyebrow.

Andie smiled. "We've talked about it. He wouldn't dare ask me without us having talked about it beforehand. He can surprise me with the 'when' but not the 'if'."

"Smart girl."

"I'm guessing we will be needing your help planning things coming up here," Andie said, "Cameron says you've had your own wedding planned since you were a little girl."

"Cam's got a big mouth. I mean, it's true. My wedding day is going to be the one event in my life I want to remember. I want people talking about it, I want it to be a moment in time where everything stands still. I know the dress, the flowers, the venue, how I want everything staged down to the centerpieces," Donna admitted almost dreaming about it.

"I hope you can help me make my wedding day at least half as spectacular as the one you're planning for yourself," Andie asked hopefully.

Nodding, Donna replied, "Trust me, your wedding will be completely kick-ass. I've been planning Cameron's wedding almost as long as my own. And I know that we're friends and know you have great taste, so I'm super excited to help you make the day ridiculously amazing. It's going to be exquisite."

"Promise?"

"Promise."

The women locked fingers in a pinky promise. As they did, they turned to walk around the lake where people pedaled the vividly colored paddle boats. Donna was already envisioning which cut of dress would look stunning on Andie. And because she was with Cameron when he bought Andie her favorite flowers, salmon-hued roses, she knew what color the bridesmaid dresses would be. Not really realizing it, Donna had been making a mental checklist of everything Andie liked. She could put this wedding together today and it would be sensational.

Donna even knew the song Cameron would want for their first dance as husband and wife, the one she would have to talk him out of; not just because it is a country tune but because Donna could say with absolute certainty that Andie would not like it.

There were many magnificent wedding venues in St. Louis, ridiculously gorgeous turn-of-the-century churches of every denomination; the Jewel Box, the Butterfly House, the Botanical Gardens, Union Station, the Peabody Opera House, St. Xavier. Donna had pulled off two under the Arch—both for well-connected families—not to mention one at the zoo, a handful of crazy weddings at The City Museum, and another handful at the ballpark, something she had sworn she would never do but what a bride wants, a bride gets.

And there were equally as many insanely cool venues for a reception. Donna didn't get to work in her hometown often enough and would be elated every day she worked on this wedding and got to come home and sleep in her own bed. The out-of-town weddings had taken their toll and she was drained even thinking about pulling off the next.

She smiled as she connived how she was going to convince Cameron and his potential groomsmen into performing a special dance number for Andie, something that would display Cameron's "killer moves." Cam's words, not Donna's.

She'd witnessed him dance. His moves could kill. But not in the way he believed.

Donna vowed to make Andie's wedding day something Andie would look back on for decades knowing it couldn't have gone any more perfectly. A mix of elegance and joy, of beauty and sentiment. This was what Donna did best. The wedding of her lifelong best friend to her new best friend would be something people in this city would be talking about.

ELEVEN

"**G**olf sucks hind tit," Cameron whispered to himself as he finished up the ninth hole, playing a foursome with Andie's dad and two potential clients whose business Henry was wooing.

Cameron questioned why Henry wanted him to join the foursome in the first place. He sucked at golf, hated tan slacks, and while he never let his boss know how much he actually despised the game, it wasn't hard to recognize the agony Cameron did his best to hide but couldn't.

"Why can't the company have a softball team?" Cameron asked Andie by cell phone when he had a few minutes between rounds. "Why can't your dad be into Mud Runs or something modestly cool? Bowling, I'd even go for bowling. Anything but this stupid game," he lamented in a hushed tone, causing Andie to snicker at his misery.

"This is why you get paid the big money," she offered, as she arrived home from her walk with Donna.

"I'm not getting paid for this! I should. This is work to me. All of it, the stupid game, the small talk, even drinks afterward. I wish I was drinking now. I should have slammed a few before I came. I'd probably play better. There is nothing enjoyable about golf. Hit, walk, hit again, miss the hole, miss the hole twice, frustration, miss again, finally put the ball in the cup only to turn around and see your boss, who is a far better golfer than you, with a sardonic smile aimed directly at my ineptness. How does anyone get joy from a game that's designed to make you feel crappy about yourself?"

Cameron preferred to leave work at the office and abhorred sacrificing his weekends to a job that already occupied more than forty hours a week. He and Andie made a vow, a vow they knew they couldn't possibly keep: not to bring their work home and even more important to keep the office politics inside the office, something Henry Hune was notorious for and openly enjoyed. But rules changed when your boss was also the father of the woman you love. Cameron toiled at steering clear of office gossip—both being involved in or the subject of.

No one viewed Henry as a horrible guy, least of all Cameron; just a man with a few peccadillos and quirks, which was a nice way of saying certain things entertained him and certain things could set him off. And according to Andie, if her father didn't like you, he could be a real bastard. So for Andie's sake, Cameron worked extra-hard to stay in his good graces and out of his line of fire.

"These guys we're playing with asked me if I was seeing someone and your dad covered for me," Cameron whispered quickly. "I'm not sure if he did that so there would be no questions or if he hates the idea that I'm with you."

"It's the former or we would have already heard about it. I'm sure he just doesn't want that being a topic of discussion while you are trying to hit a little white ball until it falls into a little manmade hole in the ground," Andie responded.

"When you say that, the game sounds even more stupid," Cameron sighed before excusing himself to get back.

Calling Donna from the car after his game of golf, Cameron first told her he called Andie but she was getting her hair cut and couldn't talk.

"So, I'm second now?" Donna asked with just enough sass to know he'd squirm at least for a nanosecond.

"Hey, she sleeps with me!" he fired back.

"Be happy about that."

"I am, I am," he said with a big breath, "Almost as much as I'm happy that my day golfing is over. The. Dumbest. Game. Ever. And then you have to go and have drinks and talk about it. I don't mind the scotch but the only thing worse than golf is talking about golf. These guys talk about pros and I just nod along like I know who they are talking about. I told Mr. Hune that I was never going to get any better at this game because I didn't care to. He looked at me like I punched his daughter for not doing the dishes or something."

"Put on your big-boy pants, Cameron, you're doing it for work. I bet I do a hundred more awful things a day because of my job. That's why they call it a 'job' and not 'fun.'"

"The only fun part of the day was when the valet pulled up Betty Blue first and Henry and those guys got all googly-eyed and moist in their tightie-whities. Right on the spot, Henry offered me twenty-five grand for my car. I think trying to impress these clients."

"What'd you say?"

"Told him no thanks. Told them all I restored this car. Took a decade of my life. I got a lot of sweat equity in her. Andie's father then turns to the guys and says, 'That car is why I hired this young man. I knew he had attention to detail and that he wouldn't stop until something was perfect.' Then he offered me thirty grand," Cameron stated, sounding slightly perturbed, "and from the look on his face, I think he was serious."

"So, you told the boss, 'no' again?"

"I told him there was no amount of money that would get me to sell her. Then one of these high-roller investment guys said, 'They say everybody has their price. He'll find yours.'"

"You should have said, 'He has, it's his daughter. But I'm still not parting with the car," Donna responded.

"Yeah, I should have. But I wasn't thinking quickly enough and it never helps when I become too big of a smartass."

"Not when you're dating the boss's daughter," Donna added.

"But it's kind of cool, you know. All my life, at least materialistically, there has never been much I've had over people. But now I have my car and my girl. Both cause heads to turn. And right now, I can see Andie's dad and the money guys in my rearview mirror watching me drive away," Cameron chuckled wickedly.

"Enjoy the moment, honey," Donna laughed with him.

"I am, I am. And in spite of thirty grand paying off a lot of my student loans, I'd never part with this car."

Cameron had offers to sell the Camaro before but he never entertained a single one. Granted, he'd never been offered thirty thousand dollars but he couldn't put a price on what it would take for him to separate from his beloved Betty Blue. There simply wasn't a number.

But as Cameron glanced back in his rearview mirror as the men watched him drive down the long country club driveway, he chuckled again.

"I may not be able to play golf but I'm driving *this*, fellas."

TWELVE

S lipping the chain around her neck, Donna allowed the cameo to fall and glanced at herself in the mirror, positioning it directly above her cleavage. She turned side to side to get a glimpse of it from different angles. Donna adored this piece of jewelry. It belonged to her grandmother and was the one heirloom she received when she passed away.

The first time Andie noticed the cameo was when they were having dinner with Cameron. Donna hadn't seen them in a few weeks, having put together three back-to-back weddings, which nearly killed her. And she quickly followed that by being out of town for two weeks in Virginia planning a "coastal wedding" for a local woman who was marrying a D.C. wonk.

Donna looked like crap when they got together for dinner, so wiped out that if it had been anyone else wanting to get together, she would have canceled.

But the weddings were successful and Donna was approached by a half-dozen young women and mothers of brides-to-be at the receptions, inquiring about her services. Can't beat that. Still, Donna was gratefully relieved when it was all over that there wasn't another wedding booked for over six weeks. She actually had some time to take care of herself.

"Do you ever meet anyone at these weddings?" Andie asked, concerned. "I mean guys."

"I can emphatically state I've never slept with any guy I've met while working at a wedding," Donna responded with a tired laugh.

"You sound like a politician denying an affair. That's not what I meant," Andie replied, turning crimson.

"I'm usually so busy until after the reception that I don't talk to anyone who isn't in the bridal party. I stay with the bride through most of it. I mean, it's her day. And then at the reception, I still have to keep an eye on the food, the liquor, the band, or DJ. Or anything special that is planned. And we always try and do something special at weddings to make them unique and memorable. Photo booths, choreographed dances, sometimes bringing in professional dancers to perform, all sorts of stuff. Thankfully, the groomsmen are usually, though not always, past the point of doing something entirely inappropriate or stupid, knowing the bride will have their balls if they ruin her wedding day."

Donna regaled them, well mostly Andie—Cameron had already heard all of her best wedding tales and now obligingly pretended to be interested—with stories about the stupid, insane things she'd put together for other people's weddings. Story after story about clowns, yes, clowns, that one groom wanted at his wedding, to dead parents in urns, grooms who came dressed in armor, a bride who wore lingerie as a wedding dress, grandmothers who got into a fistfight.

Andie found herself laughing so hard she could barely breathe.

"But the worst, the absolute worst," Donna confided, speaking excitedly, her hands waving as she did, "are horses. I will never ever again do a wedding where horses are involved."

Donna relayed the story of a couple who wanted to be married on the beach in Jamaica at sunset on horseback. Both professed to be avid riders but in truth were barely comfortable atop the big animals. "One of the horses took a huge dump right as we started the ceremony, which while funny, doesn't exactly add to the ambiance of the moment. But the worst was that the horse the bride was on got spooked as they were about to be pronounced man and wife and bolted! Ran like someone slapped it on the butt. She couldn't hang on and face-planted into the tide. Her thousand-dollar dress was ruined. Hair, makeup a hot, hot mess. She was crying, she had sand abrasions on both arms and the right side of her face. We ended up finishing the wedding in the emergency room in Kingston, Jamaica, and while it's a perfectly fine hospital, it isn't exactly scenic."

Over Andie's laughter, Donna added with a head-shaking smile, "So, please, no horses at your wedding, or I'm out."

"Promise," Andie stated assuredly, realizing she had responded as if a wedding was in the offing and tried to cover, "I mean, you know, I wouldn't want a horse at my wedding. At any wedding. So, it's safe to say, there will be no horse when I get married."

Excusing herself to use the bathroom, Andie figured it was an easy transition out of the moment. Donna smirked an 'it's okay' smile as she left, Cameron watching, his eyes following her out of the dining room.

Once Andie was out of sight, Cameron turned back to Donna, his eyes glowing with a joyous urgency.

"I want to do it," Cameron stated cryptically.

"Do what...?"

"Ask her."

"To marry you?"

"Yes. What else would I ask her?"

Even though Andie had warned her this was coming, Donna gasped excitedly at her best friend's admission, "There are a thousand things! But congratulations! It's about time!" Donna jumped up, hugging him. "I'm so happy for you!"

"I want to do it right though."

"I've never planned an engagement before. I am so in!" Donna exclaimed, her smile growing.

"I want it to be something really cool. Something even her father can't give me an ounce of grief over."

Donna nodded, her mind racing with ideas. But she found when dealing with clients —and on a certain level, that's what Cameron was now— it was easier to sit back and listen rather than bombard them with suggestions. Those would come soon enough. Usually, the more clients prattled on, the more she picked up hints at what they were truly looking for. She loved when a couple came to her and they were on the same page about what they wanted. It didn't happen as often as Donna would like, most women having planned long in advance for their wedding, while the guys shoot from the cuff, usually in direct contradiction to what his bride-to-be desired.

Donna knew it was better to listen to everything, filter nothing, then when she had a garbled mountain of information, she whittled away the grand plans down to the more-telling minutiae of the client's taste. Then she would offer suggestions as to how she would design their wedding, paring down the visions in their heads to something that actually took shape and made them more of a reality. Besides, some people, usually the guys, just like to feel they are being listened to about wedding plans.

Cameron was one of them. He'd been that way since he was a kid so Donna knew she should let him massage the vague concept of the visions in his head...and then she would convince him exactly how it should be done, making him think it was his idea all along.

Spying Andie returning through the restaurant, Donna leaned over and placed her hand on Cameron's. "I'll take care of it, you know that," was her brief but all-encompassing reply.

Cameron knew she would. That was who she was and this was totally in Donna's wheelhouse. All Cameron knew was that he wanted to surprise Andie in the most spectacular way possible. When it came to this stuff, he was all big-picture and no detail.

Donna was both. She had to be.

"What have you two been gabbing about?" Andie asked, sensing the blithe energy between Cameron and Donna.

"Our past," Donna covered, hoping Andie didn't discover that she wasn't being truthful, "When I used to help Cameron with his homework and study for tests. He's not good with tests. But you probably know that."

"He doesn't like to be challenged," Andie said, averting her eyes bouncing between them, still feeling something more was being discussed.

"Wait a minute!" Cameron protested, "Don't confuse me with your mom. I handle everything thrown my way."

"You handle what you're good at," Andie countered, "which, lucky for you, is a lot. But I've seen you completely ignore things you don't want to deal with."

"Such as?" Cameron asked.

Leaning in, Donna smiled, knowing any curiosity Andie had would dissipate faster now that they were on to this conversation. "Sorry I stirred the pot. Not really but..."

Andie sat back, her eyes locking on Cameron's. They both smiled, one of those moments where everyone else disappeared. Both loved competition, and even something as simple as a personal challenge took on a sexual charge.

"Speaking of my mother, we can start with her," Andie said.

"Your mother? What about her? I get along fine with your mother."

"Really? We've been seeing each other for a year, you worked for my dad six months longer than that. You've been around my mother at least a dozen times. How many times have you talked to her, I mean past hellos and how-are-yous?"

"Your mother is..." Cameron said before stopping to weigh his words. The pause lingered long enough for Andie to turn to Donna, both women smiling.

"How long should I make him sweat this?" Andie asked.

"I'm enjoying it. Because I know how he is."

"Your mother loves me," Cameron stated confidently.

"In my mother's world, everyone orbits her. She doesn't orbit anyone. Not even my father. Which is a nice way of saying she can be a bitch most of the time. I love her but she's mercurial on a good day. And you don't do more than walk in, kiss her on the cheek, say hello, and move on. It's not a criticism, but you don't even try to make conversation."

"That's because she doesn't like it. I'm just being considerate of her feelings," Cameron countered.

"Ah-ha! My point. It's hard, so you swerve to avoid it," Andie said, feeling she'd won.

"I respect your mother too much to try and force meaningless conversation. And she loves me for not being one of those people who is going to try and chink off some of her armor," Cameron responded, smiling because he felt he topped Andie's victory.

Until Andie smiled back. "It's not armor. It's ice," she stated without a trace of sarcasm.

"Still. Point Cameron," Cameron answered, trying to keep any sarcasm from seeping in.

Donna laughed.

"Would never hold up in front of an unbiased jury, but I'll award you a point for an interesting argument and looking good in that shirt," Andie responded, another sliver of a smile rising on her lips, her mind obviously planning her next few moves.

"Heights!" Andie piped up quickly.

"I don't like heights. So what?"

"So, you wouldn't challenge yourself and even take me on the Ferris wheel at the State Fair. You begged off even though you knew I wanted to ride it."

"I didn't stop you from getting on it."

"I wanted to ride it with you."

"You relish seeing me sweat."

"Because it happens so rarely."

Sitting back in her chair, Donna took in her two sparring friends, enjoying the ridiculous happiness they shared that allowed Cameron to battle with Andie without either getting their panties in a bunch. But she never had been audience to it playing out as vibrantly as it did right now. And though Donna didn't know for certain, she surmised that once they got home, Cameron and Andie would fall into bed and connect on an even deeper level.

THIRTEEN

I t wasn't going to be easy.
What Donna planned had mountains staggered in
its path by both logistics and Cameron, and worse than
both of those, Andie's parents. Donna broke the news of
her master plan while she and Cameron were in Leonard
Morell's jewelry store, a small brick storefront out in the
far western suburb of Wildwood that carried a selection
of uniquely exquisite jewelry. Donna loved this place. She
could point out a certain type of engagement ring to
Cameron and Leonard himself would create something
similar but one-of-a-kind, that no one else would have.

But halfway through her grand scheme for Cameron's
proposal, he blurted out, "There's no way I'm doing that!"

Donna stared at him for a moment as if he were sprouting
a second head before stating dryly, "Oh, you're doing it."

"I'm not. I'm not doing that. Come up with something
else."

"Do you know what that would say to her? Think about it,"
Donna pleaded. "You would be a man who would step up
no matter how fearful you were of the situation. You would
face your fears for her. I'm telling you that's about the most
romantic thing a man can do."

"How about I sit down and have a heart-to-heart with her
mother instead?"

"You're doing this and that's all there is to it," Donna
responded flatly, before pointing out one of the rings
Leonard held. "That one."

It was a one-of-a-kind vintage solitaire with side accents
set in white gold. The large cushion-cut diamond was
surrounded by small diamonds leading down the shaft of

the ring in a subtle wavy shape, making it seem as if the large setting was emerging like a blossom from the smaller diamonds.

"Wow!" Cameron said as he took the ring to look at it closer. "This is perfect."

Donna shot him a look. "Of course, it is. That's why I suggested it. I'm the professional and you're only doing this once, so you're doing it right."

Leonard gave Donna a bemused look, but he had witnessed her in action dozens of times before.

Cameron put his arm around Donna, giving her a hug. He couldn't do this without her. There were moments he wished he could, but he knew better. Even if Donna weren't his best friend, this was one area of life she had the hand up. And he was taking advantage of it.

"I love you," Cameron said, buttering her up before adding, "but I'm still not proposing the way you want. I can't afford it and I'll throw up."

"I've already called in some favors and you can. And you will. She will be overwhelmed and wouldn't dare say no even if there was a possibility she would, which I'm sure there isn't. And take some Dramamine, you'll be fine."

Cameron didn't respond. He knew better than to fight her on this. He was going to be proposing exactly how Donna saw it in her head because Donna believed it was what Andie would love. And he knew she was probably correct. More than probably. That was the bottom line and Cameron couldn't argue that. It didn't mean he wouldn't moan and grouse about it and he certainly wasn't about to enjoy it.

But he knew it was *exactly* the right way to propose.

"This is going to blow! Maybe literally," Cameron stated.

"Suck it up, buttercup, you're going to be fine. Leave the rest to me."

"You know, I gotta give you something for this, Donna. I mean, I can't have you working for free."

Cocking back her head so she could connect directly with Cameron's baby blues, Donna said, "You are my best friend in the whole world. I would never charge you. You understand that? Never. This is my gift to you, in lieu of a gravy boat or candle holders. But I appreciate that you appreciate what I do as a profession."

"Well, if you ever need a building designed, you just let me know."

"It won't be a building, it'll be a shrine. And you can design it. Tastefully."

Donna was over the moon that she could do this for Cameron. And Andie.

I'm a shoo-in for godmother when their first kid arrives, she thought, unable to hide a grin. She was so looking forward to spending more time with Andie as they planned the wedding. And as long as Andie wasn't overcome with a sudden love for horses, all was good. Her wedding would be beyond extraordinary. But Donna had another event to conquer first; she wanted this engagement surprise to be pure Cameron.

Which really meant pure Donna.

Now that they had selected the ring and Cameron hadn't choked too hard at the price, it was time for Donna to completely take over. The date on which Cameron wished to propose was looming, just a few weeks away, which didn't leave her an enormous amount of time for planning. Donna thrived on working on the fly and this event would certainly fit comfortably into that arena. Especially since she convinced Cameron to surprise Andie with a grand gesture.

That's a boulevard of surprises and, in spite of Cameron freaking out, Donna found pulling this off pure bliss.

The next few weeks were hell. Donna hadn't fully recovered from the last stretch working out of town and now she found herself elbow-deep in making Cam's proposal magical. She fretted every detail of every job but none more than this one. She had learned through experience that unless you demanded perfection, perfection refused to show up on its own.

"What I'm planning isn't going to be free, Cam. I'm cutting costs everywhere I can and calling in favors but still..." Donna gently told Cam while she drove down the Forest Park Parkway.

"I won't be paying for the wedding. This is it for me. So as long as you don't kill me, I want this to be as great as it can be," Cameron responded.

"I promise not to put you in debt before you get married. I know you have college loans you're paying off."

"I'll be paying those off forever," Cameron sort of laughed but not really.

"But I am going to make sure everyone present at the engagement party is talking about it right up to the wedding. And set the bar so high for the wedding that Andie's father has to hand me a blank check," Donna giggled.

"I'm all for that," Cameron chuckled, before cutting the conversation short to get back to work.

Marching toward an epic engagement surprise, Donna stumbled over one small hurdle: Cam's refusal to sit down with Henry and Caroline to ask their permission to marry their daughter.

"What is this, the 1800s?" Cam moaned.

"It's a formality. Tradition. And from what you and Andie have said, her parents are uber-traditional."

"No, I can't. Not with her mom. No way!"

"What are you afraid of?" Donna quizzed, more curious than concerned.

"Remember that first day you actually met Andie? It'd be like that revving at twenty thousand rpm."

"I don't know what the hell that means but I get your point," Donna replied.

"It means another very uncomfortable evening of sweating and fake smiles. And as soon as I take her parents out without her, Andie's going to know and the surprise is shot."

Donna drew in a long, dramatic breath, to give Cameron enough time to realize how cowardly he sounded without having to utter that buzz word, as she waited for him to recant.

But Cam knew her tricks, and he remained silent, forcing Donna to launch in.

"Okay, then here's what you're going to do: You are going to take her father out to lunch and do it the real old-fashioned way, man-to-man. That way you can at least avoid her mother, who better not be a pain in my ass when I'm putting the wedding together. And don't tell me no, Cam—you *are* going to do it!"

Acquiescing, Cam agreed, knowing that taking Mr. Hune out for lunch would be a hell of a lot easier than sitting across from his future mother-in-law on one of those stiff-backed French provincial sofas with the carved inlay on either side of the fireplace in her living room—especially without Andie there as a buffer—or listening to Donna chide him nonstop for the next few weeks.

Donna worked the next three days straight pulling things together for a wedding in Cabo. She'd done a few weddings there before and knew that any couple that wanted a Mexican wedding really wanted a ceremony followed by a drunken bacchanal. Especially if they picked Cabo. But Donna set up the hotel rooms, the flights, transportation, and insurance on everything. And she'd learned after the first wedding, where hotel rooms were trashed and a boat was wrecked, to bring lots and lots of cash; she'd had to pay off the Policia Federal to pull two groomsmen out of jail in time to make the wedding. And in Cabo, the authorities preferred the dollar to the peso.

Donna had tried to warn the bride-to-be, but considering that she asked Donna to see if she could find a tattoo parlor in Cabo so she and her bridesmaids could get a group tattoo and some piercings, Donna knew her warning was falling on deaf ears.

Her body was starting to ache, sitting at her desk in her disorganized apartment, so she pulled everything she needed over to the sofa and worked from there. Her apartment was always messy. She was there so little, cleaning it seemed pointless. Everything she needed for her business bled off her desk onto the dining table and into her living space. Even the kitchen wasn't immune. Bridal magazines, read and unread, were stacked everywhere. Donna knew where everything in her apartment was... generally. But she felt this unkempt mess cocooned her, and turned her apartment into her nest. And damn it, she was going to feather it any way she wanted.

She'd never brought a guy over, lest he finds out her little secret. Even with David, after six months of dating and he never stepped foot in her apartment. She always slept over at his. For the first few months, he thought she might be

married and he was a sidepiece. And though, intrigued as
he was to see her home, Donna would tell him her real
home was whatever hotel room she was living out of in
whatever city she happened to be working in.

She found that a satisfying answer. David never did.

FOURTEEN

The morning Cameron called and wanted her to join him for lunch, Donna's body ached even worse. She hoped she wasn't coming down with something but she also thought it might be because she hadn't left the apartment in three days. She needed to move. Andie had called twice and wanted her to take a walk around Forest Park, but she'd begged off, not feeling great and not wanting to cut into her workload. But her stomach cramped from sitting so much, especially since she'd been subsiding on 'pantry crap' and coffee. Getting up and getting out of the apartment would be good for her.

Falling into the burgundy leather booth in the back of the Cigar Club, Donna immediately asked Cameron how lunch went with Mr. Hune.

"He knew what I was going to ask."

"How do you know?"

"He made a reservation for us at Blood and Sand. You gotta be a member," Cameron said with a roll of his eyes. "He loves the place, so when I suggested lunch anywhere Henry wanted to go, he made a reservation there. Big giveaway."

"You should have picked the place."

"It would have been Leta B's, so I could have gotten a meal I loved and maybe a beer. I gave him the option of home-field advantage and he took it. Cool place though."

"Glad you liked it, so what happened? Why did we have to meet for a drink?"

"Well, he started by asking me if I asked him to lunch to tell him I found a better job. He knew that wasn't the reason and thinking back I should have said it was, just to mess with his head a bit," Cameron answered out of the side of his mouth, drink in his hand waiting to finish talking before he slammed back the scotch.

"But instead, I stuttered out some apologetic, almost-nonsensical response, which totally gave me away. So, I spent some time talking about idiot stuff, stuff that doesn't matter, playing with the silverware and fumbling through responses to things he was saying, barely listening for anything other than an opening so I could get the damn question over with."

"Okay then, how'd you do it?"

"He was talking about golf, which would have made me gag even on a good day and I just stuck my hand up and put it in his face to silence him and said, 'Sir, I'm here to talk about Andie. I want to marry her.'"

"With your hand in his face?"

"I couldn't even see his reaction because my hand was literally covering his face."

"So not like you," Donna howled with laughter. "Where's my cool, calm, and collected Cam?"

"He left the building with his tail between his legs."

"Sounds like he never arrived at the building."

Cameron dropped his head, pretending to bang it off the table.

"It was awful," he answered.

"What did Mr. Hune say?"

"He was a little shocked at my hand being in his face but I think he smiled. I mean I know he smiled because I finally moved my hand. And I asked, 'Are you smiling because you're happy, or are you smiling because you can't think of a nice way to tell me no?'"

"I wish I could have been there for this," Donna dreamed aloud. "*So, what did he say?*"

"That it wasn't his decision. That he was grateful I asked for his daughter's hand in marriage, if in fact, that was what I was doing, but that it is Andie's decision. He did say he'd be proud to call me a member of his family. "

"Well, that's good!"

"Yeah, it just...it was all weird and got weirder after that. Lots of silence. And stupid smiling. Thank God his wife wasn't there. It would have been even worse. I told you this was a bad idea."

Reaching across the table, Donna touched Cameron's hand.

"It's all good. You did the right thing. He knows it and I'm sure he appreciates it. And I'll take over from here. Give me his number, I want to call him and lay out the proposal for him."

Digging into his wallet, Cameron found a business card and penned Mr. Hune's personal office number on the back.

Donna assumed Mr. Hune would love her plans for the surprise proposal, but when she called, Henry not only brushed her off, he seemed perturbed that she called him on his private number.

"This isn't a good time," he spat out with abrupt swiftness.

"Sorry. When is?"

"Uhm, I got your number, I'll call you back."

And with that, he hung up.

Ouch.

To make it worse, Donna didn't hear from Mr. Hune for two days.

She debated calling back. More than once. If it had been anyone else, Donna would have pestered the hell out of him until she got him on the phone, gotten the answers she needed, and a commitment to help her pull off this surprise. But because it was Andie's dad, and Cam's boss, she opted to play nice but swore if she didn't hear back from him in three days, she would show up at his office first thing Monday morning.

When he finally returned her call, Donna told him who she was and how she knew Cameron-and by extension-Andie. Donna quickly interjected how close she and Andie had grown, compliments all around for everyone, before Henry cut her off, announcing he only had a few minutes until a meeting before questioning why Donna was calling him.

"I know you know Cam is going to ask Andie to marry him."

"If you know I know, then why are you telling me that information?"

Oh, that's the way you want to play it? Donna thought, taking a moment to respond.

"Because among the things you don't know is that I'm coordinating the event."

"Event? Now it's an event?"

"It's going to be when I get through with it. I've been told by your beautiful, loving daughter that you love her to the stars and back. But your responses going forward will help me believe that a little more. I need your help to make your daughter, who—let me say it again, you love to the stars and back—the happiest woman in the world."

Donna of course couldn't see it, but Henry smiled.

Enthusiastically laying out her plan, Henry listened without so much as a peep. Donna suspected he was working on another piece of business while letting her ramble on about "the great ideas" she'd come up with, including her pièce de résistance.

"This will mean so much to Andie, that I can promise you," Donna stated almost breathlessly since she was the only one doing the talking. "It's going to be something people talk about, your friends will remember, and Andie will never forget for the rest of her life," Donna announced, before dropping the bomb to see whether he was actually listening.

"And I'd like to do all this at your country club."

There was thick silence and then Henry responded with, "What?", sounding as if someone had punched him in the solar plexus.

"Good. You are listening," Donna answered slyly before adding, "I want to pull this all off at your club. Where you play golf, have drinks, do dinner. Andie's mentioned that a lot of your friends are members so it will make it the perfect place for the engagement. And Andie won't suspect anything if you invite her there for dinner..."

"Andie hates the club."

"Maybe she won't after this."

"Her mother and I have discussed Andie's eventual wedding and Caroline has always thought the club would be the perfect place for the wedding reception."

Biting her tongue, Donna wanted more than anything to snap back with utter snarkiness, "There is no way I'm planning a wedding reception at that country club. I've got grander plans than a country club for that day, a day your daughter will remember for the rest of her life," but instead opted to play the cards Henry dealt and use them against him.

"If your daughter hates the country club, your words, not mine, why would you even think of holding her wedding reception there?" she quizzed dryly.

"Fair question. Because her mother and I like the club."

"No offense, Mr. Hune, but neither you nor your wife is the one getting married. Holding the engagement party there is perfect. You get to have an event at your club, maybe even work a deal so Cameron isn't paying through the nose, which he is willing to do, but I don't want him to begin his married life in any more debt than he already has from school and let Andie pick the venue for her wedding reception. With my help, of course."

"Well," he continued, searching for a reason, "she's bound to know."

"Not if you follow my plan."

"I don't know. It sounds like a spectacle."

"It's not like I'm putting up the tallest building in the middle of Clayton," Donna fired back, knowing Henry designed the tallest building in the middle of the cherished St. Louis suburban city and that he was about to attempt to talk her out of something "too big" or "too flashy", which any wedding planner with more than a few weddings under her belt knew was parental code for "expensive".

Henry Hune again went silent on the other end of the line.

"I did something I don't think happens too often."

"What's that?" Mr. Hune asked.

"Rendered you completely speechless," Donna answered with a smile she hoped he could hear as well as the words she spoke.

After another uneasy moment of silence, Henry huffed out a single laugh as if he refused to allow Donna any more mileage out of this victory.

"Touché," was all he said.

Donna paused, signaling Henry that she had won this round. Finally, she huffed out a single syllable, "So...?"

"So....I'll talk to the club. And just so you know, I am going to ask Cameron about you."

"Feel free."

"Because I get the feeling we are going to be seeing a lot of you."

"You'll find me easy to work with, Mr. Hune. And never short on ideas."

"I hope you take as good care of my wallet as you do Cameron's when it comes to wedding expenses."

Donna laughed easily, relaxing ever so slightly.

"I promise. *If* you'll help me out here."

Mr. Hune wasn't the first difficult person Donna worked with while making wedding or even pre-wedding plans. She'd held the hands of plenty of crazy brides, penny-pinching parents, and detail-phobic grooms. While diplomacy wasn't something she would put in her top five attributes, she knew how to use her words as wrapping paper and a bow to get exactly what she wanted.

And from what she knew about the infamous Henry Hune, he fancied himself a problem-solver in life as much as at work. Donna prepared herself that it might not be Mrs. Hune who proved to be the jagged edge in the wedding plans, as Andie led her to believe. It might be Henry, a man who in business knew how to take straw and deliver gold, who was the potential stick in the mud. Donna opined that she might be a little too much like Henry, headstrong and obsequiously confrontational.

Their game of 'who can come up with the better solution' continued for almost another hour and left Donna feeling like she was trapped in a high-stakes real estate negotiation rather than planning a surprise engagement. Donna knew what was going on. Mr. Hune was testing her.

Not unlike Cameron but for a different reason, Donna never much liked tests as a kid and sure as hell hated them as an adult, especially in this situation when she knew she knew best. But if this was how she had to prove her metal to Andie's father, there was even more reason to win the battle. Because if she could win the battle, she would win the war.

Mr. Hune had already shown her the chink in his armor. Time. He was always crunched for precious minutes. All

Donna had to do was exhaust him by not caving. Instead, she compounded their conversation by seasoning it with more options, more ideas, new solutions, and opinions until she so overwhelmed Mr. Hune, he eventually sighed and said, "I'm late for my next meeting. Let me get back with you."

"Blowing me off and starting this all over again isn't going to change things, Mr. Hune."

Her laughing stopped him from hanging up on her.

"Okay, you wore me down," he admitted, "You feel that strongly, I'm going with your expertise. I promise I'll call my club and see if they will allow it."

"Thank you. You made a wise decision."

"Is it?" he asked, a smile in his voice.

"I think so. Look, if I needed a building designed, you'd be the man to go to. But for events such as these, this is my sandbox. You'll see. And you will be happy it's me planning your daughter's wedding because I'm going to prove to you that I can make things, big things, happen and get them done for a decent price," Donna avowed firmly before asking, "Trust me?"

He paused, silence escalating between them for a few seconds.

"I trust you," he responded.

Metaphorically, Donna and Henry shook hands and went to their respective corners, Henry realizing that Donna would use time against him, peppering him with options until the clock ran out or she got the answer she wanted.

Doing the happy dance, Donna said her goodbyes before hanging up.

But this event was going to have to be platinum in Mr. Hune's eyes. There couldn't be a hiccup. This wasn't one of those things they would laugh about later if it didn't impress. Donna was determined to make Mr. and Mrs. Hune coo over the entire evening. She would have it running like a Swiss watch.

Two days later, she rapped on Henry's office door. When he glanced up from marking the blueprints in front of him, he smiled at the pretty girl standing at his door, unsure.

"Your assistant had to use the ladies' room," she said.

Walking in, Donna extended her hand. "I'm having lunch with Cameron but I thought I would stick my head in and introduce myself so you could put a face with the voice."

Henry reached across his desk to shake her hand. His eyes took her in, assessing her, not giving away whether or not she was who he envisioned when she was on the phone with him.

"Am I being ambushed?" he asked.

"I come in peace," Donna joked. "It's just a hello. Yes, surprises come up all the time in the wedding and engagement planning business, but I'll take the bullet and then explain it to you covered in honey and smelling like lilac. But rest assured, Mr. Hune, I'm not an ambush type of girl. I'm the straightforward type."

Donna noticed something clicked in Henry's eyes as soon as she said it. Maybe it was being face-to-face, allowing him to see her as she spoke, but something certainly changed. Trust? Or at least some sort of registration that she was not out to get him. It allowed Donna to plant both heels on the bamboo floors of his office which she was reluctant to do in case one of them started shaking.

She was never intimidated by clients but Henry Hune was different. This entire situation was different. There was a personal investment on her part as this engagement and eventual wedding were for people she loved. There was history. Donna couldn't recognize it at the moment but she wanted Mr. Hune to not just trust her, but to like her.

"Well, it's good meeting you, I'm late for---"

"A meeting?" Donna piped in, cutting him off. Smiling she added, "You used that excuse on me before."

Their eyes locked. Henry didn't smile but steam didn't come out of his ears either and Donna took that as a good sign.

"Is it still an excuse if it's true?" he quizzed, his expression never changing.

"As long as you're not trying to shuffle me out the door, it's all good, Mr. Hune. We're going to be seeing a lot of each other, or at least talking, so I thought it was a good idea since I was here to get a little face time with you," she muttered as she headed for the door.

"I'm sure we will have plenty of chances, considering you're Cameron's friend."

"And Andie's," Donna responded as she turned toward him at the door.

He smiled back, recognizing this was a thrust and parry as Donna was sizing up the fight in his game. He knew better than to engage. Henry did what he did with Caroline; he smiled without another word until Donna understood that was her cue to exit. The only difference was that with Caroline, she was happy to exit, feeling she won. Donna knew better than that and was always willing to engage.

But as far as Donna was concerned, the connection had been made. And she was sure Henry Hune was now wondering just how the hell he was going to manage her. But she was also certain he would allow her to do what she needed to do to pull off a beautiful surprise engagement—and a spectacular wedding that their friends would be talking about for years.

On Donna's way out, Henry's assistant stopped her, giving her the name of the person to contact at Mr. Hune's country club, adding, "Mr. Hune will call them today so that your call won't be a surprise."

Always better to forgo the victory lap and make a graceful exit, Donna thought as she took strides down the hallway, a noticeable jig in her step.

As she climbed into her car, her phone rang. Cameron.

"I thought we were meeting at the restaurant?"

"We are."

"Andie's dad just told me you were in his office."

"I was. I wanted to meet him, so I stopped by. Heading to the restaurant now. I hate to sound like a schoolgirl but did he say anything about me?"

Cameron fell silent for a moment. "He said he likes aggressive people."

"I wasn't aggressive. I was...pleasant."

"He thinks you have a passion for what you do."

"I do."

"But don't do that again," Cameron said.

"Do what?"

"Drop by his office unannounced. At least without giving me a heads-up. First off, Andie could have seen you which would have blown this whole thing, and second, he's mercurial. Mr. Hune can love you one moment and snap your head off the next. I don't think he's happy about doing this at his club, which I told you he wouldn't be. He doesn't really love the place. He likes to golf, drink, eat, and leave. He's only agreeing to the place, well, because you think it will be a good place for this, which I'm still not sure about either. But just...be cool around him. He can be tough and I don't want you to be surprised if he gets tough with you."

"Do you think he is the only tough person I've dealt with, Cam? The only wealthy person? The only one who thinks they are right and I am wrong?"

"You know what I mean."

She did. Cameron was stuck at work with this guy, his future father-in-law, with no escape from any potential problems should they arise. He'd hear about it every day. Other potential sons-in-law don't have the same proximity to the man who will be ultimately paying for their wedding as Cameron did, and he wanted to keep the waters from getting choppy because his lifeboat at work was mighty small.

"I won't do it again without telling you first. Are you heading out to lunch now?"

"Getting in the elevator."

"I guess this means lunch is on me?" Donna half-joked.

"Yep," Cameron smiled as the elevator descended. "And I'm hungry."

FIFTEEN

B efore Mr. Hune had second thoughts, Donna contacted Peter Franlinn, the country club manager, as well as the caterers, to briefly outline her grand plan. They were either enormously respectful of Mr. Hune or very afraid of Mrs. Hune because they didn't bat an eye at Donna's plan, offering to facilitate the event, even with the mild insanity she had conjured up to make it a night to remember. They even took her on a tour of the club grounds, selecting a site for the party to happen. Fingers crossed the weather cooperated but other than that, this might actually be pretty cool if she said so herself.

Now Donna needed to entice another co-conspirator into the fold. She needed Caroline Hune.

With Mrs. Hune's husband a reluctant ally, Donna felt that if she could sweep Mrs. Hune into the surprise party inner circle there would be fewer bumps along the path to the wedding. Besides, after every tidbit Donna had heard about this woman, she wanted to meet her in the worst way. She had formed a vision without ever laying eyes on her and, if nothing else, wanted to see if what was in her mind's eye was accurate at all.

And while Mr. Hune was difficult to win over, Donna believed Mrs. Hune would be twice as precarious and persnickety because the woman wouldn't invest unless the outcome could cast her in a favorable light. So Donna had to spin the event into a compliment for the future mother-of-the-bride. It wouldn't be the first time.

Experience informed her that mothers and daughters were either best of friends or worst enemies. Donna's mother had been both at different points in her life but according to Andie, Mrs. Hune seemed to be more of an annoying distraction, a mitigating influence on her life, rather than a nurturing mother who had guided her daughter into adulthood.

At least, compared to her father.

Most young women at one point or another compare themselves to their mothers, for better but too often for worse. Love-hate. But it perplexed Donna that Andie didn't, considering it was her mother who came from wealth and status, not her father. Which made it all the more intriguing for Donna to sit down with Mrs. Hune.

As Donna stepped into the Hune home, her hand extended to Mrs. Hune, she stifled a sharp gasp as if jabbed between the ribs. The put-together, stylish woman with her blonde hair pulled back tightly, highlighting her cheekbones, was instantly recognizable. The cool blonde who attended the weddings with the handsome, gray-maned "favorite uncle".

A man who was certainly not Henry Hune.

Her head now spinning, Donna could feel her teeth clench, a smile frozen on her lips as she followed Caroline down the foyer, stumbling slightly as if all the blood had shot to her brain and her legs were wobbly from lack of circulation.

From Caroline's demeanor, Donna could not ascertain whether she recognized her as she led her, in silence, to a formal sitting room most people don't use in their homes but once or twice a year.

Caroline didn't give anything away, her coolness keeping whatever was going on hidden well behind her eyes. It threw Donna off her game; she needed to sit down before she fell down. Donna knew she had to watch what she said even more than she had planned. But holding this in and tempering her words would be infinitely harder; this revelation just brought it to a different, much headier level.

As if she didn't have reason enough to feel her skin was crawling, after sitting with Caroline for thirty minutes, Donna concluded why Andie seldom spoke of her mother and when she did, it was less than flattering. While Andie's father was cagey in a business sense, her mother was absolutely what Donna previously surmised from Andie's comments, but hoped wasn't true, that Caroline Hune was wildly egocentric.

But what really pissed Donna off was that Caroline offered nothing as Donna entertained her with all the plans for the engagement surprise. Usually, the mother of the bride would be as effusive and excited as Donna, adding their own panache to the plans. Caroline's silence felt judgmental as if it were a vague comment on Donna's work.

And knowing she would have to see this woman more than she would like tightened a knot in her stomach. *How do I keep this secret? Especially from Andie. Is it even a secret? What's this woman's deal?* All Donna really knew was that she didn't want to be part of it.

Yet, she was, without volunteering.

When the few sentences Caroline did utter began with "If it were my engagement..." Donna knew she didn't gain an ally; she gained an exasperation. Caroline Hune was a woman not only entirely narcissistic but who believed what she was saying was a bellwether for all of humanity.

Making this meeting more uncomfortable, every so often Donna believed she saw a flicker of recognition from Caroline. Not much scared Donna, but for some reason this did. Caroline came off too self-absorbed to notice "the help", so Donna felt secure that Caroline never paid her a lick of attention or caught her staring at her and the handsome, gray-haired man. Donna didn't want Caroline's eyes to widen in realization. That would screw up so much. Whatever she did or didn't do could come between her and Andie, manifesting in very weird ways. Secrets always do.

That confrontation could be saved for a later date, Donna thought. *Like never.*

Recognizing that Caroline was used to speaking at people not to them, Donna accepted that that was exactly what was happening; that Mrs. Hune would weigh every aspect of this engagement event as something that would reflect on her. Even from the little Caroline contributed, the more Donna believed this beautiful, well-put-together woman was insanely insecure and overtly concerned with appearances and how others perceived her.

This bitch is made of sugar glass, Donna thought, *and yet she is still cheating on her husband as if people wouldn't judge that above all else!*

Even more interesting to Donna was that Mrs. Hune made little attempt to hide her insecurities. Donna made absolutely sure no one saw the chinks in her armor. But not Caroline. She didn't seem to care. Nor did she ask Donna a single question about herself. Something uncommon in these situations. People hiring Donna wanted to know her. At least the glamourous aspects Donna enjoyed showing off about herself. Caroline didn't seem to have the time or interest to be focused on other people; she just let her selfish nature shine through.

"I'm relieved you're handling this. My daughter and I, we don't see eye-to-eye on much, which if you're really as close as you say, you already know. She never misses a chance to tell people what a horrible mother I am," Caroline said, her eyes drifting off as if trying to understand why her daughter unjustly felt that way about her. "So it's all the better to have a neutral third party making the arrangements. I don't get that girl. More like her father than me. But they've always been close."

Donna didn't have a clue how to respond to that except to continue to smile and nod at Caroline's never-ending waving of her opinionated, myopic freak flag.

Which made it even more confusing for Donna what Mr. Hune could possibly see in this woman. Andie had explained it but Donna knew from working with families that every child had a vantage point on the parents, and their marriage, good or bad, was what the children measured their relationships against.

Certainly, Caroline Hune was beautiful. Donna could see it was her cheekbones Andie inherited. But from her, albeit limited, interaction with Mr. Hune, Donna couldn't for the life of her grasp what connected him to this woman. Maybe thirty years ago she was different; more carefree, less concerned with image, more engaged and active?

Actually faithful.

Who knew? Maybe he loved that she brought him status to couple with his obvious ambition. Something had to connect them, and something more had kept them together all these years. But damned if Donna could figure it out. Having been around enough couples making the biggest commitment of their lives, Donna could state with absolute certainty that there was absolutely no logic to falling in love.

She believed if there were logic to it, she would have uncovered it by now.

She often felt the couples for whom she had created "the best day of their lives" were utterly mismatched. And yet, they wouldn't be hiring her if they weren't getting married. For better or worse. For richer or poorer. There were a few times she thought with solid certainty, *these two won't last a year!*

The rest, despite her inability to sometimes understand what brought them this far in a relationship, had a spark, even if at times volatile; it was a connection.

Perhaps she would sense it when she saw Mr. and Mrs. Hune together? Or maybe it had become a marriage of convenience and they lived private, separate lives. That would make sense. Maybe their faith made divorce out of the question. Donna didn't know nor did she know what to say. Did Andie know? This was different than a usual wedding because her best friend was marrying into this mess.

By the time Donna exited her home, Mrs. Hune was at least not going to stand in her way. She wouldn't be an ounce of help, but at least Donna didn't get the sense that Caroline would be a thorn in her side. She would stand on the sideline and cheerlead, probably from somewhere comfortable. Rah, rah, sis boom bah! Perfect, actually. *My type of gal*, Donna thought, a slim smile sliding onto her lips as she walked out.

Parents were often the hardest to deal with because they, most especially Midwesterners, held onto their cash with a vice grip. And if you wanted to know what you were going to get in a bride, Donna believed you had to feel out her mother and father first. The bride usually followed the mother's emotional lead and rebelled against the father's financial plan.

In Andie's case, she was one of the rare birds who, instead of becoming her parents, which most young adults start morphing into much to their own self-loathing, she reacted to her parents; cherry-picking their best attributes and running away from those she could never imagine herself turning into.

That took guts.

And it was also very hard because most people don't see themselves slipping down that slope until they hate who they've become. Any woman who could scoop up Cameron was someone who was more aware than most. Maybe that was why she and Donna became fast friends.

This engagement surprise had to be right. It could not disappoint. From the engagement party to the wedding night, this was going to be Donna's biggest and best. For Cameron. For Andie. And to let Mr. and Mrs. Hune know that when they hired her, they hired the best.

No pressure. No pressure.

SIXTEEN

I t's going to work. It has to work!

That was Donna's new mantra and she muttered it continually to herself, thousands of times over the past three weeks, as the epic engagement party had grown into a Jenga tower threatening to topple over at any moment. Accommodating the Hunes' invitation list alone had been monumental. Even Cameron was surprised at the number of people his future in-laws added to the party, making the day more about them than Andie.

And making it impossible for Cam to afford.

"Shouldn't this engagement party be just immediate family and our friends?" he asked, wishing to hear the answer he wanted, but knowing he wouldn't.

"You keep telling yourself that," Donna chuckled. "They never are. Parents always make these things about them. There's a lot to be said for eloping. But trust me, I'll contain it. They're going to hate me but I'll contain it."

In spite of feeling crappy, with cramps and a slight fever, which probably meant another urinary tract infection, something Donna was prone to, she put on a brave face and ambushed the Hunes just after dinner, asking for help paring down the guest list to something manageable.

Besides, it was her chance to see them together. Something she'd been craving.

"This isn't the wedding, you can invite as many as you like to that, but this is the engagement and should be crowded with Andie's and Cameron's friends and a few of your closest friends who know Andie. We have to trim your list," insisted Donna over the Hunes' objections.

Of course, getting them to agree wasn't as easy as laying out the logic of why it was the smart thing to do. They spent the better part of the next three hours, Donna wishing she was home living in her mess, rather than in the Hunes' immaculately clean and organized study, cutting the guest list from over two hundred people down to under a mere one hundred, allowing Andie and Cameron an equal amount for their friends.

The outdoor space at the club where the event was to take place was certainly large enough to house a massive tent. Donna insisted on one in case of weather, which in St. Louis is never predictable. As everyone who lives there knows: if you don't like the weather in St. Louis, wait fifteen minutes, it'll change.

But Donna would have to give the kitchen a number so that appetizers and a buffet could be arranged and the bartenders would have enough liquor for the night. She didn't like packing a space to capacity; she believed there should be room for people to mill about, relax and enjoy themselves. Andie and Cameron were going to have to make their rounds and thank everyone, so it couldn't be too vast or too intimate.

"Surprises grow exponentially more difficult to pull off with every name on a guest list," Donna stated, her eyes staying on Caroline. "People have big mouths, friends don't think before hinting or completely spilling the beans, an odd person out of place or unable to cover in a conversation could ruin what is supposed to be a blindside."

Donna held her gaze on Caroline so long that she looked away. Donna liked that. And even though a few times, when Caroline protested about taking names off the guest list, Donna wanted to end the debate by asking about the gray-haired guy. As much as it made her itch not to, she knew she could never do that to Mr. Hune. Never.

Later that evening, sitting in the tub surrounded by bubbles, trying to relax away the pain in her abdomen, Donna reluctantly picked up her phone when it rang. Cameron. She would have loved not to answer, exhausted from her evening at the Hune home, but she knew he wouldn't sleep until she gave him the news that she had reigned in Andie's parents and cut their list down to ninety.

"You're bothering me during a bubble bath," she barked, not even saying 'hello' first.

"Was it that bad?"

"Wasn't easy. They're crazy. Not the craziest I've ever dealt with but..."

"I warned you. Two hundred people on their list alone. Who do they think their daughter is marrying, heir to the Busch fortune?"

"I got it down to eighty-three by the time we were done. Told them they could invite whoever they wanted to the wedding since that was coming out of their pocket. But this should be close friends. Seriously, who has ninety close friends much less two hundred?"

"I do. On Facebook," Cameron joked.

"Great. I'll be sure to add them to the list for the wedding. But I did what I set out to do, which was talk her parents out of their quotient of crazy. And I succeeded. Strangely, I'm getting to like the Hunes. Well, Mr. Hune."

"You don't like Andie's mom?" Cameron asked. Donna was unsure whether he was being sarcastic or not.

"I just...she's..." Donna paused, couching what she should say considering what she knew she shouldn't. Donna's suspicions about Caroline weren't something she ever wanted to say to Cameron because he would be required to tell the woman he loved.

"Let's just call her a very complicated person. And not in the way I wished she was," Donna flatly added.

"That's an understatement," Cameron chuckled, not picking up the intention behind Donna's words.

"Compared with some of the parents of brides I've worked with, they're not as stubborn as some of the others. They caved to reality which isn't as common as you might think," Donna quickly asserted, opting to steer the conversation away from what would be a difficult conversation, even though she could practically hear Cameron roll his eyes. She knew he didn't view them that way. They submitted a ridiculously long list of people and if he didn't have Donna, Cameron was acutely aware he would probably be cajoled into inviting every last one of the people on their original list. Ka-ching! Ka-ching!

"That's why you make the big bucks," Cameron chided his best friend.

"I never make the big bucks. I make a few bucks. Most of the time for the hours I put in, I could work at Ted Drewes and make more money. I just love what I do."

Determined to make this one of those times, in spite of the almost daily texts from Caroline Hune, always about something trivial, Donna relished texting Mrs. Hune back "If two of your friends have shellfish allergies, then they shouldn't eat the shrimp".

It became increasingly clear to Donna how someone as direct and big-picture as Andie could be driven crazy by her mother who was all about the image and none of the substance.

Still, Donna couldn't help but be fascinated by her best friend's future mother-in-law. It would seem that, if you peeled back the layers, you would find simply more layers of nothing to peel, but Donna saw it differently. She recognized that, underneath the veneer of selfishness, was a human car wreck. Donna would never know what caused it, nor was it any of her business, but it allowed her to cut Caroline a little slack. But just a little, because she knew that whatever injured Caroline, the fallout spread to everyone in her life.

The closer this engagement inched, the more Donna's excitement blossomed. She loved surprises as long as she wasn't on the receiving end. And creating this surprise in cahoots with her best friend made it even more sublime. Donna was positive that Andie would love it. How could she not? The man she loved was going to pop the question.

Even if the tent caught fire, she would still have that amazing ring on her finger and be in full wedding planning mode. There are very few women who do not get caught up in that and Donna already knew Andie was ready, willing, and able.

The night finally arrived and Andie almost derailed everything when she phoned her parents and tried to beg off having dinner with them, harrumphing about how she had a long day at work, fighting the union on some project they were working on, continuing on with her father about all the work she still had on her desk that she had to dive into the next day. But Mr. Hune insisted. And when her father insisted, Andie felt obligated.

"Just dinner. Then I'm heading home," Andie stated flatly, before sighing to let him know how really pissed off she was about it.

But at least she was coming and Cameron could stop sweating, which was the only thing about the phone call Mr. Hune enjoyed.

Both her parents and Cameron talked to Andie on her way over. It was a tag team; each calling to make sure she wouldn't pull a Houdini at the last moment and not show up. Cameron being the last person she talked to—while he was standing next to Donna on the club grounds—got the brunt of her displeasure about having to eat dinner with her parents at a place she disliked, around people she disliked even more.

Cameron kept trying to salvage her mood by slapping a happy face on the call, but clearly from what Donna could hear Andie had a far different emoji to represent the evening she was sure she was going to have. The word "sucks" was peppered in liberally. She had to endure it when all she wanted to do was go home and take her shoes off.

"She is royally pissed," he stated to Donna after he hung up.

"Then her swing from angry to elated when the big moment happens will be all the grander."

"That's putting a positive spin on things," Cameron added, a little less giddy about Andie's upcoming reaction.

The party under the tent was in full swing when Cameron received word that Andie had arrived and was with her parents in the dining room. And according to his spy inside she was not looking all that pleased about it.

"You wanted to rock her world. Well, this is gonna do it," Donna shared with absolute certainty.

Even though she was ordering dinner, unbeknownst to Andie, she was not getting served. Any hope for a quick meal with the folks leached away with each passing moment as she eyed the tables around her getting served but nothing was reaching their table. Her parents' pre-planned chatter didn't interest her in the least. And though, knowing Andie, it made her somewhat suspicious because she could pretty much talk about anything, especially with her father, she was too preoccupied with her own agitation to realize she was being played.

Mr. and Mrs. Hune were quite adept at this game of subterfuge, something that didn't surprise Donna. They'd had lots of practice at their country club, with the phony smiles, handshakes, and hugs. The more Donna thought about it, the more she surmised that Caroline was a pro at playing a role and relished slowly crawling under her daughter's skin only because, under these circumstances, she would be forgiven for it.

According to her man inside who whispered a play-by-play into Donna's ear, her plan was working exceptionally well.

"Showtime!" Donna said into her iPhone, giving him permission to cue Mr. Hune.

She listened as her guy, dressed as a waiter, told Mr. Hune their meal had been delayed because of Mrs. Hune's special order. And that it was going to take another thirty minutes to prepare. She could hear Mr. Hune pretend to get worked up and Andie sigh.

"Forget dinner," Mr. Hune said, agitation rising in his voice. "My daughter is in an awful mood, and we're hungry. Just have them bring my car upfront."

The faux-waiter then relayed that their cars had been moved to the rear parking lot because of a private party and it would take at least fifteen minutes to retrieve them.

"Do you have the spare set of keys, Caroline?" Henry asked his wife.

"Yes."

"We'll get it ourselves. Andie, come with us, we'll drive you to your car."

"You and Mom are going to walk? Seriously, Mom is going to walk? In heels?" Andie muttered incredulously, causing Donna to burst out laughing.

"Yes, we're going to walk. Let's go," she heard Mr. Hune respond sharply.

Donna signaled her team to turn down the lights in the tent and then pointed to Cameron.

"You're on," she announced to Cameron, giving him a kiss on the cheek.

Cameron jogged through the waiting crowd, friends, and family patting him on the back as he passed, like a quarterback heading into the game. He was terrified, for a few reasons, and was taking deep breaths as he headed into the darkness behind the tent.

After a few minutes, Mr. Hune, still pretending to be furious, arrived at the tent with his wife and daughter. Donna had instructed him to keep talking so she could hear him approach. He was complaining about them moving his car to the rear parking lot when a party was going on. Once Donna saw him, she spoke softly into her microphone.

"Hit it!"

Suddenly, behind the tents, carnival lights illuminated the area, almost blindingly so. Donna could see Andie cover her eyes as she and her parents froze in their tracks. Andie stared, confused, as she looked at a one-hundred-foot Ferris wheel looming overhead.

Suddenly a canned, tinny melody began to play from the Ferris wheel and it started to move. Sitting in a seat, holding on for dear life, and sweating profusely, Cameron rose into the sky until his chair was at the apex of the ride.

The confusion on Andie's face grew as she stared up, not sure she was seeing what she was seeing, especially knowing Cameron's phobia of heights.

Slowly Cameron stood in the rocking chair, steadying himself.

"I am in love with you, Andrea Hune! I have been in love with you for a long time now!" Cameron called down to her as her father and mother locked their arms in Andie's, holding onto her. Their smiles gleamed in the carnival lights as everyone in the tents stepped out to join them, shocking Andie even more.

"And I didn't know how to show you just how much I love you but I'm hoping you can understand because I am standing up here, WAY, WAY up here, to express my love to you. To show you just the lengths I will go to, to have you in my life."

The blinking lights illuminated the tears in Andie's eyes.

"I am terrified. Not of being up here...okay, I am, I'm really scared, but I'm more scared of living my life without you. So, I have something I've been wanting to ask you."

Though she couldn't see it from where she stood, Cameron opened the jewelry box and displayed the engagement ring.

"Okay, light it up..." Donna whispered into her microphone.

Four words lit up across the circumference of the Ferris wheel.

WILL YOU MARRY ME????

Donna could see Mr. and Mrs. Hune tighten their hold on Andie as her knees nearly buckled.

"Will you marry me, Andrea Hune?" Cameron yelled. "Please say yes or I'm never coming down!"

Everyone laughed as if on cue, genuinely and supportively.

Andie gently pulled free of her parents' embrace and took a few steps toward the Ferris wheel.

"I know what it took for you to do this from up there! But that's not the reason I'm saying this. I'm saying this because I can't imagine my life without you anymore," Andie said, backhanding tears from her cheeks. "I love you. And I would love to marry you!"

A round of cheers and applause rang out. Cameron bolted forward, rocking the chair, losing his balance. Everyone gasped as he lurched forward in the metal seat, quickly grabbing hold of the side of the chair. Steadying himself, Cameron chuckled slightly, nervously, taking a petrified breath.

"Get me down to my girl, please..." he called down, plopping in the seat and holding on as the Ferris wheel revolved again, the music playing as he descended. Andie rushed to meet Cameron as he gently dropped toward her. A carney opened the safety bar and escorted her into the chair with Cameron where they kissed to more applause. Again, the music played as the Ferris wheel took them up in the air together to the applause of friends and family—the majority of whom Cameron had never met.

Cameron waited until they were at the top before slipping the ring onto Andie's finger and kissing her again. She hugged him, holding him tightly as the Ferris wheel spun, this time with the two of them kissing lovingly, going for a ride on the Ferris wheel, like two kids at a carnival.

Overwhelmed with emotion, Donna's eyes filled with tears at the palpable love between her oldest friend and her newest. She thought to herself that maybe she wasn't as jaded as she liked to pretend, but this almost never happened.

When Mrs. Hune gave her a surprised, side-eyed glance, Donna smiled stiffly and said, "Wait until their wedding. I'll be a puddle."

"I won't cry," Caroline responded almost proudly. "Certainly not at their wedding."

"Because it's a happy occasion?" Donna asked.

"I have my makeup done professionally. I'm not ruining that. I'll wait until I get home, have a bourbon, and then a good cry," she answered in an almost clinical tone as if what she was saying should be how everyone handled their emotions.

"I have to give you credit," Mr. Hune jumped in, causing Donna to turn from Caroline, realizing Mr. and Mrs. Hune were actually holding each other tightly, "This is about as beautiful a moment as we could ever want for our daughter. Thank you."

"Thanks to both of you for helping me out," Donna responded.

"I can't wait to see what you do for the wedding," Mrs. Hune added.

"Going to be hard to top this," Mr. Hune said, nodding in agreement with his wife.

"No Ferris wheels. But it will be gorgeous."

They both hugged Donna, which surprised her although it was rather awkward. Soon the Hunes were whisked off into the crowd of well-wishers as Donna turned to the Ferris wheel to watch Cameron and Andie descend, still holding tightly to each other. Andie held up the ring, admiring it in the blinking lights of the ride, before kissing Cameron again.

Donna smiled. This was exactly what she wanted for Cam. And Andie

Damn, I sure know how to throw an engagement party! Donna thought to herself.

SEVENTEEN

C ameron and Andie barely let go of each other all night. Andie was overwhelmed, especially as she introduced Cameron to virtual strangers whose names she couldn't remember. Regardless, she was walking on clouds and every time Donna passed her, she whispered "thank you" and gave Donna's hand a squeeze.

It wasn't hard to see that Andie's gratefulness was completely genuine. If Donna didn't love her before, she did at this moment. And for Andie, to have Donna pull off what she pulled off without her knowing felt like a miracle, but even more to get Cameron to agree to the Ferris wheel. Andie knew that took some real convincing.

It was clear by everyone's comments that the night was an overwhelming triumph. Donna doled out business cards like she was dealing Blackjack on the Casino Queen. Everyone wanted to know who put this together, and how Donna made Cameron face his fear of heights to prove his love to Andie. The guests felt that they witnessed an event. That's exactly what Donna wanted for Cameron and Andie.

As Andie circulated the tent, thanking the guests for coming, Donna caught sight of her kissing someone on the cheek. As Andie backed away from the embrace, Donna's eyes stayed on the man. It was the handsome gray-haired man Donna had seen at the two out-of-town weddings with Mrs. Hune. He was here. Vacillating between being relieved and being anxious, hoping he was a close friend or relative of Caroline's and not a family friend or former neighbor, Donna watched as Cameron joined Andie and was introduced to the man. They shook hands, pleasantries passing between them. Donna waited until

Cameron walked away, moving to another person to thank before she crossed through the tent and walked over near him. After Cameron thanked a couple of co-workers for coming, Donna slid in next to him with a smile.

"Pretty great night, huh?"

"Yeah. Amazing. Thank you!" Cameron responded.

"I'm thrilled it worked out as well as it did," Donna answered, giving Cameron a squeeze. "Question...that guy Andie just introduced you to, the gray-haired guy. I've seen him at a couple of weddings recently."

"He's part of the moneyed crowd here. They all know each other," Cameron answered.

"What's his name?"

"I think Andie said it was Hal. Hal Something...uhm, don't know if he said what he does for a living. Too many new people, too many names."

"Did Andie say how she knew him?"

"What, you want to date the guy? That's what you want, some older guy with a lot of dough?" Cameron fired back.

"No!" Donna reacted quickly. "Just...this is the third time I've seen him this year. Which, while I agree is not a complete surprise in St. Louis, I usually don't see people at weddings that often, especially out-of-town weddings, without kids of their own who are getting married or have a ton of friends getting married."

"Let's go talk to him, you can ask," Cameron said, taking Donna's hand.

She quickly wrestled lose from Cameron's fingers. "No, no...not that big a deal. Just thought he might have said."

"Hal!" Cameron quickly waved to the gray-haired man before Donna could stop him.

Hal smiled in Cameron's direction. Donna froze, wanting to protest, but knowing if she did, it would only put a laser on the moment as Hal strode toward Cameron in an easy gait, a smile widening on his face.

"Hal, this is Donna. She's my lifelong friend, I love her like a sister, she put this together," Cameron said, making introductions.

Hal stuck out his hand toward Donna. "Hello, Donna, lifelong friend, and sister from another mister," he said, his voice an octave lower than Donna expected, making the awful joke slightly more palatable.

"Hi, a pleasure to meet you," Donna said, offering nothing more.

"Donna told me she's seen you at a few out-of-town weddings in the last year," Cam added, trying to initiate a conversation.

Hal's eyes focused on Donna, trying to make the connection. He nodded briefly before speaking, "Everyone I know seems to have a son or a daughter getting married. I do get invited to quite a lot of them, so that doesn't surprise me. I enjoy the ceremonies out of town because I can turn them into mini-vacations."

"A lot of people do that," Donna inserted.

"Why not? You're usually somewhere beautiful, surrounded by friends...why not extend it a couple extra days or so?" Hal agreed with another winning smile.

"Do you have kids, Mr....?" Donna asked bravely, trying to tear through the lining a little more.

"Dennison, Hal Dennison. And no, I don't. Which is one of the reasons I'm surprised at the number of invitations I receive. Why these kids would want this old guy around, God knows. But I've known so many of them growing up. I feel like everyone's favorite uncle. My sister has six kids, my brother has six as well. So, I know all of them, their friends, most of the friends' parents...and I've met many more over the course of my life."

"What do you do, Hal?" Cameron questioned, thankfully staying away from the ubiquitous question, "Where'd you go to high school?", which was too often asked when St. Louisans met for the first time, to suss out both their mutual acquaintances from those schools, but also social standing.

Hal smiled. Donna quickly assessed that he found it amusing that Cameron didn't know who he was. Donna didn't either. Who was he?

"Now I do motivational speaking. I coached swimming at UCLA for many years. Assistant-coached two Olympic teams. Actually, swam in the Olympics in Seoul, and before you ask, no, never medaled. Was a decent swimmer but a better coach. But since coming back to St. Louis, I've written a few books and speak around the world. I speak a lot here, high schools, colleges, businesses large and small. Next engagement, I'll invite you."

"I'd love that!" Cameron jumped in with a smile. "Wow, I didn't know the Hunes knew someone famous!"

Hal laughed. "Hardly famous. Infamous, maybe. Not famous."

"We're monopolizing your time," Donna said, smiling warmly. "I'm sure your wife or girlfriend is looking for you."

"Solo this evening," Hal nodded, sizing up Donna's statement. "You two are the busy ones tonight."

"I guess that was my polite way of saying I have a ton of things still to take care of," Donna responded with a chuckle that wasn't entirely convincing, "But it was great meeting you. I'm sure I'll be seeing you at other weddings soon, including Cam and Andie's," she added, leaning on Cameron's shoulder. "And hopefully one out of town, somewhere fabulous!"

Hal laughed. "Look forward to it."

Donna walked away, leaving Cameron talking with Hal for a bit longer. Pulling out her phone, she turned, taking one more long, hard look at them. Usually next to Cameron, other guys pale, but not Hal Dennison, motivational speaker, ex-Olympian, and coach. He was ridiculously good-looking and you could see he was still in excellent shape under his expensive Tom Ford suit. Good taste.

Was Caroline Hune having an affair with this guy because she thought he was better than Henry Hune? Was he really all that more successful? Henry was handsome, actually more refined, so being better-looking was up for interpretation. Could that be it? Was Hal unobtainable, even for Caroline? Or the perfect match, equally aloof and self-involved? This guy could easily attract women; what would he want with someone like Caroline who, while certainly beautiful, was not exactly low maintenance?

Googling him, Hal popped up. The books, the swimming, some photos from back in the day when he was an Olympic swimmer.

Wow, yeah, he was even more gorgeous then, Donna thought, bringing a smile to her lips, as she quickly perused his Wikipedia page.

"He's a remarkable man," Donna heard from behind her. Turning, Caroline was standing a few feet behind her, near the edge of a table, her hand toying with the centerpiece.

"Cameron?" Donna asked, even though she knew exactly who Caroline was talking about.

Caroline smiled, not liking games and knowing that was exactly what Donna was playing.

"Did you think I didn't recognize you the first time I saw you?" Caroline asked. "The weddings you've put together have been special. Remarkable, actually. That's a gift. Everyone asks who you are, including me."

Donna didn't thank her for the compliment.

"I have been to a few that were magical," Caroline slipped in. "I find the events you put together are often better than the people actually getting married."

"Ouch!" Donna said, almost laughing at the harshness.

"It's true," Caroline said without an ounce of self-reflective humor, leaning towards Donna and adding conspiratorially, "and some of the parents of those people are here tonight."

Caroline moved to face Donna so neither was looking in Hal's direction.

"I've known him a long time. We actually swam here on the country club team when we were kids," Caroline remarked, before pointedly saying, "he's my Cameron."

Donna hung Caroline's final statement for a long moment, weighing whether or not Caroline was begging for some understanding from Donna over an affair.

"I'm really uncomfortable keeping secrets. I'm not very good at it. And I love Cameron and your daughter," Donna stated. "Not telling either of them what I know has been really uncomfortable and well, I hate it. And both of them would be pissed at me if they knew I kept this a secret."

"Did you do that for me?" Caroline asked.

"I did it because what I assume is the truth would hurt Andie. She loves her father. And knowing that you're...doing whatever you're doing with Mr. Dennison, would infuriate her. And I'm sure your husband as well. I don't know your marriage, and that is not my business. Point is, I don't know you or Mr. Hune all that well, or whatever arrangement you two have. Again, not my business. But it's put me in a terribly uncomfortable position. I hope you understand that."

Caroline turned in Hal's direction. He was talking with a couple over near the entrance to the tent. Dejection, years of it, wiped across her face as if she were removing all her makeup with a thick towel.

"Hal...beautiful, smart, wonderful Hal, could never accept himself. Fifty-three years old, and still can't. He still thinks people don't know," Caroline said. "What that Wikipedia page you've been looking at on your phone doesn't tell you is why Hal left coaching at UCLA."

Donna's eyes scanned the tent, making sure neither Cameron nor Andie nor Mr. Hune, were not striding in their direction.

"He and one of his college swimmers...had this thing. The young man wanted something more permanent, more intimate I suppose. Hal has difficulty in that area," Caroline said.

Damn, if you're saying that about someone else, you must be the iceberg the Titanic hit! Donna thought.

"Fearing everyone would find out that he was gay and in whatever kind of relationship he was in with one of his swimmers, he quit and moved back here. Can you imagine leaving Los Angeles, where you're a bit of a celebrity, where no one gives a whit about your sexuality, quitting a job you love, a sport that's been a part of you since you were a child, and coming back to prehistorically provincial St. Louis? That's how much Hal dislikes himself. He told me once he thought it would be easier here, he'd be less tempted. It's very sad."

"It is."

"So, when he gets invited to a wedding, or actually any event, I am his plus one. And yes, Henry knows all about it. He's fine with it. We've actually tried fixing Hal up, hoping that age would open him up and allow him to accept himself and find some happiness with someone else but..." her voice trailed off. "My daughter does not know. I mean, she knows he's gay, I think everyone who is in Hal's orbit knows, but she doesn't know I travel with him so he can keep up the façade he thinks is working for him."

Donna felt there was something left unsaid and it showed in her eyes. Caroline looked away from what she felt was a judgmental gaze and turned to peer at the crab apple tree in the front yard that just started to bloom.

"He loves me," Caroline almost whispered.

Donna shifted uncomfortably. "Why are you telling me this?

"Because you've seen us. Actually, you've been watching us," Caroline stated accusatorily. "And I love him."

She then turned back and met Donna's eyes.

"I know. You don't hide it," Donna said without an ounce of fear in her voice.

"So, you've judged us," Caroline hardened.

It took every ounce of decency in Donna to force a smile as she continued to shift her weight from foot to foot.

"You're lucky, Mrs. Hune. You have something many people want. You married someone who absolutely adores you. When Mr. Hune looks at you, he lights up. You know how rare that is? You two created a beautiful child who has grown into the most incredible woman. Yet, you pine for something that can never be. I'm sure Mr. Dennison loves you but, well, to be frank, so what? He can't be Mr. Hune. He can't give you what Mr. Hune can. And has. Never ceases to amaze me how people always want what they can't have. Especially when they have so much."

"Considering your relationship with Cameron, I thought of all people, you would understand," Caroline responded defensively.

This pissed Donna off. She nearly laughed but swallowed it, speaking sharply, "I love Cam. But I'm not in love with him. Andie is. And she's going to marry him. That's what people do when they're in love. And be sure, love...real love...takes effort. I see it in every couple I work for that truly loves each other. Like Cam and Andie. So, let's focus on their wedding. Which I intend to make a thousand times more incredible than tonight."

Though Caroline didn't like the curtain being pulled back, she barely reacted. She had trained herself since she was young to keep criticism at an arm's length. Even when the truth scared her to death.

Waving at an exiting couple, Caroline spoke to Donna without even glancing at her. "I admire Henry. He's a wonderful man. A great father. Which Andie needs considering she got me as a mother," Caroline said softly. "Only reason I had a child is because Henry wanted to. I did it for him. Crazy, I guess. Maybe not, I mean Andie is remarkable."

Donna refused to say another word. She'd already overstepped. It was clear that Caroline needed to tell someone this, tonight. A secret that haunted her life. And a near-stranger was far safer than a pseudo-friend. As she turned again and watched Hal, Caroline's aura shifted. Almost cruelly. "We would have been perfect. Henry and I look perfect, but…" Caroline spoke in a whisper. Caroline took a step away, moving almost in front of Donna. She turned her head so Donna could hear her as Caroline forced a smile; a show for anyone watching.

"I'm dubious about my daughter marrying Cameron," Caroline said. "I know he's your friend but he's not who I would have picked for my daughter. Marriage is about a lot more than love. My daughter won't accept that there are other aspects. It will catch up to her. And when it does, Cameron will have you to lean on. Who will Andie have?"

Donna wanted to respond but there was no point in continuing what had already turned insidiously negative.

Turning once again to Donna, Caroline pursed her lips, a face that Donna could only assume was something Caroline did when she felt she overstepped. "I'm sorry. Please don't tell Andie or Cameron what we talked about," Caroline implored. "Not that I'm wrong. But I keep betraying everyone."

Caroline's last comment floored Donna. She was happy Caroline was looking back at Hal when she uttered it because Donna couldn't hide her shock. She recognized that Caroline's love was very select. Whatever capacity she had, she needed to spend on herself, Donna thought. Unfair, probably. But from everything she'd seen and heard, Donna was sure she wasn't far off about a woman who suffered from unrequited love and lifelong disappointment.

"Certainly," Donna answered Caroline.

"And for the record, not that I need to explain myself to you..." Caroline added, "I love Henry. And I love my daughter. Maybe not in an idyllic manner, but I do. I may not be the model candidate to be anyone's wife or mother, but that doesn't mean I'm a shrew either. One day you might come to understand that about me."

As Caroline walked away, Donna sighed in relief. Holy hell... Donna thought, focusing again on herself and realizing how drained she was, what was that about?

She hurt, pain from lack of sleep, and cramps where she didn't even know she had muscles. Donna vowed to sleep for three days and then meet with Andie so they could start planning the wedding. But she had never felt so tired, not even after back-to-back weddings in different locations.

Donna knew she didn't give her body enough time off, always running from event to event, in town, out of town, going, going, going, planning, planning, planning, and the stress of the actual events knocked her down like she'd been punched by a prizefighter.

"You're astonishing," Andie said from behind her as she pulled up a chair and plopped into it, putting her feet up on another.

"I like when things go off without a hitch," Donna chuckled.

"There wasn't one tonight. Not that I saw."

"There were a few but I fixed them quick."

Andie took Donna's hand, holding it.

"I can't thank you enough for making this happen. First, I was surprised. Which doesn't happen too often. Completely and totally blindsided. And how the heck did you talk him into getting on a Ferris wheel?"

"That was the hardest part," Donna answered.

"I can only imagine."

"But I knew you would get it. I knew if I could get him up there it would mean something."

"It did. He faced a fear for me, that's pretty awesome."

Donna laughed as Andie squeezed her hand.

"That's what I told him! But credit where credit is due, he did it. Tonight, I didn't have to drag him over there and tie him into the seat. He did it on his own. Granted, I don't think he wanted to weenie out in front of this many people, but Cam stepped up and did it."

"He really is the best man I've ever met," Andie responded.

Donna turned to face Andie, their eyes locking as she nodded.

"I would agree."

"It's not a surprise that you're his best friend. Because you are pretty awesome yourself," Andie added, emotion creeping into her voice. "In spite of the people you saw here tonight, I think you know that I don't have many girlfriends. Not real ones, ones I can count on, anyway."

"There were a few here tonight," Donna replied, testing.

"These are girls I know. From high school. From college. A few through work. I'm talking about three-in-the-morning-I-need-help friends. I don't have those. I have friends I can go have a drink with. But in the short time I've known you, you'd be the woman I would call if I was in a jam. I hope you take that as a compliment."

"I do. And you know what, Andie?" Donna asked, smiling. "I feel the same. I told Cam that. Think it frightened him a bit. I think he wanted us to be friends but you know, not that good of friends."

Andie laughed, wiping a tear before it fell. Real friends were so rare for Andie; trusting other women wasn't easy, she assumed it had something to do with her relationship with her mother. And if she had been told a few months ago that the woman she trusted the most was Cameron's best friend, Andie would have walked on. But they were friends, she and Donna, and while it was odd for her to hear herself say it, it also felt really comforting to know it was true.

"And I saw you talking to my mom. That must have been interesting," Andie said.

"You have no idea," Donna laughed, quickly covering by adding, "She's...a complex soul. And I don't have the same relationship with her you do. I don't know how to say this without it sounding bad, but I think she's the best person she can possibly be. I often get to see a different side of the mother-of-the-brides than the brides do. I see what they want for their daughters—their hopes, aspirations, wishes—that the daughters don't get to see for whatever reason."

"I know who she is. She's damaged. Dad helped fix her. He taught her some compassion. Some semblance of humanity. Maybe having me did too. But even when I was little, I had to fight for any attention. She was incapable of reaching out to me. Toughened me up for sure. And explains why I'm such a daddy's girl," Andie admitted freely. "I wish my mom could have tried harder, fought harder for that good that other people say they see in her. And honestly, Donna, when everybody else feels an obligation to tell you that there's some humanity in your mother, isn't that a clue there isn't?"

Donna didn't answer.

"But in spite of it seeming otherwise, she wasn't created in a lab," Andie continued. "My grandparents weren't good to her, I know that. She can only be who she learned to be. Thank God for my dad...or who knows who she'd be, or who I would have become."

Donna knew. "Conveniently" married to Hal, allowing him to roam on the side for a secret dalliance, while she kept up appearances so that other men would be envious of Hal for his wife's beauty and poise. Secretly wishing a man would touch her, would make her his. But basking in Hal's handsomeness, his past victories, his lectures, and cocktail banter, but always secretly wondering where he was the night before or watching his eye follow the young man bartending at whatever gala they were attending.

Donna reached up and grabbed a bottle of champagne out of a bucket.

Holding it up, she said, "Something great happened here tonight. To friendship. Our friendship. And the future."

Donna took a swig from the nearly empty bottle and handed it to Andie, who followed suit.

"So...when should we start planning the big day?" Donna quizzed, spinning in the chair to face Andie, wincing as she did.

"I guess we should start soon. I'd love a spring wedding."

"This coming spring? As in next spring?" Donna couldn't hide her incredulity.

"I'm not waiting a year-and-a-half to get married. This coming spring. I'm done pretending Cam and I aren't already living together and paying for an apartment I'm never in."

"Does Cameron know you want to get married next spring?"

She glanced over her shoulder at Cameron all the way across the tent, bouncing from person to person, shaking hands, thanking them for coming.

"He wouldn't care if it were tomorrow. What's he got to do with it anyway, other than show up?" Andie laughed. "I know he doesn't want to drag out this engagement."

"Well then, we need to get real busy, real fast."

Just then, Mr. Hune retrieved his daughter to escort her over to meet an older couple whose names Donna didn't remember, which was rare for her.

I must be tired. I usually remember names, she thought to herself. It was a learned skill and something she'd had gotten very good at. But at this point in the night, she didn't care. Donna just wanted to finish up and go home.

Mr. Hune returned to where Donna was sitting and pulled up a chair facing her. He nodded for a long moment before speaking.

"I'm impressed."

"No, your friends were impressed, which makes you relieved," Donna answered, grinning, but tired enough and feeling bad enough to willingly edge into the conversation with a little confrontation.

"Touché."

"But I'm glad. I'm glad the evening went well for Cam and Andie, and I'm glad you're happy. Seriously. I worked hard so you could see what I can put together."

"You impressed me. And you impressed my wife, which is much harder than impressing me. The night impressed us both," Henry stated, standing and extending his hand toward Donna.

They shook, both with smiles. Donna knew then, she had hooked a fan. It was then that Hal caught Donna's eye as he kissed Caroline on the cheek, clearly saying goodnight. Henry turned. Then turned back to Donna and allowed a smile to cross his lips.

"Amazing guy. I saw you and Cam talking to him. You should read his books, he's quite a motivator," Henry said. Maybe it was that she was utterly exhausted, but Donna didn't know how to respond to that. "I'm sure he is," she uttered with feigned enthusiasm. Insincere enough for Henry to recognize Donna's suspicions.

"The first rule of Fight Club..." Henry said as he started to walk away from Donna. Hearing her laugh loudly, from deep within her chest, he couldn't help but turn back to give her a desolate smile.

Donna was more than ready to pull her blankets up around her neck and burrow into her sheets. But in spite of how crummy she felt, she was aware that was not possible until the Ferris wheel was disassembled by the carnies, loaded on their truck, and driven to a school carnival about a hundred miles away. Until the chairs were stacked and the tables rolled into the awaiting catering trucks. Until the tents were taken down and stowed into the storage room in the back of the club. Until everything was cleaned up and the country club had no footprint that this celebration ever happened.

Tomorrow, Donna promised herself, there would be no phone calls for an entire day. She planned on sleeping. Recovering. She had way too much coming up to feel this crappy. She could not afford to get sick.

Never in her life did she get sick, Donna believed it was by the sheer desire not to. And whatever was running her down, which Donna assured herself was too much stress, too many things to get done and never stopping until they were completed, had to disappear. Pronto. But at this moment, she wanted to bask in the afterglow of success as the dishes were being carried in and the tablecloths were coming off.

Giving herself a few minutes to breathe, Donna continued overseeing everything being broken down and taken away. One of the carnies made a fumbling, crude pass at her as they finished loading the Ferris wheel onto the truck, which Donna only chuckled over. With everything finished and the tents gone, Donna walked to her car.

I wish I just felt less exhausted by the whole thing. Good Lord, what is this wedding going to do to my stress levels?

Unlocking her car, she slipped in. The seat seemed to swallow her as she felt she could finally let go. She slid the key into the ignition and was just about to turn the engine over when she sighed. Five minutes before I drive home, Donna thought. She just needed five minutes to allow her body to relax. Jacking the seat back, she lay there and shut her eyes.

Waking up, the sun was streaking across the country club grounds. Donna sat up, blurry-eyed, confused. "Oh shit, you're kidding...!" she said aloud to herself, wiping her face, realizing she had slept through the night, the keys still in the ignition. Embarrassed and still exhausted, she turned the key and started her car, spinning it out of the parking lot and pulling away, as the first tee-time members began arriving for their morning round of golf.

EIGHTEEN

C aroline didn't sleep. She'd like to believe it was from all the excitement from the evening, usually, events like this would drain her and she would curl up in the warmth of her bed and sleep until the next afternoon. But this was different. Donna's words were stuck in her head.

Hal was Caroline's first love. A few years older, tall, athletic, with an aura of detachment that only drew her in further. They grew up a few blocks away and since their parents were members of the same country club, she and Hal saw each other daily at swim practices every summer. When Hal took a summer job as a lifeguard at the club as well, Caroline could stare at him all day from the anonymity of her chaise lounge. Hal was all shoulders, chest, abs, and a sweeping mop of chestnut hair. As far as she was concerned, he looked like a movie star, carried himself like a celebrity, and treated every woman, young and old, like they were his favorite fan.

Being a few years younger, Hal didn't truly notice Caroline until he was in college out west, swimming on a scholarship, and Caroline was finishing high school. The summer before she went off to Stephens College in Columbia, she made the feelings she had for Hal known. He remained elusive, which should have been Caroline's first clue. At eighteen, she was stunning and smart. Guys were tripping over themselves to date her. She was still a virgin, having never found a man she felt was worthy of her. As if she'd been saving herself for Hal because she knew that if he as much as intimated he wanted to go there, to be her first, Caroline wanted that to happen.

Her world tilted. How could this man not want her? He claimed to have a woman he was serious about at Stanford. Some track star. Carried a photo of her in his wallet. They were discussing moving in together. The hotter summer turned, the more her longing for Hal seemed to expand. She wanted him. After the final swim meet of the country club season, Hal, who was now a coach for the team, making him feel even more of a luminary in their insulated world, showed up at a party thrown by one of the team parents. While the parents drank cocktails on the back patio by the inground pool, all the swimmers hung out in the house, eating generous amounts of catered food and playing video games.

Caught between both groups, Hal vacillated between inside and out, never staying in any conversation for too long. He would allow himself to be fawned over by the swim team moms, glad-handed by their rich husbands, adored by the kids who he coached. But it was all betwixt and between.

Caroline felt the same way. Nearly all of the swimmers were younger than her. She wouldn't have joined the team if Hal weren't a coach. Plus, it was a great way to stay in shape. And she didn't like the way all of the dads stared at her. She wasn't impervious to the glances and ogles of her dad's friends from the club, all wishing they could be eighteen and forty pounds lighter again.

Latching herself to Hal, playing on them both feeling out of place, Caroline snuck an armful of beers from a cooler and they went out and sat on his car down the block from the party. Hal told her how disappointed his father was since Hal announced he wanted to coach swimming for a living. His father had bigger plans. But Hal loved the sport. He wanted to make it his life.

After Caroline finished her second beer, her head was spinning. She knew Hal had been drinking since he walked into the party, one of the dads shoving a drink in his hand almost immediately after he walked onto the pool deck. He didn't appear drunk, but Caroline sensed he was fairly lubricated.

"So, did I hear right? You're moving in with your girlfriend?" Caroline asked.

Hal chuckled, taking another swig from the Heineken in his hand. "She's not...," he started, but then stopped speaking, catching himself. "Yeah. She's already got a place. I'm moving in."

"Do you love her?" Caroline wanted to know.

"Oh, man. The big questions, huh? I guess, yeah. You know...it just feels right. We're both busy. She's got her thing, I got mine. And school. We support each other."

Caroline began playing with the lace on his tan deck shoe. "That's good. You need that. Especially being so far away. I'm going to Stephens. Part of me wishes I was going further away," Caroline opined.

"It's a good school," Hal offered.

"But the guy situation there..."

Hal laughed. "Mizzou is right there. And all of those guys would like to nail a Stephens girl."

Realizing what he said, Hal threw up his hands and laughed.

"Sorry, sorry," he exclaimed, reaching out and touching Caroline's bare leg. "I didn't mean it like that."

"It's okay," Caroline laughed. "It's true!"

"When you're as beautiful as you are, there are always guys. Probably too many," Hal opined as Caroline's hand drifted from his shoelaces to his tanned leg.

His compliment was the opening she'd been waiting for. Caroline leaned up to him, her lips going to his. She didn't wait for him to kiss her back, her hand crawling into his hair and holding him there. Setting down her beer, her hand cupped him between his legs, massaging. She'd never done this before and fought her self-consciousness at the clumsiness of it all. But once she could feel him respond, she pulled away and took his hand. Hal slid off his car with her and they got inside.

Caroline cringed every time she thought about losing her virginity in the back of an Opel.

Hal never spoke to her after that night. Being her first time, Caroline only had a vague indication of how bad the event was. The only image that stuck with her was Hal on top of her, staring out the window, keeping watch for anyone coming while he was having sex with Caroline. But she was making love to the man she'd dreamt about for years. That was all that mattered. It wasn't until Caroline's second partner, a grad student at Mizzou, that she understood what great sex could be.

Hal and Caroline reconnected almost two years later, while he was home visiting his family for Christmas. He still took her breath away when she saw him in Frontenac Plaza. And he greeted her affectionately, pulling her close, almost making a show of it. He told her he and track star broke up and she was in Europe, while he was doing some grad work at Berkley and helping out with the swim team there. Caroline's world had opened up enough to realize that a lot of what Hal was saying was bullshit. He was gay. And even if he didn't know it yet, she did. She never brought up their twenty minutes in the back of his Opel. Neither did he. But he did ask her out. To dinner. That led to him asking her over for Christmas dinner with his family.

The show began. Hal would fly her out to California for different events. She became his out-of-town girlfriend. Which was just fine since she really wasn't meeting anyone to her liking at college or back home. And as Hal's coaching career took off, including a short stint as a model, Caroline enjoyed being with the man who needed her. Their mutual detachment, the monied separation from everyone else, only seemed to make them more alluring to the California crowd.

Until she met Henry. His exotic handsomeness was juxtaposed against her patrician beauty. Henry knew from their first conversation that he wanted her. Caroline had Hal as an escape. But she was tired of simply being the beautiful, poised woman who whisked into his life for the adventures and disappeared for the day-to-day. And while he never came out and told her he was gay; it remained a silent fact that harbored itself between them. Safe from both sides.

Henry's pursuit coupled with Caroline's need for a man who not only loved her but desired her, wore her down. But she wasn't about to abandon Hal. She idolized him. But being unable to ever have him only twisted that into a necessity she couldn't shake, making Henry's craving for her less potent. The harder Henry tried, the more of himself he gave, the less she required him. She wanted Hal to touch her the way Henry did. To love her the way Henry did.

Never did it occur to Caroline that if she simply turned that around, longed for Henry the way she longed for Hal, she'd have everything she ever wanted. Not once. Until Donna threw it in her face.

Caroline sat at the kitchen counter and sobbed. She would never stop loving Hal. But she'd been chasing a phantom for decades. Hold back a vital piece of herself to the man who truly loved her. To the point, she didn't even know if it was possible. It neutralized their marriage. Even as hard as Henry worked to make it wonderful. It kept her from enjoying her daughter. Not even willing to get close to her baby girl, because she wanted something else. Someone else.

'It has to be different,' Caroline thought. It had already destroyed decades of her life. Upstairs was a gorgeous man who loved her in spite of herself. She may never be able to repair the relationship with her daughter but if she could salvage love with her husband, maybe the second half of her life wouldn't be marred by the same sins.

Climbing the stairs, Caroline stepped silently into the bedroom. She slipped into bed and snuggled beneath the sheet. Next to her, Henry was asleep. He always slept shirtless, wearing only pajama bottoms. In the shadows, she could see his back was to her. *We didn't use to sleep this way,* Caroline thought. They used to sleep curled up into each other. But that ended years ago when Andie was young. Because she would often sleep between them. Now after cursory 'good nights' they rolled away from each other, both sleeping near the edge, Henry's arm often hanging over.

In the darkness, Henry's back looked big, like a wall. Caroline wondered if it was to protect his heart or to keep her out. Slowly, her hand reached over and touched him. A light sleeper, Henry's hips shifted and he turned towards her, awake.

"What's the matter?" he asked, her touch startling to him.

"I...I just wanted," Caroline began, stopping herself from saying more, hesitant. She pulled her hand back. "Nothing. I'm sorry I woke you."

Through the near darkness, Henry could see Caroline's eyes. There was something.

"You can tell me."

She remained very still for a long moment. The weight of her fear battling the girth of her need.

"I'm sorry," Caroline finally said.

"For?"

"Would you hold me tonight? Like you used to," she replied softly.

Without another word, Henry shifted his body towards her, his arm going around her as he sidled up and turned onto his back, so her head could rest on his chest. Neither of them spoke. Caroline pressed her face against his skin, breathing in his scent, hoping that would bring back the reminiscence of being first married. At that moment she felt she could put her unrequited love for Hal behind her and be in love with this man. Her hand slid down, feeling that her being close to Henry aroused him. When was the last time? she thought, not being able to remember but wanting that now more than she ever had.

Sliding his pajama bottoms down, she slipped her body on top of his and kissed him with both the passion she wanted, but also the passion he deserved for always loving her in spite of how she treated him. She allowed him inside her and submitted to his power and tenderness. She had forgotten what a masterful lover Henry was.

Henry seized this moment to remind her.

Considering how rarely she said the words to Henry, Caroline felt too ashamed to utter the words "I love you" to him. She let her desire speak for her. Overwhelmed by the pleasure and emotion Henry gave her, Caroline buried her face into his neck and held him tight. She didn't want this feeling to end.

Neither did Henry.

NINETEEN

Donna slept all weekend, only crawling out of bed a couple of times to eat and take a shower. It felt glorious. Cam called. Andie called. A few other clients called. She didn't answer.

Arriving home in the morning after the engagement surprise, she needed forty-eight hours away from the noise in her head and the achiness in her body. Donna-time was hard to come by and she knew she'd have to force herself to take it. The time was now and it was long overdue.

Because once she called Andie back after the weekend, explaining her radio silence, Donna knew they would jump right into the stratosphere of wedding planning mode, leaving Cameron back on earth waving up at the sky. Especially since Andie insisted on a spring wedding. That ratcheted up the plans considerably.

Organizing a meeting with all involved—Andie, Cameron, and Mr. and Mrs. Hune—Donna accepted the role of general in charge of this operation. And like any good leader, Donna started the evening by explaining that pulling off a wedding in six months would mean they had to move at a sonic pace. Some of the venues, as well as music, catering, and florists, were booked months, if not years, ahead.

It meant the Hunes would have to call in favors from friends or companies they had relationships with. It could be done but, like all good operations, it would have to happen swiftly and with precision.

Luckily, they had a woman in charge who knew exactly how to make these things pop. Yet, Donna still found herself saying, "You have to trust me," a few too many times for her liking. After the talked-about success of the engagement party, Donna felt she earned that trust. Since this was a preliminary meeting, she didn't have specifics, just general ideas she could share. She couldn't offer Mr. and Mrs. Hune anything other than hope.

And Donna hated offering hope. She much preferred grounded realities: venue, menu, music. She promised the amazing but preferred to have more pieces in place with a wedding a mere six months away, most especially this one. Weddings, by their nature, only need a bride and groom, someone to legally preside, and a pair of witnesses. Anything past that is icing. But it's the icing that's remembered. And Donna liked to lather it on thick and have it taste incredibly sweet.

Over the next few weeks, Andie and Donna came to a consensus on details, leaving out Mrs. Hune as often as possible, and relegating Mr. Hune to writing deposit checks. Cameron was on board as long as Andie was happy. He kept telling Donna, "It's her wedding," which was something Donna had been drilling into Cameron since they were young. The groom is secondary, it's the bride's day.

And Cameron relayed to Donna that he grinningly joked with Henry Hune, "Got carpal tunnel from writing checks yet?"

Off the record, Cam relayed to Donna that Mr. Hune sometimes bemoaned the amount of money this wedding was costing, but his other assessment was that deep down Henry was delighted to pay whatever it took to make the day extraordinary for his only child.

Of course, there wasn't a chance Mr. Hune would never tell his daughter that and, if Cameron hadn't divulged the information, Donna would never know it. Though honestly, she could always sense with a father-of-the-bride if he was determined to keep spending to a reasonable limit—or it was more of a blank check. Donna only had one father ever tell her upfront that his daughter's wedding would be a blank check. And yes, the bride and Donna spent like they won the lottery and were at a half-off sale at Neiman's.

"I also need the deposit for the florist," Donna told Mr. Hune, stopping by to pick up checks to drop off at vendors.

"I remember the exact moment..." he said pensively, apropos of nothing, sitting at his desk in his sun-filled home office.

"The exact moment...?" Donna quizzed.

"When I knew I'd spend like a madman on my daughter's wedding."

He glanced up at Donna, their eyes meeting as she smiled. She was really starting to like Mr. Hune and felt this was one of the moments that would make her like him even more.

"When?" Donna asked.

"Andie was, I don't know, maybe five could have been four. Anyway, I was sitting in here, I had a different desk, but Andie loved playing in here. I had blueprints spread all over, and she came skipping in, all happy, wearing a towel on her head like a veil and had taped napkins to the back of it and said, "Daddy, I want to marry you."

Donna's smile grew. "Do you remember what you said back?"

"Yeah. I said, 'I'm already your daddy, isn't that enough?' And she answered, 'No. I want to marry you so you can build me a castle.'"

"I remember her climbing all over my papers so she could sit on my lap as I asked her, 'Is that what husbands are supposed to do?'"

Donna remained silent as she watched Mr. Hune go back into his memory, joy causing him to smile. "She looked up at me, very serious, and said, 'Yes. They take their mommies to a castle to live.' She was so sure of her answer, not a doubt in her mind. And I remember saying, 'Well, you know, you already have a mommy, and I'm married to her.' But Andie was completely undaunted by that and answered, 'Then you have to marry us both.'"

Henry fell silent for the moment, and Donna thought he might cry. She kept her focus on his eyes, expecting tears to form.

"I told her one day she was going to marry a man who loved her. Not for a long, long time, but that it would happen one day for her like it did for Mommy," Mr. Hune said, still caught in the memory. "And then I said, 'Do you know what Daddy's going to do?'"

He paused and finally Donna could see the tears she was anticipating, "I said, 'I'll make sure that day is the most amazing of your life until the day you have your own child.'"

Again, he fell silent, reaching across the desk and handing Donna the check.

"Did she say anything to that?" Donna asked.

Henry smiled. "She responded 'Okay,' kissed me on the cheek, jumped down out of my lap, and went running off."

"You made it all okay for her," Donna nodded.

Henry returned the nod. "And it's still okay," he told Donna, closing his checkbook.

After collecting the checks, Donna walked across the circular drive to where she parked her car. As she opened the door to slide in, she felt a sharp dig under her ribcage. Donna grabbed the door, her knees almost buckling. She managed to twist her body and drop into the car seat. The intensity of the pain mushroomed and it felt as if she was being stabbed between her lower ribs.

Her mind clear, Donna wished the pain was from the outside, but she knew instinctively it was from somewhere deep within her body. She looked up at the Hunes' home, debating whether she should attempt to get back to the front door, knock, and ask for help.

No. I don't want anyone to know, was the mantra that played in her head, over and over.

Closing the door, Donna fought to get a deep breath, hoping that would untwist whatever was wrenching inside her and allow her to take a full breath. Clutching her phone, she quickly debated calling 911. Or Cameron. Her hands were shaking as she pulled the phone toward her, her eyes swelling with tears, blurring the screen.

"Breathe, I need to breathe," Donna managed to say aloud, her mind racing as panic seeped in.

Starting the car, she rolled down the window to let the brisk air of early winter slap her in the face. Donna squeezed her eyes closed and focused on getting air into her lungs. The pain gradually started to subside, allowing her to finally pull in a real breath.

Lying back, Donna shut her eyes for a second. She certainly was not going to fall asleep again. God forbid, not in the Hunes' driveway. Besides, she was too frightened, her body electric with adrenaline. Letting the phone drop into the passenger seat, Donna began to get her bearings as she backhanded away tears. She just wanted to get out of the Hunes' driveway before Henry or Caroline realized she was still there and come out to check on her.

Weaving through the back streets to avoid the highway, Donna meandered her way back to her apartment. She wasn't the best driver on a good day, and with how tingly and weak she was feeling, she didn't trust she wouldn't cut someone off or cause an accident. Once more along the route home, the stabbing pain inched into her side, this time a little lower. She almost pulled over but the pain never reached the level of the first episode. Gritting her teeth, Donna kept driving.

Maybe I should just drive to the emergency room? she thought. Barnes Hospital wasn't that far. She wasn't sure she had her insurance card in her wallet though. She always had it when she traveled, you just never know. She was unaccustomed to getting sick.

And this wasn't sick. This was something else. Anxiety? Hypertension? A cyst? Blockage? Donna went through the Google list in her head of what this pain could be.

When she finally pulled into her garage, Donna sent up a quick prayer of thanks.

I'm home, she thought. Just a short elevator ride, a few doors down a hallway, unlock the door, a few more steps, and she could collapse on her sofa.

Which is exactly what she did. And then she sobbed.

TWENTY

The next morning, Donna called her doctor. She wasn't big on regular visits other than to the gynecologist, which she felt obligated to do just because that's what a woman does. But her general practitioner hadn't seen her in at least two years, and Donna felt that going to the doctor too often was tempting fate. Wasn't their job to find something wrong with you? Other than being exhausted by work and an occasional urinary tract flare-up, she was great.

Until recently. But still, Donna was without a doubt-positive that these pains were a manifestation of just being overworked and overtired.

Donna surmised, after checking off the litany of possibilities, that she had some sort of infection in her bladder. She could not get sick now. She had far too much to accomplish for something to slow her down. *I'll get sick after Cam and Andie are married*, she reassured herself. Right now, she just wanted to get some antibiotics and knock out whatever was going on inside her.

As Donna drove to the doctor's office, Cam called.

"Hey, you okay? Andie said she called you last night and didn't hear back," he said.

"I'm fine. I have a doctor's appointment this morning. Tell her I'm sorry. I saw her father last night to pick up checks. I didn't hear the phone."

"She worries about you," Cam added. "So do I. You work too hard."

"I never had anyone whose wedding I was planning say that to me."

"We're not 'anybody' and we know you do. You're our friend first. So, I'll just tell her everything's okay."

"Tell her not to worry if I miss one phone call. And yes, I'm fine and I love you guys for caring."

"Well, you were smart not to pick up. She has someone she wants to fix you up with."

"Who?"

"Mel Toomy," Cameron said with a wince in his voice that Donna couldn't miss.

"Pray tell, what's the matter with him?" Donna asked, entertaining this conversation to get off the subject of why she didn't return Andie's call the night before.

"He's alright, I guess," Cameron responded less than enthusiastically, "I just don't think he's the right guy for you."

"I'll ask again. What's the matter with him?"

"He's not funny. He thinks he is but he isn't. He's sort of stuck on himself and doesn't take criticism very well and you're not one to hold back if you don't like something," Cameron answered. "Andie says he's smart which she thinks is something you would appreciate, but I just don't see it."

"But Andie does?"

"She also thinks he's a 'gentleman'. I didn't even want to ask her what that meant because it would have started a big debate. One I'm sure I'd lose."

"I'm sure you would," Donna laughed, before adding, "Okay, so, the big shallow question: What does he look like?"

"Andie thinks he's good-looking..."

"You don't?"

"You might think so. I don't know..." Cam sighed, adding, "I think my friend, Doug Marker, would be a better match."

"Doug Marker? That guy I've never seen with the same girl twice?"

"He's not that bad. He's a lot of fun and girls think he's hot. Got a good job."

"Oh, Cam, he sounds perfect! Fun, hot and got a good job! What more could a girl ask for," Donna chided. "Two questions: How long have you known me? And in what world do you think someone like Doug Marker would be a good match for me?"

"I used to date around. A lot."

"But most of your exes actually like you. And all your dating led you to Andie."

"Maybe you could be Doug's Andie?"

"I'm not anybody's Andie. But thank you for thinking of me and, no offense, but Andie probably has a better sense of who is right for me."

"Because she's a woman?"

"You have a problem with that? No. But also yes. Because she's got a more critical eye when it comes to men and she's not as heavily invested. Doesn't have our history. You want a guy for me that you could also hang out with."

"Whoa. You think I'm that selfish?"

"Yes."

"Well, I see nothing wrong with fixing you up with a guy I think you would like AND I like."

Donna laughed again, "My God, I haven't trained you well at all. We'll talk later," she said with a sigh, before adding, "But thank you for the laugh. I needed it."

Telling Cam she was heading into the doctor's office, Donna said her goodbyes and hung up. Truth was, she didn't want to continue this conversation. She needed some alone time and didn't want to talk. Donna certainly didn't want to worry anyone over something that was most probably nothing and she was afraid she might slip.

The doctor's office. Was anyone even slightly happy when they walked in? Donna certainly wasn't going to be the first. There was a creepy sameness to all of them, even the smell which made the nose wrinkle in disgust. And more to the point, she would have to get out of her clothes to get checked over for something she was sure was nothing.

She hoped she could talk the doctor into giving her some sort of antibiotic for what she was sure was an internal infection and maybe a B-12 shot for a little added energy, and let her get on with what she had to do. Which was a lot. It wasn't that Donna didn't like her doctor. Dr. Frank was just starting to gray and quite handsome, with a face that tanned easily from all the golf or tennis she assumed he played, and he had pictures of his family everywhere.

"So, besides always being happy to see me," Dr. Frank said with a half-grin, "why are you here?"

"I've been exhausted," Donna answered, smiling. She believed smiling would make him think this appointment was simply preventative. "I'm having pains," she continued, her hands moving down the sides of her torso.

The doctor asked her to explain what the pains felt like. Donna shook her head, not sure what to say. Which was rare. "I don't know. Like pain. Sharp pain. Runs down my sides to my..." she gestured down to her groin.

Dr. Frank said nothing. Just nodded. Which infuriated Donna into continuing. "It's like my insides are the biggest rubber band ever, and someone sets it on fire and then snaps it. Over and over."

Donna explained how "having my own medical degree from Google, it must be related to how hard I've been working," making sure her voice stayed cordial, almost girlishly delightful.

Nothing to see here, just tell me I'm okay and send me on my way, she thought.

But Dr. Frank leaned against the door, eyeing her in silence.

"Are you going to talk? Or am I going to have to diagnose myself?" Donna blurted out, causing the doctor to smile.

"Let's do a blood panel," Dr. Frank announced. "This might be anemia but I want to rule out other things."

"Other things?" Donna asked.

"I'm a doctor, I like to be sure," Dr. Frank answered with a sly smile.

Not unexpected, Donna thought, relieved it was nothing more.

And as easy on the eyes as Dr. Frank was, Donna just wanted to get out of there.

"Can we do this like now? I have an appointment with a bride-to-be," Donna asked, not telling the doctor her appointment wasn't until the following day.

Dr. Frank explained that they no longer did the blood draws in the office but the front-desk people would give her a list of labs, the kind that dotted grocery store shopping malls in St. Louis. She could make a convenient appointment and, as soon as he had the results of the labs, he would call.

Perfect. Find out, get me well. I need to be going at one-hundred percent energy again.

As she drove, Donna called a blood lab near her house and with a bit of fast-talking and begging, convinced them to let her come right in. They scooted her in quickly; the tech taking her blood had a big smile and a few jokes that helped Donna relax, and she was in and out of there in less than 20 minutes, minus eight tubes of blood.

Donna manned the phone the rest of the day, trying to find venues that weren't booked the last weekend in March or the first weekend of April. Yes, many of the managers and event coordinators at the venues laughed at her, but she was used to that when working on a wedding less than a year out.

Donna wasn't above pulling in some favors, cajoling, whining, offering to outbid; pretty much everything in her arsenal to get a list of locations she could confidently present with pictures on the iPad to Andie and her parents. And Cam. Not that he would have much to say about it. This decision had to be made first and fast. Donna was already thinking outside the box, which is usually where she did her best thinking and got the best results when someplace unique lit up her mind with possibilities like a pinball machine. St. Louis was loaded with cool, unexplored, and underutilized locations.

In spite of its reputation to anyone outside of the city, St. Louis isn't some depraved, crime-ridden den of iniquity. Sure, crime exists, as it does in any metropolitan area but the stats are misleading. Donna was always trying to quell the unease with people coming to St. Louis for an out-of-town wedding. She reminded them that like any urban area, you had to be smart about where you went, especially at night.

Being aware of your surroundings was paramount, and only an idiot would go anywhere alone. Thousands and thousands of people come here throughout the year for ballgames, hockey games, a million different conferences, concerts, gatherings of all sorts, and thousands upon thousands go home happy. Since the city is relatively small, the local news makes a heyday out of the latest crime. That is the world today.

Donna would tell visitors, ad nauseum, that St. Louis wasn't just downtown. And while downtown had a cool vibe, with the riverfront, the Arch, the ballpark, museums—the City Museum was probably the coolest place in the country—it was a city with the most amazing, eclectic architecture. But what people in 'the Lou' knew, St. Louis also extended, quite beautifully, out to the monied western suburbs.

Part of the beauty of St. Louis is that you can find almost any sort of location. There are places that still have 19th-century charm all the way up to the most ultra-modern venue. The right place was here, the right church was here, the right banquet hall, taproom, party house, they were all here. And best of all, in comparison to most of the other cities where Donna had planned weddings, St. Louis was one of the most affordable. Never a bad thing.

Getting the Hunes to agree on what they wanted for this wedding and extremely quickly, even with Donna's guidance, was going to be the hard part. While she had a feel for Andie's parents, Donna felt much more secure that she knew what Andie wanted far better, and though Mr. Hune was no longer a mystery to her, Mrs. Hune still was.

Donna and Andie had already peppered Henry Hune for down payments on a number of venues, wanting to hold what they could until a final decision was made, but Donna felt less secure that they would all agree on what they wanted in time to get the deposits back on the ones they didn't select.

Also, Donna wasn't sure that Mrs. Hune wouldn't undermine the process. Luckily, she didn't seem to do anything quickly. It just wasn't her speed and she wasn't going to change for anyone, even her daughter. Donna needed Mrs. Hune to understand that she had to get an answer on one of the six wedding venue options she'd presented. Like yesterday. All the venues she held in reserve wanted an answer; they had other people interested and were only holding them because they'd worked with Donna before.

The number of guests they planned on inviting limited the possible venues for the reception. And Busch Stadium wasn't an option. Sitting all of them down that evening, including an uncomfortable, fidgety Cameron, with an open bottle of Cabernet, Donna wasn't leaving until she made a call and said, "Book the space."

As she sat on the cream-colored sofa in the formal living room, or as Caroline called it "the sitting room", Donna sent up a prayer that this wouldn't be a long night. She was still tired. Surprisingly, other than hellos, Mrs. Hune was almost silent through much of the evening, clearly more interested in keeping her wine glass filled and one eye on her phone, than engaged in the locations Donna was showing her on her iPad. Mr. Hune was as mildly engaged as Cameron, both more interested in Andie's reaction to each venue, which suited Donna fine. If she had to only please Andie, it would be a much easier and faster night.

Andie quickly had her heart set on The Ridgeley House, an architectural stunner of a location with expansive lawns and a ballroom inside the old mansion that could handle up to five hundred people. The Ridgeley House was originally built in the early 1900s by a cattleman, Ernest Ridgeley, who had something to do with milk industrialization. During the 1960s, the place fell into disrepair but was bought by the Martin family, who owned mortuaries. They restored it but used it as a home until they sold it in the 1990s when it became a wedding destination. The ballroom was actually enlarged to hold bigger receptions and the lawn reconfigured so the river could be seen in the background.

The photos Donna showed Andie of sunset weddings, with the Missouri River to the west and the sun setting over it totally won her heart. She wanted a sunset wedding, outside on the vast green lawn, weather permitting. It would be spring in Missouri, which could mean rain or the unwelcome remnants of winter hanging around.

The Ridgeley House was about thirty minutes out of St. Louis but the small winery village it was located in had a dozen rooms as well, which the bridal party would easily take up. It was surrounded by small bed and breakfast inns, hotels, and the like, so if people didn't want to drive home, there were plenty of charming places to stay for the night. Which was important when people were drinking.

"I'm booking it before someone else takes it," Donna said, picking up her phone as Andie's eyes lit up. As Donna spoke with the venue catering managers, Andie glanced at her parents, hoping to get some feel for their take. Henry nodded easily, happy his daughter was happy. Caroline stood and touched her daughter on the shoulder as she walked out of the room, giving no real indication of whether she was happy or not. Donna fired Andie a "don't let it get to you" look and Andie nodded.

Walking out of the Hune home, Donna was actually giddy. She had accomplished one of the biggest and most pressing tasks in a little over an hour, booked it, called the other venues to return Mr. Hune's deposits, and sipped a glass of wine while doing so. An impressive night, if she did say so herself.

Even Cam called on his ride home to thank Donna for getting him out of there so quickly. "I thought I would be there for hours," he said, "and I never got dinner, so I was hungry."

"You were smart," Donna answered, feeling victorious, "you kept your mouth shut. You might make a good husband after all."

"Did you notice Mrs. Hune looking at you all night?" Cameron then asked.

"At me?" Donna answered, surprised. "All I saw was her looking at her phone like she was expecting a call and making sure her glass never went empty."

"No, no...she was watching you most of the night."

Donna shrugged. She hadn't seen it. But she tried never to make eye contact with Caroline Hune, knowing that would be an invitation to jump into the conversation and from the conversation, into the plans, and inevitably slow everything down by half.

Falling into bed, Donna thought she might actually sleep well. Now that she had booked the venue, and the wedding and reception would be in the same location, she could hit the ground running with the other details to get them handled sooner rather than later.

Cam and Andie were still debating the size of the wedding party, with of course some pressure from their folks to include relatives, which neither wanted to do. But they needed to give Donna a final number. Tuxes were easy. Bridesmaids' dresses were a whole other megillah. Andie had to first pick her wedding dress so Donna could get a picture in her head of a few options for their style.

She also had to find out how extravagant the Hunes wanted the meal. The Ridgeley House had a menu, and hopefully either chicken, steak, or vegetarian would be good enough for them but if they desired something over-the-top or exotic, they were going to have to bring that in from somewhere else and have it prepared there, which most venues hated to do, and usually charged more for on top of their standard, exorbitant bill. But if Andie, or more likely her parents, wanted a specific caterer, and there were a plethora of award-winning, talented chefs in St. Louis to choose from, that was completely up to the Hunes. Donna just needed to nail down details, pronto.

Sometimes having less time to think about details was the best option for all involved. Your gut answer is usually correct before your head gets involved and screws everything up.

Donna's phone rang early. Positive it was either Andie or a vendor, Donna sent up a quick novena that it wasn't Andie. If it was, that probably meant she or her parents had some change that Donna would have to implement quickly. Pulling her cell phone off the nightstand, Donna blinked a few times to clear her eyes to see exactly who was calling.

Dr. Frank.

Donna let the phone ring four more times before she answered.

TWENTY-ONE

Sitting in the doctor's waiting room at 8:20 in the morning was not on Donna's to-do list. He wouldn't tell her anything over the phone other than that he needed her in, first thing; he found something in her bloodwork and he wanted to talk to her about it. The fear made it difficult for her to pull in a full breath.

I can't be pregnant, she thought, which was about the only thing she could rule out. That at least made her smile at the front desk nurse, who returned a warm yet suspicious smile.

"The doctor doesn't call patients in this early with good news, does he?" Donna asked.

Again, the front-desk nurse gave her a warm but suspect smile. "I don't know. I don't know what it means," she stated, though Donna was sure she was lying.

Dr. Frank pushed through the door, briefcase in hand, a couple of folders under one arm, and a travel cup of coffee in his hand. He smiled at Donna, almost as if surprised she was waiting for him.

"Hi Donna, come on back to my office with me."

Following him down the hallway, each step Donna took made her increasingly nervous. Dr. Frank walked ahead of her and not next to her, though he did keep glancing back over his shoulder at her as they made their way to his office, in which she had never stepped foot before.

"Sit, sit..." he insisted, again nodding, this time to one of the chairs across his cluttered desk, as he dropped his briefcase and pulled the folders from under his arm, falling into the chair behind his desk. He looked tired.

"This is bad," she stated flatly.

"I don't know if it's bad, but the results of your bloodwork...I need to ask you a few things."

"Okay."

"Do you have any vaginal bleeding?"

"You mean other than...sometimes. I have. I mean....when I'm stressed. That's why I thought I had an infection of some kind."

"And discharge?"

"I don't...I guess...you know, I am out of the country sometimes, and once or twice there's been---"

"I want you to do a cancer screening," he said, cutting Donna off.

"Excuse me?"

"Today."

"But---"

"Today," he repeated with such finality Donna almost burst into tears.

Dr. Frank announced he would set up an appointment for her but Donna's head was still swirling around a murky haze with the word "cancer", and she didn't hear the details, other than she'd have to drive over to Barnes Hospital to see some other doctor who would perform more specific tests. Donna's hand went up as if she needed to ask a question in class, silencing him.

"Can you write this down? I'm not going to remember."

Dr. Frank went silent for a moment, nodding.

"I am sorry. I hit you with this pretty hard. You just seem to be the type of person who prefers the facts, no matter how cold or difficult. This is a lot to take in. And just because you have symptoms and the blood tests came back with some abnormalities doesn't mean you have cancer, Donna. You're young. It could be a lot of other things. Or nothing. Sometimes the body does funny things when it is under stress.

But we need to be sure. We need to know what it is and what we can do about it *if* it's anything at all. I'd tell you not to worry but you'd think I was being an ass. Worry. You have a right to. But hopefully, it won't be anything at all, and I'll be recommending that you take a couple of weeks off somewhere sunny and warm, with doctor's orders to rest."

"Not until next spring," she blurted out.

"Excuse me?"

"I'm planning my best friend's wedding. I can't do it until the end of March."

Dr. Frank sighed as if she were the dumbest person he'd ever met.

"Cancer doesn't work around your schedule."

Walking out to her car, Donna couldn't feel her feet. There was no goddamn way she could be sick. Especially cancer-sick. Yes, she had pain in her side, pain in her abdomen, that's all. A few pains did not equal cancer. Cancer. Damn! It didn't run in her family as far as she knew.

She was way too young for this. Yes, she was aware that children get it too, but she was almost never sick. Never. But she worked too hard, and too often, and she couldn't say no to things. She didn't know how to delegate well and she loved being in charge. This had to be something else. But if it was cancer, a plan formed in her mind: catch it, treat it, and let her get on with life.

Internally, Donna kept repeating over and over that she was a busy woman and this nonsense wasn't going to stop her. She had to keep repeating it. It was the only thing that would help her get across this parking garage and to her car.

As she slid into her car and jammed the key into the ignition, the mantra stopped in her head and she broke down in tears. And she couldn't stop.

What the hell? Oh my God, I need to call The Ridgeley House about some of the details, I hope I can do it from the hospital. I should have time. They're not going to knock me out or anything, I don't imagine. Tests. What kind of tests? I should have asked, she rambled in her head, each individual thought tumbling over the next.

Glancing at the card Dr. Frank gave her with the name of the oncologist she was going to see, she noticed it was a woman. Dr. Dorothy Muliski.

Sounds old, Donna mused. But at least a woman would be looking at her lady parts. Donna knew she needed to pull herself together, post haste. She didn't want this new doctor to find her in a puddle of her own tears, she wanted to be as together and professional as possible, even in this shitty situation. Before she threw the car into reverse to back out of the parking spot, she prayed aloud, "Please God, there cannot be anything wrong with me. Please God, please God, please God!"

On her way over, Donna realized she was being extra-cautious.

What the hell? I don't have an overwhelming need to be safe at this moment. I mean seriously, I may have cancer or something.

At least it brought a smile to her face. And in the damp fog she was locked in, even that was a victory. Thankfully, Dr. Muliski's office wasn't too far, because the morning traffic that seemed to push in on either side of her made her claustrophobic and uncomfortable. She wanted to shove every car away from hers because she absolutely needed more space. She just wanted to get into that parking garage and find a spot. And sit, at least for a minute, by herself, before she headed in to meet this new doctor and do whatever she wanted her to do.

Damn it, more tears.

"Stop. Stop! Not now, I'm close, the garage is up ahead," Donna said aloud, seeing the garage a half-block up through the tears rimming her eyes. She just had to cross traffic, which she hated, but with tears blurring her vision, it was even more dangerous. "Back the hell off and give me space!" she yelled at the oncoming traffic.

As the traffic lightened, she shot across the street without anyone honking at her. Sucking in a deep sigh of relief, she took the ticket from the gate machine.

They better validate, she thought, figuring it was the least they could do with how much just this visit alone was going to cost.

Finding a spot on the third level, Donna turned off the car and sat, taking deep breaths, trying to hold them but each time she again felt that pain in her abdomen. Or she thought she did, wanting to believe it was now psychosomatic, only happening because of the stress of being sent over here when she had a thousand pressing things that needed to get done.

Maybe all of this is because she is as crazy as people tell her she is? Thinking she was feeling the pains now because of what was going on, she couldn't be sure. Gripping the steering wheel as hard as she could, Donna gritted her teeth and screamed through them as loud as she could until she ran out of breath.

"This is bullshit!" she screamed, pounding the steering wheel.

She got out of her car, tightened her lips, and set the alarm. Wiping the tears off her cheeks with her palms, and with the validation card in hand, she marched toward the doctor's building.

"Let's get this over with. I'm busy," she said aloud through her pressed lips.

Another bland waiting room, Donna sighed to herself as she walked in. She suddenly missed being a kid when at least they had fish or colorful toys lying around, something to keep you occupied while you were waiting, instead of sitting in these nondescript hospital chairs with faux-art in tacky frames on the walls, which you look through but never at.

Who makes this crap? Donna thought, wincing as she perused the pastel modern art in its cheap gold frames.

"Hi," Donna said, forcing a smile at the woman behind the desk. "I'm Donna Morgan, Dr. Frank set up an appointment this morning with Doctor Muliski."

"I'll let her know you're here."

Wow. Not even a 'Take a seat, she'll be with you shortly.' She is going to let her know I'm here. Like pronto, right this moment.

It didn't take but two minutes for a very tall, very young nurse to come and retrieve Donna from the waiting room. Donna wanted to ask where she went to high school and if she played basketball, but she opted not to; the nurse didn't seem the type for small talk. As she led Donna down another pale hallway, Donna noticed more art as they rounded the corner and arrived at a nurses' station.

Height, weight, paperwork to fill out. Donna parked herself in the examination room, to fill out the pages, her hand shaking as she wrote. She was barely able to concentrate on what she was doing but knew she had to get this done so she stared at the clipboard and paperwork.

Damn it, damn it, damn it, another hospital gown! Perfect. Donna hated her legs; they were short, needed sun, and her thighs were heavy. Thankfully, she was smart enough to wear a simple pair of panties today; nothing the least bit provocative, nothing too granny. But at that very second, Donna was hating everything about her life and every responsible decision she'd ever made that could have been filled with something fun, provocative, or wildly inappropriate.

Dr. Muliski was not as old as her name suggested. Although she was expecting a woman with gray, naturally wavy hair pulled back so it ran down her back, the lines around her blue eyes aiding the warmth and serenity she liked to exude to patients, Donna got a woman of maybe forty, tops.

Pretty, in a patricianly sort of way, black hair, probably dyed, fingernails painted, pale lipstick. She was more matter-of-fact than Donna would like for someone she'd never met before who was about to invade her body, but she explained everything she was about to do before she did it, which helped some. And the nurse assisting her was a woman too, younger, blonde, with one of those tight smiles people give you when they know you're going to hate what they do to you.

She told Donna that the tests she runs are a little more conclusive and that, while cancer was a possibility, she often discovered that cancer wasn't the problem. The doctor never said what the problem then turned out to be, but Donna guessed that weighing everything else against cancer, the other things were a sunshine-filled picnic in the park.

With liquor and a very handsome date.

More blood draws, then feet up in stirrups and some other fluids and samples were taken that Donna didn't care to talk about. She kept her eyes closed through most of it. She couldn't really see what the doctor was doing anyway; and even if she could, she wouldn't want to. Feeling it was more than enough.

And she did not want to see whatever looks passed between Dr. Muliski and her nurse. If they were shocked, Donna didn't want to know while she was lying on this table, legs up, in a paper gown. If they were terrified, she did not want to know that either. If they were bored out of their skulls, she wasn't much interested in finding that out as well.

Donna only wanted to lie there, making wedding prep lists in her head, until she was told she could get dressed and go home. Or at the very least sit up and be finished with whatever the doctor was using to probe her body.

The doctor then sent Donna down to Radiology to have a scan and x-rays of the inside of her body. God knows, she'd seen pretty much all of the outside and more than Donna would have liked of the inside. Donna was moved through three different machines, in all of which she was expected to lie perfectly still. She jokingly asked the surprisingly handsome medical technician if it was possible for her to make some business calls while she lay there.

He didn't laugh, which didn't bode well for him ever asking Donna out.

Back up in Dr. Muliski's office, finally dressed and making a couple of calls while she waited for the doctor, including one to the event coordinator at The Ridgeley House, Donna confirmed Cam and Andie's wedding date and time. At least one thing got done that day besides her getting in and out of her clothes.

Dr. Muliski rushed into her cramped, crowded office and slid around her desk to sit. She gave Donna either a wince or a smile, Donna couldn't tell which, but she knew it all depended on the news that was coming.

"I'm still waiting on one of the tests, but I have the results of three of them and I have the scans."

"Okay?"

"There's no easy way to say this..."

Those words slammed Donna back in her chair, blinking back tears she knew would come. She tried to clear her vision, hoping to listen just as clearly.

"It's cancer. Cervical."

"You know already? You're sure? I mean, you just ran these tests," Donna blabbered, between taking breaths. "This is bad."

Dr. Muliski nodded.

"How...how bad?"

"I cannot give you a definitive answer. Yet. But my best judgment from the images and the test results so far: Stage Four. And it's spread."

Donna opened her mouth, not sure whether words were supposed to come out or she was supposed to scream, just to help her keep breathing. Her head was swimming in what felt like mud, words not connecting into a sentence for her to utter. Stage Four. Spreading. Stage Four. Spreading. *That's bad, that's bad, that's really, really bad*, kept repeating in her brain.

Donna could hear her pulse.

"Am I going to die?"

Donna expected Dr. Muliski to take a deep, easy breath and assure her she was in fact not going to die; instead, she locked her eyes on Donna's. For what seemed like a thousand years, she didn't speak. She just stared deep into her eyes as if trying to burn the cancer out of her. Donna heard Dr. Muliski's painted nails clicking off of each other. The doctor was scared.

For Donna.

"We will do everything we can."

Those were not the words Donna wanted to hear next.

Dr. Muliski continued, explaining that once she understood how far and where the cancer had spread, she would design a course of treatments, which could include surgery but most certainly would include chemo and radiation to shrink the tumorous masses. Every word the doctor spoke made Donna's head whirl, like when she was a child, and would twirl around and around to make herself dizzy.

I need to call my mother. I need to call Cam. And Andie. I wish someone were here who could actually listen to all of this, to take notes, to explain it to me in an hour or two when I'm not just hearing my heart beating, Donna thought, everything again falling all over each other in her mind.

What the hell? How does this happen to someone like me? I'm not sick, not really. A few sharp pains, and yeah, they hurt but.... okay, a few other things I didn't pay much attention to but, but, but suddenly I'm the walking dead? No, no! It doesn't happen like this. There has to be a larger sign, something grander. More telling. A way I would have known. Should have known. Telltale signs. Something. The thoughts cascaded over each other in Donna's mind, jumbling until they were pureed.

Finally, a coherent thought broke through the pack and lodged itself in front of all the others in her brain. "This is going to ruin my business," Donna uttered aloud, eliciting a wincing look of confusion from Dr. Muliski. Yes, in the darkest moment of her life, that's what Donna worried about the most. Dying was still abstract. But her job, what she'd built over the last few years, and how this would affect that, was what was paramount in her psyche, crazy as Donna knew that must have sounded to the doctor. She had Cam and Andie's wedding to do.

I'm not dying until after that. As far as I'm concerned, whatever this doctor wants to do to me will have to wait until I pull that off. Sorry. That's the one thing I'm not bending on. A few months one way or the other isn't going to matter from what Dr. Muliski is saying. And I'm not spending my last months being sick from chemo or whatever, slowly withering away in a bed somewhere because of all the drugs they are giving me to fight what they say is trying to kill me, Donna vowed to herself. *I'm sorry, I just have too much to do to die any time soon. Way too much.*

TWENTY-TWO

"**I** don't want anyone to panic because I'm not."
Donna paused after saying that out loud and listening to it.

Okay, I'm not saying that. It makes it sound worse, she thought.

Donna had no idea what she was going to tell people. Or whether she was even going to say anything. She'd rather not have people know. At least until she knew one hundred percent, without a doubt, what was going on in her body. Dr. Muliski hadn't given her definitive results or what course of action she wanted Donna to take so she was hoping she could keep this situation on the down-low until she straightened out in her own mind what it all meant and exactly how serious it was.

No, no. She was suddenly sure she didn't want anyone to know. Not even Cam, who she usually told everything. He would go crazy, demand she quit working as their wedding planner, and probably abandon the wedding to sit with her and hold her hand while she went through whatever it was she was going to go through, for however long she was going to go through it.

Donna would have none of that. She couldn't let Andie in on the secret either because Donna knew Andie would agree to postpone the wedding as well.

Death never crossed Donna's mind. Why should it? Even when her father died, the impact was on how much he loved her, not that he was gone. But her own death, her own mortality? She honestly hadn't thought about it once, even when she was in that bad car accident back in college. She didn't see her life flash before her eyes; she didn't decide to go climb Mt. Kilimanjaro; she didn't join a cult religion searching for God.

The thing that made her saddest about the possibility of death was that her one long-standing dream, her own wedding, would never take place. That day she had envisioned for so long would die with her. It was the only thing she had ever really wanted. Maybe she should have focused less on other people's relationships and weddings and placed more attention on finding someone for herself?

Woulda, coulda, shoulda, she thought, closing her eyes tightly, struggling not to cry.

Tears came at strange times throughout the day. It didn't follow rhyme or reason. But she was overcome with emotion whenever things slowed down and she had an excessive amount of time to let her mind go to these dark places. She needed to keep busy and she wished the damn doctor would call, so she could know exactly what was going on in her body and what she should prepare for.

She felt like she was trapped in a box and heavy walls were falling in on top of her. There were times she couldn't breathe, like someone was sitting on her chest. Yet her heart pounded as if trying to punch through her chest. Stress. Anxiety. She was used to them but had never suffered from them to this degree so this was a completely new and unwelcome experience.

Donna recognized that she needed to tell her mother, Geena. She didn't want to but she also didn't want to spring this on her mother later. If this thing that was devouring Donna from the inside was as bad as the doctor alleged, the more heightened the angst would be when she finally did reveal the news.

Donna knew Geena would take this upon herself. Her mother did that, and it had bothered Donna all her life. Everyone's issues became Geena's burden. In a personal, melodramatic operetta that played to the cheap seats long after the orchestra had finished. Donna loved her mom, but Geena reveled in drama, and right now, Donna had more than enough to deal with. She didn't need her mother's drama to swamp her own, and Donna knew it would as soon as she announced her diagnosis.

Yes, Geena would be sympathetic; yes, Geena would be there for her; yes, Geena would help her and hold her and make sure Donna was as comfortable as possible, but it came with a show. And it would cause Donna to push her mother away. "Jesus, Mother, you should have a two-drink minimum," she would tell Geena when the breast-beating histrionics would start.

"I'm in the wedding business, mother, it's drama on the best of occasions. I don't want to play a role in your soap opera," Donna would announce to Geena when her mother started on whatever was the most recent overblown calamity.

Donna knew Cam would never forgive her when or if he found out she was keeping this a secret from him, even under the guise of protecting him. But she also knew telling him would impact his and Andie's decisions about their wedding. She was not going to disrupt the progress they were making. Physically, she didn't feel terrible. Yes, there had been a couple of episodes but that was all. But Cam, being Cam, would insist that Donna step back, get rest or whatever the hell people do when they get cancer, and take care of herself. Andie would be the same.

What they wouldn't understand was that Donna needed the stress of the wedding arrangements and the blinding pace of putting it together. This was stress Donna thrived in; it made her feel good, and it was something she believed she could still manage.

And it would keep her mind off of the stress she couldn't manage.

The only thing certain was that Donna's life would be a mess over the upcoming months. She had no idea what that mayhem would look like once the doctors decided what they were going to do to help her through this. And she hated not being in charge of her own life. That scared Donna more than anything.

Stage Four. If it was Stage Four, Donna rationalized, the doctor didn't say definitively. She was pretty sure, but she could be wrong. She could be. Who knows? It is just pain. Pain doesn't have to mean cancer. Cancer. How does someone like me get cancer? How could I have functioned with it, and what does Stage Four mean anyway?

There was too much she needed to find out before she blabbed. Too many sequestered tears she wanted to shed while she held tight to this news.

She decided right then that until they gave her a definitive prognosis, she would keep all of this to herself. There was absolutely no need to wig anyone else out with something that might not be real. Right now, today, the drama was Donna's. And hers alone

Donna wanted to cry a little more.

TWENTY-THREE

I t took another eighteen hours of avoiding phone calls and canceling plans for Donna to stop crying. She wasn't sure what the catalyst was for her to finally stop; it was more like she just couldn't anymore. And thankfully, though she had come close a couple of times since, her dry streak had lasted six hours.

Taking the small amount of time off left Donna with a list of phone calls to return, not the least of which were from Cam and Andie who had each called a half-dozen times. They'd gotten used to Donna returning phone calls within the hour. She could only imagine that her not returning calls for two days scared them. She was surprised they didn't show up at her door. That, she didn't need. She didn't want to face either of them. Donna knew she would break down.

Dr. Muliski also called, wanting her to return to the office for some more conclusive findings. The fact that she wouldn't tell Donna over the phone pretty much announced that the news wasn't something that was going to be a relief. Donna set an appointment for two that afternoon because she had to drop off checks at a couple of vendors to reserve their services. They had called too and she didn't want to lose them for Cam and Andie's wedding or the other two she was finishing up.

"Where have you been?" Cam demanded when he finally got her on the phone. When he added, "Andie and I were coming to your place tonight if you didn't call one of us back," Donna laughed.

"Can't a girl have at least a little mystery?"

"Mystery is highly overrated when I'm worried," Cam responded. "So why the mystery?"

"I'll leave it a mystery. What do you need that's so important?"

"Nothing. I was just calling. Like I do all the time. I need to know you're okay. A single girl in the big city, you know."

This made Donna smile for the first time in two days. It was nice to have friends who worried about you.

"Tell Andie I'm okay. I've paid the deposits to the vendors we've agreed on and we need to sit and get the rest of the details nailed down asap. You should be there as well, Cam."

"Do I have to?"

"You don't have to, you have me looking out for you. But it will show your bride-to-be that you are invested in this."

He didn't answer her.

"Did you hear me?"

"Yes. Invested. I am. You know I am. Marrying Andie is what I want. More than I deserve actually."

"I think she would disagree with that assessment and so do I, but I think it's wonderful that you feel that way. Tells me you are going to treat her like a queen."

Donna instantly had a pang of regret. Not at the words but again, selfishly, that she would never experience it. She would never have that guy that put her first. After a dry day-and-a-half, she felt like crying all over again.

"I gotta run," Donna spoke quickly. "Will you tell Andie you talked to me and I'll call her later?"

Donna hung up and took a deep breath, fighting emotions that were again surging. Seeing the hospital up ahead, Donna pulled it together. God knows why; seeing the building where she was getting more news, most likely not good news, should have made this that much worse. But being the practical one, at least Donna would have something definitive and hopefully, the doctor would hold her hand and walk her through the practicality of fighting whatever was going on inside her.

Dr. Muliski tried to mask her dismay with what she probably thought was a warm smile but it came across as the smirk of someone who smelled something awful and was trying not to let on.

"Unfortunately, these results confirm my diagnosis," Dr. Muliski began, causing Donna to bite her lip as she took a deep breath and held it. "There's no easy way to say this. You're Stage Four."

"Meaning?"

"We have to treat your cancer aggressively."

"What does that guarantee me?"

"At this point, I don't believe we can eradicate it. It's already spread. What we can do is give you more time."

"Time for what?"

"Life," Dr. Muliski said pensively.

"What kind of life? Just being alive or a real life where I can do something? And how much time?"

"A lot of questions I can't answer. If we go in and attack this, it will take a lot out of you. But it will give you maybe another year. Maybe two."

"But I'll be sick and weak and won't be able to do much?"

"I won't lie to you, that's probably true."

"And without aggressive treatment?" Donna asked, feeling as if they were playing ping-pong and neither was scoring a point.

"Well," Dr. Muliski muttered, sitting back in her chair as if it were easier for her to take Donna in from that position, "I'd imagine a total of six months. It's been my experience with patients that cancer will eventually take over your body and you'll be bedridden for the last couple of months. But six months on your feet, feeling okay."

Donna sat. Silently.

Six months. Six months of okay. As opposed to a year or two of shitty. Life versus time.

"You don't have to decide right now," Dr. Muliski said with a calm warmth, sitting erect again, putting her hands on her desk.

"I don't think there is a decision," Donna answered, her head swimming but something becoming crystal clear. "I'm not going to wither and die. I mean, I don't want treatment that's going to make whatever time I have left miserable. I'd rather just live as long as I can, as best I can. My best friend is getting married in a few months and I'm putting together his wedding. I want to be on my feet and smiling when that happens. After that...come what may, I guess. But if I'm dying, I would rather enjoy what time I have, even if it's less, then go as quickly as possible. I've never been big on long goodbyes."

"I don't think you should make this decision right here, right now. You need to think about it. At least sleep on it. Pray."

"Are any of these treatments or medicines going to allow me to grow old and gray?"

Dr. Muliski shook her head.

"Is any of that going to give me a year or longer of living? I mean, actual living? Like up and out of bed, doing things?"

This time, all Donna got was a shrug.

"Alright then. My answer's still the same."

Dr. Muliski stared at Donna across her desk, not sure whether she was being brave or crazy but saying nothing. Her head nodded as she studied Donna more, her young face, the curls in her hair, the eyes that seemed disarmingly alive, wondering if Donna was responding out of some misguided nobility, or if the pain scared Donna even more than living.

There were no good answers. Just insane ones. Which, when a doctor tells you you're dying and it is looming large, a little insanity leaking in shouldn't be much of a surprise.

Maybe it was that Donna appeared so calm, which even she didn't understand. But she couldn't cry. Not here. Not anymore. She felt dazed and numb as if she and the doctor were plea-bargaining a prison sentence. She would love to scream and fall on the floor, sobbing uncontrollably, and maybe that would happen again when she got home, but right here, right now? Nope, she couldn't muster the strength for that in the doctor's office.

"Would you like me to set up a consult for a second opinion?" Dr. Muliski asked.

This time Donna shrugged. Getting news like this once was hard enough, did she really need an encore?

"How sure are you that I'm dying?" Donna asked in an almost-monotone voice.

Nodding before she spoke, Dr. Muliski answered, "I'm sure about this diagnosis. I already shared the results with two colleagues. With someone your age, I didn't want to give you the wrong information. I didn't want to frighten you or get your hopes up. I wanted to present only the diagnosis and prognosis, as informedly as possible."

"And they both agreed with you?"

Again, the doctor just nodded.

Before Donna realized it, she was out of the chair, standing, staring down at the doctor.

"A vital six months sounds a lot better than a crappy year or two. Maybe I'll change my mind, maybe I'll regret this decision but I doubt it. I want to be able to dance at my friend's wedding. I'm really close with him and the girl he's marrying. This will be the last wedding I put together. I want to do it right."

"You should tell them," the doctor said with enough insistence in her voice for Donna to know it was more of a demand than a request.

"I will. When the time is right. Same with my mom. Family. Friends. They'll all know. But it's going to be on my time, doctor. And while I know what I want for treatment, which is none, when and how I'll tell them, I'm not sure."

Thanking her, Donna shook her hand. Dr. Muliski asked Donna to schedule an appointment for the following week. She intended to monitor the progress of "the disease," which in Donna's mind meant monitor her demise; to "help you make the right decisions at the right time."

After making the appointment at the front desk, and once she was in the hallway, she realized that once again, she couldn't feel her legs. It was like she was floating; only not on air, but rather through the muck that slowed her down. She couldn't land on a single thought, battling different snippets of the doctor's diagnosis, things she needed to accomplish today, rehearsing what she was going to say to people about what was going on with her. She alternated between feeling completely shut down and feeling so much all she wanted to do was slink off into a corner, tuck her knees to her chest, and hold herself so tight her arms went numb.

Donna's car was becoming her sanctuary. As she sat behind the wheel, she wished she had a blanket to hide under. Not to cut out the world, but to cut out having to look at herself. It was her reality she wanted to hide from. She wanted to be someone else so she could feel sorry for the girl with terminal cancer, and have that girl not be her. The worst thing about hiding from the world was she had to do it alone. And as much as being alone suited Donna, she really didn't want that right at that moment. She wished someone was there, holding her hand.

But if someone were there, they would know too. And Donna didn't want that.

That's the last thing I need, she thought, *Well, next to cancer...*

Stopping for gas on Clayton, Donna decided to slip inside and grab a diet Pepsi. She didn't drink much soda, actually almost none at all, but she loved it, especially from a fountain. The fizz, the bittersweetness, the aroma. She knew it wasn't good for her and they always made her feel bloated and kind of sluggish, but considering what she just found out, she figured what could it hurt? Bad-schmad. At this point, what the hell? Wasn't like the soda was going to kill her.

Paying for the gas and the soda, Donna almost made it to the door when David walked in; his tall, thin frame slipping through the door as it started to close after someone walked out. This was the last thing Donna needed today. Shit. And standing not more than ten feet from the door, there was no way to avoid at least exchanging some sort of very awkward pleasantries.

"I didn't know you were in town," David said slowly, more slowly than usual. He never seemed to talk rapidly like Donna.

"I live here, remember?" Donna responded, wishing she had something pithier to say.

"I thought you didn't drink soda," David responded.

"A treat. Long day. Already."

"And it got longer when I walked in?" David asked.

"Pretty much," Donna answered, nodding uncomfortably, taking in David, that tattoo on his arm peeking out from under his sleeve.

Donna loved that he was so tall. He wasn't powerfully built, rather long and reedy. The first time they had sex, she was intimidated that he didn't seem to have an ounce of fat on his body. Just long muscles covered with pale skin. He had a lanky walk she found incredibly sexy, his long legs always moving very deliberately and with a certain grace that many guys didn't possess.

She remembered when she first saw him, walking across Delmar toward the art gallery, where she was at an opening for an artist whose wedding she planned. He saw her looking at him and even though he wasn't invited to the opening, decided to crash because he wanted to see if there was anything there.

There was.

"I'm sorry how I broke things off," David nudged into a conversation he wished he were having elsewhere, and Donna wished they weren't having at all. "It was stupid and I was kinda drunk and...it was bad. Sorry."

Taking him in as if looking at something alien, and feeling as vulnerable as she was, Donna had to steady herself. Nothing would have made her more satisfied at this moment than him leaning down and kissing her, her following him back to his place, and them falling into his bed.

She didn't know if she'd ever have sex again, and here he was, the last guy she had sex with, all one hundred and seventy-five pounds, six-foot-three of him. In that instant, Donna fantasized about what it would be like to spend a few hours in bed with him again, her body in pain but feeling wonderful from his touch; admitting to him everything that was going on with her, the finality of it all, and having David pull her onto his chest and kiss her, telling her he would be there for her. All the way to whatever the conclusion might be.

Donna took a sip of her diet Pepsi. The fizz tickled her nose, effervescently snapping her back to reality. While she appreciated what he was doing, awkward as it was, she couldn't anoint it with any gravity.

Hell, after shitting on me the way he did, it's the least he could do, she thought. And more to the point, it was water under the bridge. His leaving her the way he did was so far down on Donna's list of concerns you'd need to hop in the car and drive to it.

"What happened, happened. It was shitty. You were shitty. But I've let it go, David. And I'm sure if I told you I forgive you and miss you, you'd ask me out again and we'd end up in bed, but you know, there is so much other...there's so much...I got other things that...that I have to... deal with. I mean, I thought you liked me better than you treated me but what the hell. I'm a big girl. And there's just so much more."

"More what? What do you mean?" David asked, his eyes squinting like they did when he didn't understand something, which Donna realized was a lot of the time even though she found it strangely sexy.

"I mean larger. In the scheme of things. If there is such a thing as the scheme of things. I'm finding life more random and less schematic than ever before," Donna said, her eyes glancing between him and the diet Pepsi in her hand.

Thrusting the large cup of soda into his chest, Donna smiled and said, "Here. I don't really need this either. I just thought I deserved it. It's diet. Drink it. I've already lost my taste for it."

As his hands instinctively grasped the plastic cup, Donna looked him up and down once more, accepting that she couldn't even muster any residual anger or resentment toward him. David wasn't a mean guy; he was just weak. And she wasn't in love with him anyway. Why waste any more energy on something that really, truly didn't matter?

Bigger fish, bigger fish... Donna thought in a mantra as she scooted past him and out the door into the sunshine. She knew he was still watching her even without glancing back, and she couldn't resist swaying her backside a little more evidently, just as a reminder to David, as she made it to her car and drove away.

TWENTY-FOUR

Picking up her cell phone to call Cam, Donna immediately set it down. Like she had a dozen times prior. She wanted to share this information with her best friend, but she couldn't. She needed to protect him from worrying. And that need was far stronger than her need to release this demon on someone else. She couldn't tell him. Or Andie. Or her mom. Or anyone else. She just couldn't.

I'm the strong one all the time, for God's sake, Donna thought, *I've always prided myself on that.*

This was the first time she had been the needy one. The one living the horror.

The concept of dying clobbered her yet again. This time, the concept of what comes after this life...if there was an after. Where do people go? Heaven. Hell. Or was it just over? The end. Nothing. Donna wasn't sure if she should go back to church and pray for forgiveness. Forgiveness from what, she wasn't really sure. She hadn't done anything too horrendous in her life.

But maybe all my minor transgressions add up into one big black mark in God's big book? she thought.

But when people find out they're dying, she assumed a good portion of them start praying for the absolution of their sins, so maybe she should join the crowd. Just to be on the safe side.

She was also quite sure some people just go out and start having crazy fun for as long as their bodies will tolerate. And Donna saw some merit in living the time you got left to the max. If only she had learned to do that before this, she'd know-how.

Rather, Donna mused, *I wonder how many others like me just want to go back to work without saying a word to another soul?*

That's where she felt in control. Planning weddings was her domain. She knew what worked, and she was good at it. It not only gave her an identity but being good at something gave her a sense of worth. And since she now felt her body was no longer in her control, it belonged to something that was going to kill her, having a sense of control and worth was absolutely necessary, paramount for Donna's sanity.

Sitting down with Andie and Cam, pretending the last few days never happened, Donna dodged questions like "What is going on?" by telling them she had a slight touch of the flu and while she tried to work through it, it kept knocking her down; and that until she was sure she wasn't contagious, she refused to see anyone. It was obvious that Cam suspected she wasn't telling them the whole truth, but he opted not to say a thing while Andie was there.

Donna caught them up on the details; what was ready to go and what still needed to be done. She noticed Cameron giving her the eye a few times but brushed it off as paranoia. He couldn't know anything and Donna felt secure that she was very good at faking her way through meetings like this. She had worked with enough horrible brides-to-be who made her skin crawl, yet she managed to keep a smile on her face throughout.

Donna was no expert in what it felt like to be as sick as she was told she was. Especially since, at this moment, it was nothing more than inconsistent, yet surprisingly sharp, pains. She didn't know what she would look like through this, and yes that was a concern, but more importantly, what it would feel like to slowly die.

With Cam gazing at her with weird suspicion, Donna couldn't help but wonder when he would actually know. Would it be something Donna gave away that he couldn't see or would he notice something physical about her that would be the telltale? She just wished he would stop staring at her, with his chin pointed at his chest, his eyes cast up, like some old English teacher in the midst of a conversation with a student about an essay he knew the student plagiarized. Donna wouldn't match his look. He could have his suspicions but he didn't know. Not yet. Nothing must change.

Well, except she had a medical anvil dropped on her head. But Cameron could not possibly know that.

By his wedding, he would. But not now, not today.

When they finished up, Donna gathered her bag and coat, wanting to make a swift exit without having to make any excuses as to why she wasn't lingering to chit-chat. She went so far as to prepare an excuse because Cam may not know what was going on, but he knew Donna. She was usually blabbing all her business to him.

Quickly hugging Andie, Donna told her she was late for another appointment.

"Who is he?" Cam asked.

Turning, both Andie and Donna fired quizzical glances at Cam.

"You've been anxious the entire time you've been here. And now you say you're late for an 'appointment,'" he uttered, making quotation marks with his fingers.

"Why can't an 'appointment' be an 'appointment'?" Donna asked, mimicking his air quotes.

"Because you'd tell me what it was and you haven't. All you've done is rattle off what's gotten done and what still needs to be done but at the pace of someone that's been holding in pee or something."

Andie winced at that one.

"Really, Cam," Andie groaned.

"You're marrying him," Donna added, trying to throw the scent onto Cam and off of herself.

"And the only thing I can think of is you have a date with someone you don't want to tell me about yet. Which leads me to believe you either don't think I'd like him or I already know him. Or both."

"Neither. It's an appointment. Nothing more, nothing less," Donna spoke as she slipped into her coat, heading toward the door.

"It's a date," he replied with sureness, as Donna made her way to the door.

"Believe what you want," Donna said. "I'll call you," she said to Andie, not Cam.

Andie gave Donna a wave as she cracked open the door and slid out, letting Cam believe she was heading out to meet some mystery guy rather than heading home to fall onto her sofa and pull the afghan over her. She wished it were a guy. She might not feel as if she were being swallowed alive then.

For the next two weeks, Donna worked with Andie almost every day. And attempted to avoid Cam, irrationally believing that, because they'd been friends forever, he would be able to somehow sense her impending death. She was looking forward to seeing her best friend marry this wonderful woman who had become her closest female friend. Having something to hang onto, to focus on, helped Donna keep her attention away from the inevitable. An inevitable that she hadn't quite made real for herself, and honestly didn't want to.

It was only those times, in the middle of the night, when she roused from the few hours of sleep she was able to get, that she'd fret over a future that wouldn't be hers. Or when she felt a pull or a pang in her back or side, wondering whether it was the beginning of something much worse. Since she had no idea what would be worse, everything scared her, everything made her hold her breath.

But Cam being a guy, and yes, Donna was blaming it at least partially on that, he was pretty much oblivious to anything odd with her physically. Which buoyed Donna's hopes that she could keep her secret until this wedding was over. Then, after Andie and Cam returned from their honeymoon, she would sit them both down, break the news, have a few good cries, let them take care of her, and then die. That simple.

As much as they would both be angry at her for keeping this from them, Cam was most likely livid, she knew they would understand why she did what she did. Not only for them but also for herself; because she needed to have something to do instead of chemo or any of the other possible Band-Aids that could do nothing more than prolong her life.

Again, she thought he would deep-down understand, but being upset over that would give him a place to settle his distress. Her dying would be hard on him. But Donna felt better knowing he had Andie. If she couldn't be in her best pal's life forever, there was some contentment in knowing he'd be taken care of and had someone he loved by his side.

When her cell phone rang as she was dozing on the sofa at about 8:30, after a day of wrestling with the seating arrangements and trying to find out why Andie's bridesmaids' dresses hadn't been started on yet, as well as simply feeling run down, Donna glanced at the phone, hoping she didn't have to pick it up. It was Andie.

She debated for a couple more rings before answering, knowing she was going to have to calm a bride-to-be's nerves about something and not really feeling up for it. But it was part of the job and the job was what she was trying to stay focused on to keep her mind off everything else.

Answering, Donna asked, "Everything okay?"

"I was going to ask you the same thing," Andie responded, catching Donna off-guard.

"What do you mean?"

"Can I ask you something personal?" Andie quizzed flatly.

"Yeah, of course," Donna responded, wanting to say "no" but knowing that would set off alarm bells.

"Are you pregnant?"

Okay, Donna did not see that one coming.

Donna went dead silent. Completely. Entirely. Not even breathing. Then a laugh bellowed up from deep inside, so deep it had to come from somewhere near where the cancer was whittling away at her body; a laugh that deep hadn't happened in weeks, a laugh so freeing and joyous and painfully happy. The only thing that stopped Donna's laugh was that it caused her to cough so hard she couldn't catch her breath.

"I'll take that as a no," Andie responded, chuckling slightly.

"No, no...certainly not pregnant."

"I'm sorry. I had to ask. It's just...I noticed something different over the last couple weeks."

"What do you mean different?" Donna asked.

Donna could actually hear Andie shake her head, trying to come up with the right words.

"It's hard to pinpoint, you know," Andie finally answered, trying to figure it out herself. "It's not like you haven't paid attention to every detail of this wedding, because you have, but you still seem distracted. And you're dodging Cam. I can see it. He can't but I can. And I thought, *Oh my gosh, she's got something she doesn't want to tell him. She doesn't want to upstage my wedding with news. And I racked my head and well...a pregnancy would certainly do that.*

"A pregnancy would," Donna agreed. "But I'm not. Thank God. And if I seem distracted, I'm not. I just...you know, have a couple of weddings like yours, which is my total focus, believe me."

"Donna, I don't want you to think I'm complaining or that I think you're not doing an amazing job. Even my mother thinks you walk on water with the attention to detail you give everything. I just thought something was going on and wanted to say if you need help or need to talk, I'm here. Before I'm a bride you're working with, I hope you look at me as your friend."

Donna's primal instinct was to jump on this offer, to answer swiftly, to come clean, to sob and tell Andie everything she was going through; her confusion, her terror, the horror of what was happening to her body. Even while she lay there, it all hit Donna like an electric shock. But just as immediately, Donna stopped herself. She realized she needed to talk to someone and if it were any other time, Andie and Cam would be the people she would go to first. But not under these circumstances.

She closed her eyes tightly as tears squeezed out the sides. She couldn't, she just couldn't.

"I love you for that, Andie. And you know if there were something other than work, I would tell you. But there isn't. I just want to get every detail of your wedding perfect, but I also have to start paying some attention to the other weddings I have upcoming."

"Are you sure?" Andie quizzed again, the concern in her voice telling Donna it was not that she didn't believe her; she was simply being thorough.

"Positive."

Andie and Donna finished the conversation with the usual girlfriend inconsequentials, but the more they gabbed about nothing the more Donna felt a clench in her throat and wanted to break down in tears. How the hell was she going to keep this news from her friends for six more weeks?

TWENTY-FIVE

D onna couldn't get out of bed. This was the first day that her entire body ached to the point of tears. She wasn't sure whether she should call the doctor or just suck down a few pain relievers every couple of hours. But if this was cancer taking hold, she hated it already and it was making her rethink how she was going to deal with this.

The phone rang a few times, which she let go to voicemail as she stood in front of her open refrigerator, debating whether milk would be good for how she was feeling, or if she could have what she craved, which was coffee. She was sure it wouldn't make her feel good but might give her a lift psychologically.

She certainly wasn't hungry but knew she should eat something or she was going to be dragging until she did.

Why does my body hurt so bad? If this is the flu or a bug of some kind, I can't be running to the doctor or to Urgent Care every time I'm feeling crappy, and the cancer wasn't supposed to start messing with me for months, according to Dr. Muliski. She said I had time. More time to feel good than I would have if I chose chemo.

Checking her calls, she saw there was one from Andie, two from people she didn't have to call back, and one from Andie's mom, which surprised her. She hadn't really been in touch with Caroline for the last couple of weeks.

First things first, Donna called the Chinese place down the block that delivered and ordered three bowls of soup. It wasn't chicken noodle but it was soup.

Hedging a bet, Donna returned Andie's call first. Andie called to give Donna information about one of the bridesmaids. Her cousin, Cynthia, who lived in New York, sent Andie her measurements for her dress, which Andie regretfully questioned, believing her cousin was trying to "diet down a size" rather than just give her actual measurements.

"If you have her number handy, give it to me. She's not the first bridesmaid I've had pull this 'I'll be a four by the time of the wedding' crap," Donna responded, trying not to let Andie hear the weakness in her voice.

After she did, Donna asked if she knew why her mother had called.

"My mother called you?" Andie quizzed, surprised. "I have no idea why. I haven't talked to her in a couple days. But I bet it's about the seating chart. She's had some calls. Requests."

"Dealt with it before. Many times."

"From relatives."

"Dealt with it."

"Relatives I wish weren't coming."

"Dealt with it."

"Then I'll let you deal with this too."

This made Donna smile. And she needed to smile.

At the end of the call, Andie asked, "I know I've asked before but...are you sure you're okay?"

"Tired. Not a good night's sleep. Too many things in my head. I get like this when I feel like time isn't on my side when putting together a wedding. Especially this wedding."

"I appreciate that," she said, "and can relate."

Donna announced she was going to call Caroline, so Andie wished her well and hung up. Lying on the sofa, Donna closed her eyes. Before she tackled Mrs. Hune, Donna needed a minute. Parsing the truth was more exhausting than it should be. But suddenly, her phone rang again and her eyes popped open.

It was Mrs. Hune again.

Either it's urgent or she's going to be unable to talk the rest of the day, Donna mused.

"How are you, Mrs. Hune?" Donna answered instead of saying "hello" It usually put someone in a better mood even if they were calling to complain.

"I'm sorry to keep calling," Caroline sighed as if it were a burden.

"Sorry I didn't call you back earlier. I was tied up with some things. What can I help you with?" Donna asked, cradling the phone in her neck, closing her eyes.

"I don't mean to be forward, so excuse me for saying this if I'm wrong, but I don't think I am," she stated, then paused long enough for Donna to feel her body tighten. "I had cancer. I know what it looks like."

There was a breath-holding silence on both ends of the call.

TWENTY-SIX

As horrible as she was feeling, Donna agreed to meet Mrs. Hune at a Starbucks in Town and Country. Nestled in a strip of little brick storefront shops on Clayton Road, it more often than not catered to high-end clientele residing in the area's ritzy suburbs.

After she announced to Donna she had had cancer, Donna couldn't speak. Her breath was trapped in her throat as if someone were strangling her. And she never said anything else but "Do you have time for coffee?"

Sitting across the small bistro table from Mrs. Hune, Donna looked like hell warmed over. But she didn't have time, nor was in any shape, to do much more than jump in the shower—the water actually painful as it hit her skin—pull her hair back and shove it under a hat.

Not my best look, Donna thought. But on a day where every movement ached, who cared?

For the first time since Donna had met her, Mrs. Hune was wearing little makeup, which allowed Donna to notice Caroline's beautiful bone structure which Donna noted was almost flawless. Like her daughter's. Donna understood what Mr. Hune saw in this woman and she imagined Mrs. Hune was probably slightly more beautiful than even Andie in her twenties, and as always, put together with a precision of upscale glamor no matter where she was going or who she was meeting.

She's one of those people who does everything for herself, but she does herself for everyone else, Donna thought.

"I had cancer. Liver cancer. When I was young. Andie doesn't know. Henry knows, we were dating then, but he doesn't know how bad it was. I went away that summer. Not to France, like I told him; I had chemo and radiation, which is what people did in those days. There weren't the drugs they have today."

"Again, I find myself asking this, but, why are you telling me this?" Donna asked, already knowing the answer but wishing she didn't.

Caroline smiled. "I'm not very good at much. Certainly not a very good mother, as I'm sure Andie has mentioned more than once. I haven't been a very good wife but thankfully Henry loves me, God knows why. And I'm not a very good friend, though my friends would never tell you that because either they're afraid to or because I come from money and people generally like the proximity to money. But one thing I have going for me is I'm surprisingly intuitive when it comes to things like this. I know illness, weird as that may sound. I saw so much of it for years and then lived through it. I can feel when it's around me."

Great, the cancer-whisperer, Donna thought.

And here she was, sitting across from her with a cup of tea and a half-eaten scone.

"Do you have cancer?" Caroline asked.

Donna wanted nothing more than to bolt from the table and dash out of this crowded coffee emporium, but her body ached too much.

"Yes," Donna said softly, wishing she didn't have to entertain this nonsense.

Mrs. Hune stiffened, sitting taller in her chair, a look of disbelief and surprise mixing on her face. Surprised that Donna hadn't denied it.

"Where?" Caroline asked, and then waved her hand ever so slightly as if erasing an imaginary chalkboard. "You don't have any reason to tell me," she quickly added.

"Cervical."

Again, she sat up in her chair. Donna was sure Caroline was patting herself on the back about being right as she let a whisper of a smile form on her lips.

Caroline nodded, before stating, "It can be dealt with. It's not fun, that I can assure you, but it is treat---"

"It's Stage Four. And it's spread."

That shut Caroline up.

Damn me, Donna thought, wishing she hadn't blurted that out, her need to skewer this woman stronger than her ability to shut her own trap.

But it worked. Caroline nearly spit her tea, a little actually dribbling off her lip which she instantly wiped with a napkin.

"Tell me you're just trying to make a point," Caroline said quickly in a breathy tone that made Donna realize she was actually trying to have a human emotion.

Donna smiled softly. *What do you say after you've told the truth?* she wondered.

"I wouldn't make up something like this for a 'gotcha' moment. Whatever intuition you have, it's good. Damn good, and a little freaky. But now you have to do something for me."

Mrs. Hune nodded without a word.

"Andie doesn't know," Donna admitted.

"Does Cameron?"

Donna shook her head before speaking. "No," she stated definitively. "And I don't want either of them to know anything about this. Not your husband, or anyone else. Hell, I haven't even told my own mother, so I'm not even sure why I just didn't lie to you. Please don't make me wish I had. I want to do their wedding. I want it to be phenomenal, as it will be my last. My doctors have told me I have about six months. So far, I just feel crappy but not life-alteringly so.

So, I'm still working and I'm keeping this a secret until I simply can't, which come hell or high water, I'm going to make sure is after the wedding. Because as stupid as it sounds, there's nothing I'd rather be doing right now than planning this event and getting to see my best friend marry your daughter. I'm asking you to keep a secret. Tell me now, right now, if you can do that. I need to hear you say it. Be honest. Because if you don't think you can, I need to know that too."

Caroline's eyes seemed to widen with each word Donna spoke.

"Can you keep this a secret?" Donna repeated emphatically.

There was a rim of tears in Caroline's eyes. Donna wasn't sure whether it was because she was sad for her or because

Donna had entrusted her with a secret she didn't think she was capable of keeping.

But Mrs. Hune nodded.

"I need to hear your voice, Mrs. Hune."

"You kept mine about what I said at the engagement party, I will keep your secret," she said, before her hand jutted across the table, grabbing Donna's, squeezing it tightly with a strength Donna couldn't believe Caroline possessed.

"But you're dying. How...how do you go on knowing that? I never believed for a minute I would die. Never. But you... where do you get that strength?"

The two women sat at the table, Caroline holding Donna's hand as her words smacked Donna across the face.

Donna was dying.

Even if the doctors hadn't put it in such blunt terms. She was dying. Hearing Caroline actually say those words, seeing the empathetic pain in the eyes of a woman who was probably the least compassionate person Donna had ever met, made it more real than it had ever been.

"I don't have strength," Donna gasped harshly, "I don't!"

Feeling the heave in her chest, Donna closed her eyes. Tears. They fell. She couldn't look at Caroline. And she couldn't stop the tears. Caroline wouldn't let go of Donna's hand, actually tightening her grip.

"Goddamn it, I'm dying..." Donna wept softly.

Mrs. Hune let Donna cry for a good ten minutes without saying a word. Every time Donna opened her water-logged eyes, Caroline was glancing around. Donna was sure hoping no one knew who she was. Donna thought it must look like Caroline was either firing her or cutting off her trust fund, and she was now inconsolable. But Donna was unconcerned about what people thought; in six months it wouldn't matter if they were gossiping about her.

After the tears subsided, Donna sipped her lukewarm tea without saying much. Neither did Mrs. Hune, now that she proved her intuition was accurate. And while Donna didn't believe she would divulge the secret, Donna believed Caroline was actually feeling her pain as she held her hand.

Donna recognized this was not a woman who went to sleep carrying the burden of anyone else's problems. She was not built for that. Even her own daughter's trials and tribulations probably didn't keep her up nights. And though Andie had never said that, it now made more sense to Donna.

Walking out to their cars, Donna filled Caroline in on the wedding plans and the items that still needed to be finished. Including the dress. It was a way to fill the moment. As they arrived at Mrs. Hune's Lexus, Donna extended her hand and thanked her. As she took it, Mrs. Hune's face scrunched up and she pulled Donna to her, her arms wrapping around Donna tightly, holding her.

"I hope I'm not being presumptuous, but if you need to talk, you know how to reach me," she half-whispered in Donna's ear, still hugging her.

The intimacy stunned Donna. She wasn't sure whether this was the sisterhood of cancer or the fact that she had oozed herself into the Hunes' family life by planning this wedding.

Probably both, especially when the hug lingered longer than Donna was comfortable with. Though she imagined it was Caroline's way of telling her she was serious about the offer.

"Love is an effort, Mrs. Hune," Donna said.

"I'm learning that," Caroline admitted.

"It's an effort worth making. Your husband. Your daughter," Donna said, nothing to lose. "I wish I had more time to make that effort for the people that love me. But until I can't, I'm going to keep making the effort."

They locked eyes a moment before in silence before Caroline slid into her car and motored off with a brief wave. Donna stood in the parking lot, allowing the warmth of the day and the smell of early spring to overtake her.

She'd been to many places around this country and beyond over the past couple of years but nowhere else in the world had the aromas of St. Louis in spring. The damp perfection of the air, cleansed by frequent rain, filled the nostrils with something that could best be described as comfort. Winters could be tiring in St. Louis; the gray lingering for too many days, making you feel as if you were living in a small frozen jar. It can be claustrophobic.

And summers always had a stretch that would be sweltering; your body couldn't help but perspire continually, your clothes always sticking to your skin. People lie to themselves that the humidity is sexy, the skin glistening, but it really isn't, certainly not for Donna. It's just brutal and damp. She ran from the air conditioning of whatever building she was in, to the air conditioning of her car, to the air conditioning of her home. And in each place, with every friendly person she would meet, there was a signaled understanding about the humidity. A sigh, a roll of the eyes, a weak smile as you wiped away the spritzing beads of sweat on your upper lip or hairline.

But spring is amazing in this city. As is fall. And while she loved fall more, Donna adored the spring because of the aromatic newness to everything. Seeing the greenery budding and the crocuses and daffodils pushing up from the dirt and opening into whites, yellows, and purples coddled her soul and gave her a renewed sense of hope.

Not for Donna this spring, but she had been indoctrinated for so long, even at this moment in her life, it felt right and more importantly, safe. Even telling Mrs. Hune her secret seemed to have carved away some of the burdens she had been holding onto.

"The moment this wedding is over, I'm going to rent a billboard on Highway 40 and make a public announcement," Donna said out loud to no one. Adding in her head, *at that point I'll take all the sympathy, soup, and prayer people are willing to offer as I face whatever is to be.*

Maybe even a miracle.

TWENTY-SEVEN

The next two weeks shot by. Donna's hopes were buoyed by the fact she didn't feel any worse. She didn't feel any better either, but the pain certainly didn't graduate to anything she couldn't tolerate while working, as long as she choked down a couple of Aleve or the oxy Dr. Muliski prescribed. The oxy scared Donna to death but considering she was already dying, that scare didn't hold as much dramatic weight as it used to.

And though she had waves of regret for admitting the terminality of her cancer to Mrs. Hune, each day that passed let Donna breathe a little easier since Caroline hadn't divulged her prognosis to anyone else. Especially her daughter.

Speaking to Dr. Muliski almost daily and seeing the doctor religiously once a week, Donna realized she spoke to Dr. Muliski as much, if not more, as anyone else in her life, except for Cam and Andie. And so far, she'd been able to keep her secret hidden from them.

Donna had also been calling her mother more often. She sensed something was amiss since Donna hadn't been faithful about their contact for years. Donna passed it off as a change of heart; this was her attempt at being a better daughter. She didn't think her mother believed her, but Donna could tell she was grateful for the calls, so she didn't ask any more questions in spite of her suspicion.

I had to have inherited that trait from someone, Donna thought with a smile.

With exactly one month until the wedding, Donna sat down in a favorite place of Cam's, Leta B's in the Southwest section of St. Louis, about a half-mile or so off of Hampton.

Leta's infectious laugh, and her sarcastic husband, Vic, who bussed tables as he dropped smart-ass comment after smart-ass comment to anyone and everyone, endeared Cam to this place. And if you could give Vic shit back, as Andie learned to do quickly, he loved you.

Cam and Andie arrived in Betty Blue and he carefully pulled into the small parking lot, parking his pride-and-joy in the very back spot where no one could put a scratch in it by opening a door too swiftly.

Andie climbed out, shaking her head over his fawning concern for his "four-wheeled girlfriend" as she had come to refer to the car.

"God forbid it ever comes down between me and that car," she said as she hugged Donna before they sat down at a table.

They ordered another terrific meal. Leta had gone back to the kitchen to prepare Cam's steak herself, which made him feel important, while Andie, who was freaking out about looking amazing on her wedding day, ordered grilled fish and salad. Donna opted for a creamy pasta, something she would never eat under different circumstances but thought, *What the hell, an urn is one-size-fits-all,* as she closed the menu.

Cam was a bit surprised, and Andie side-eyed Donna as she ordered, which only made Donna roll her eyes.

"I'm not the one getting married," Donna said, sluffing off the concern. Changing the subject, she quickly jumped into the problems she was having with two of Andie's out-of-town bridesmaids, both cousins. Andie had asked them to be in the bridal party out of obligation to appease her mother and father.

The first bites of Donna's dinner were exactly what she hoped any creamy, garlicky pasta would be; almost melting in her mouth as she savored the flavor, the noodles sliding down her throat. *If there is a heaven, this, toasted ravioli and St. Louis-style pizza is what they serve,* she thought, trying to amuse herself, in love with every bite of the pasta. It was exactly what she needed, old-fashioned comfort food, and her joy played on her face.

"You act like you haven't eaten in a while," Cam said, referring to the rapturous glow on Donna's face.

"I'm hungry, shut up and stop being judgy! I never get food like this. God knows I don't know how to make it," Donna replied, before turning to Andie. "I think it's a good idea to cut the cake before the toasts; it gives the servers plenty of time to get the cake cut up before and have it ready for the old aunts who will rush up and wrap a half-dozen pieces in napkins to take home," trying to throw off any suspicion about anything else going on but the wedding plans.

"Does that really happen?" Andie asked.

"Every wedding. Every parent there who has a little kid will take cake home as well."

Already having downed a couple of cold Lites, Cam laughed loudly, causing Andie and Donna to break up laughing themselves.

"Did that amuse you?" Donna chided him with a huge grin.

But that's when she felt it. It hit her on the right side as if someone had taken a molten hot piece of glass and shoved it through her ribs and into her lung. She couldn't breathe, in or out.

Grabbing Cam's arm, the smile washed from her face, sweat beading up instantly as her eyes widened in terror. As she reached for Andie, her arm smashed into the wine glasses between them, sending them crashing to the floor.

Cam stood, trying to grab Donna as she shifted out of the chair toward Andie. Andie caught her and held her from behind, laying her on the floor as tears flooded Donna's eyes and she began shaking involuntarily.

"Are you choking?!? Are you choking?!" Donna could hear Cam scream at her.

But Donna couldn't speak; she could only shake her head side to side, not sure what to do, still unable to draw a breath, panic surging through her body.

"Call 911!" Cam screamed as Andie laid her on the floor.

The pain subsided slightly and Donna was able to pull in a few short breaths which kept her from passing out. But she was now completely terrified. She feared she was dying. Right here. Right now.

Through the tears she attempted to blink out of her eyes, seeing Andie leaning over her.

"Can you hear me?" Andie asked, desperate to remain calm.

Donna nodded.

"Can you breathe?"

Again, Donna nodded but barely.

"Can you talk?"

Donna wanted to say something, though it wasn't anything close to "I'm fine," which is what she wanted everyone to believe, but she couldn't speak. There was not enough air to push out to form a word. Andie could see the terror in Donna's eyes and it frightened her more than even she realized. All Donna could do was signal with her hand and, while Andie held tightly to the other one.

Donna could see Cam dash away as other faces peered down at her.

"There's an ambulance on the way," Andie told Donna and Donna nodded in response.

A siren. Faint, but Donna could hear it as the usual chatter in the bar was almost silent. Though she couldn't make out faces, Donna counted the heads of the people she could see surrounding her over and over, trying to keep her mind busy and not focus on the reality of what this very public episode was going to mean.

The wail of the sirens actually shook the floor she was lying on. Donna heard the rush of bodies through the door, the clatter of a rolling gurney, people talking. The faces standing over her backed away, except for Andie who would not let go of Donna's hand.

Paramedics peppered Donna with questions but she was still unable to speak so Andie handled most of them. The pain in Donna's side waffled from unbearable to absolutely excruciating and she couldn't help but show each spasm on her face. Andie let the paramedics know Donna was having a very difficult time breathing.

"And she's in pain," Andie added quickly. Donna pointed to her right side, below her lung, as she winced again, fighting tears as the pain got worse. She squeezed Andie's hand tighter.

"Could you stop with the questions and get her to a hospital?!" Cam begged, moving up next to Andie, looking down at Donna, saying, "I'm here, Donna. Andie and I are with you. I know you really liked that pasta, you want us to get it to go?" he joked, trying to alleviate the fear on his best friend's face, which Donna found oddly comforting.

The paramedics rolled Donna on her side and then back down on a board, then quickly lifted her onto the gurney. She could hear them talking with their dispatch team and the response, but the pain was so severe she couldn't make sense of what they were communicating.

She just wanted them to get her into a building where someone could make this pain go away. She dearly wanted to take a deep breath, feel her lungs fill fully. Her brain swam.

As they walked next to Donna out of Leta B's, sobering up with every step, Andie refused to let go of Donna's hand. Cam's hand stayed on Donna's arm, only letting go momentarily so they could slide her into the back of the ambulance.

In the ambulance, they placed an oxygen mask over her face and though Donna still couldn't breathe deeply, she took comfort that there was oxygen being directed into her lungs.

Donna felt the prick in her arm, she assumed starting an IV. She kept her eyes closed. She was feeling claustrophobic enough without visually seeing the tight space she was in. She wished she could pass out, so as not to even hear what was going on.

She knew Andie was in the ambulance because she hadn't let go of her hand. In a moment of clarity, Donna was relieved she hadn't even finished her first glass of wine, fearing they wouldn't give her painkillers to dull the pain ripping through her.

I don't care. Give them to me, Donna thought, *just make this go away!*

Lights of a hallway. Donna saw Cam; she saw Andie.

Then she saw nothing.

Did I die? Is this what it is? Nothing? No heaven? No hell? I'm not getting that pasta again, am I? No toasted ravioli. I should have eaten more of that stuff when I was alive. Damn it! There's no singing or dancing angels. No fire and people wailing. Death is just this? Donna hallucinated as she felt her body floating further and further away.

Then she fell asleep.

Finally coming to, the walls of the room were almost opaque white. There was a whiteboard across the room with the name of a nurse and doctor written on it. Donna recognized that she dreamt all that stuff about the emptiness of death. She was alive. And from the beeping monitors surrounding her, she was hooked up to a lot of stuff that was supposed to make sure she stayed that way.

Perfect.

Her neck was stiff, so Donna's hand patted around, searching for something to drink. She came across one of those weirdly oversized Styrofoam jugs with the corrugated plastic straw. Lifting it from the table, it was either heavy on its own or full. She took a sip, and the dryness washed down her throat in a lump as if she had swallowed a wad of tissue.

It was then she noticed Cam asleep in a chair off to her right.

"Cam," Donna muttered in a hushed, harsh voice not loud enough to rouse him. Taking another sip of the water, Donna cleared her throat before making another attempt.

"Cam!" Donna spoke as loud as she could muster, able to get his name out at a reasonable volume.

Cam's eyes fluttered open and he sat up, smiling as he did.

"She lives," he uttered, his smile growing.

Standing, Cam moved to the side of Donna's bed.

"You scared the shit out of me," he admonished, his voice stern but soft.

"Yeah," she responded dryly, "scared me a little bit too."

After calling for a nurse, Cam told Donna that Andie had left a few hours ago to get some sleep. And that Donna's mom was there most of the night as well. Not knowing when she was going to come out of her stupor, they planned shifts, with Cameron taking the first one.

As the nurse arrived and checked Donna over, asking her a handful of questions and checking the monitors and her vitals, Cam remained silent. His eyes locked on Donna and she suspected he knew and wanted some verification.

"What hospital am I at?" Donna asked the nurse before she left.

The nurse smiled. "Barnes."

Turning to Cam, Donna winced slightly. "What did they tell you?" she asked, her entire body achy, adding to the overwhelming feeling of exhaustion. She was able to take a full breath though not a deep one.

Cam shook his head.

"I know you've been seeing some doctor here at Barnes. That's all I really know. I was hoping you would tell me..." he said quickly, before pausing and adding, "...the truth."

A couple of weeks before his wedding. Donna didn't want this to happen. Certainly not now. But she was trapped in a bed with tubes and wires. And her best friend needed the truth.

"Sit..." she mustered, patting the bed next to her.

A grimace settled on his face, making Cameron look like a boy about to be scolded for something he was trying to hide. His chest rose and fell quickly with each shallow breath he took, knowing what Donna was about to say could not be good.

"I'm going to cut to the chase because it's all going to come out anyway," Donna began. "I have cancer. And it's bad."

"How...how bad?" Cam stammered, his throat closing as he fought tears.

"To the point I'm not fighting it. Because to do so would ruin the time I have left."

Donna held her breath as tears filled Cameron's eyes. Cameron didn't make a sound as they fell down his cheeks, soaking into the sheet Donna was lying on. He took her hand and held it to his chest, almost as if wishing he could give her his own breath. They said nothing, each trying to comfort the other in silence for a long moment.

"How...long?"

"Six months."

"Six months?!" he gasped, trying to bite back the words as he spat them out, "Are you sure? Are they sure? Why aren't you gonna fight this? I'll be there. Andie will be there. We'll take care of you. Whatever you need."

"That's what I don't want. To have to have someone take care of me."

"That's bullshit," Cam snapped before calming himself. "Have you told your mom?"

Donna shook her head.

"Only one who knows is Andie's mom," Donna replied, almost laughing.

Cameron reared back to get a better look at Donna. As he did, he realized she wasn't joking. Donna sighed.

"She's weird. She figured it out. She had cancer before," Donna said, again having to clear her throat. "I don't even think Andie knows that. But Mrs. Hune's got like some sixth sense about it. She confronted me. I didn't want to lie to her. I made her promise not to tell anyone. I didn't want anyone to know until after your wedding. I wanted to get through the wedding, for you and Andie. It's really important to me that I put this wedding together for you, Cam. Next to my own, this is the wedding I've always dreamed about. Yours. I know that sounds stupid or whatever, but it's true. I want this to be an awesome day for you and Andie."

"You've already made sure that's going to happen."

"And I'm going to continue to."

"You can't---"

Donna stopped him from speaking another word of that sentence by squeezing his arm with every ounce of power she had in her grip, which wasn't much physically. But he got the point.

"I can. I have to. And you have to let me. If not for you and Andie, then for me. This is what's keeping me alive, Cam. I'll never have my own wedding to plan. I'll never walk up the aisle to meet the man I love at the altar. But seeing my best friend get married, knowing I had a hand in the day, that's a gift. You have to give that to me."

Cam's face scrunched up and his lip protruded as tears flooded his eyes. He'd made the same face every time he cried since he was a kid, and right now, he looked like a little boy again.

He pulled his feet up onto the bed and slid next to Donna, his arms going around her as he sobbed. It felt like Cameron himself was dying. Donna couldn't remember ever hearing a man cry that hard, much less Cameron who wasn't prone to huge emotions. He held her tightly against him, his chest heaving with each overwrought breath.

There were a thousand things he wanted to say at this moment, but he just needed to get this out. And Donna was grateful he couldn't speak. She wasn't sure she wanted to hear the words he had to say, as there were a thousand things she wanted to say to him as well. But as she started to cry, everything could be expressed with tears. It was all here; they were in each other's arms, Donna's head against his chest. Both now crying uncontrollably.

She'd known this man, her best friend since forever, loved her. And she loved him. The hardest part about death as Donna could see it at this moment would be losing this friendship that had been the most vital, valuable, consistent thing in her life since she was five.

Closing her eyes, Donna let Cameron release all the emotions this news had bluntly forced out of him. She knew trying to shut this down would only cause it to boil up again some other place, some other time. Donna had been through it, trying to contain it as if the anger and pain were toxic. It was going to happen and you had to ride it out, even if you didn't want to be bawling at whatever particular moment the urge took over.

Donna would let Cam hold her and cry for as long as he needed to. And she would cry with him. Not for her own death; she'd cried over that, and would again, but for the finality of their friendship. She was learning there were no boundaries when it came to this depth of pain.

The door from the hallway made a whooshing sound. Figuring it was a nurse on her rounds, Donna glanced over as Andie came through the door, immediately stopping in her tracks as she witnessed the man she intended to marry holding his best friend, his eyes water-logged, his cheeks tear-stained.

Andie's face dropped and she actually took a step back toward the door in fear, her hand going to her mouth to silence any sound she might make. She had never seen Cam like this. And she automatically knew that whatever it was, if it was bad enough to break the steadiest person she'd ever known, it was going to floor her.

As tears filled her eyes, not even sure what she was crying about, Andie moved to the bed. She touched Donna's shoulder as Cam reached over and took Andie's other hand, holding tightly. She needed to feel the warmth of his grip.

"What...are we dealing with...?" Andie forced out.

"It's real bad..." was all Cam could get out before fighting his tears again.

Donna laughed. Not hard, but it was a laugh or maybe a cry with a little laughing involved. But the two of them crying made her laugh. There were going to be way too many tears coming up in the future.

"It's not funny," Cam protested.

And again, Donna laughed through tears.

"Yeah, it kinda is."

"What is it?" Andie asked, now confused as to the severity of things. "What am I crying over?"

Donna made a C with her fingers and held it to her head. Andie's look only grew grimmer.

"They've given me six months," Donna said in a voice so even, the tears still flowing didn't shake.

Andie gasped again, this time more deeply, finding it hard to let out a breath. She looked directly at Donna and the tears fell furiously down her face.

"My mother knew, didn't she," Andie said, more than asked.

Nodding, Andie continued, "I knew there was something she wasn't telling me. A reason she was hugging me, asking how I was feeling. I didn't know what it was about and I didn't want to ask.

"Don't be mad at her, I made her promise not to say anything. I didn't tell her, she just sort of knew."

"The one thing she's good at," Andie answered, "knowing illness."

"It's weird," Donna chuckled.

"I know, right? And though it was a little scary, it was kind of nice having my mom make an effort," Andie said. Donna smiled, knowing she had at least a little something to do with Caroline's affection towards her daughter.

Andie climbed next to Donna, and she and Cam held her, all three crammed into this hospital bed. Donna didn't want anything more at this moment. Feeling these two people love her with everything they were, caring for her, and sharing the fear and horror of her prognosis wouldn't heal her body, but it would help heal Donna's soul and her spirit. And both were in desperate need of relief.

Over Donna, Cam and Andie stared into each other's eyes. Donna didn't have to see it to feel it. Being between them in this bed, Donna felt the depth of their love. But even more, she felt something she couldn't explain, a physical current between Cam and Andie. Something willful. Definite. A communication of the heart.

If this was what love felt like, Donna regretted that she would never get to experience it.

But whatever was happening between them, Donna felt blessed to be part of it, to feel the energy between them. She hoped they would always speak this way—with an electrical, inaudible connection—because it was the most powerful thing she had ever felt.

She closed her eyes, wishing it could heal her but she knew it was just between them.

TWENTY-EIGHT

She didn't want to be continually reminded of the inevitability. She knew she was dying. No, she wasn't giving up; she was just trying to take every day and live it, enjoy what she could, and keep moving forward. The pain subsided, and her doctor prescribed a medication that would help Donna manage any future discomfort. She was so antsy to get out of that bed, mainly because the cat was out of the bag. The people who came in, all wanting to know why she didn't tell them made every moment emotionally painful, most especially when she was alone with her mother. Donna felt trapped, having to explain her rationalization and feelings about what was happening. And the finality of it all.

The tears were overwhelming; everyone else's, not Donna's. Hers had dried up just a little more with each person she saw. She had at least partially come to grips with her future. Or lack of it. It simply was. Donna intended to stay as busy as her body would let her, accomplish what she intended and find a reason to smile. It wasn't like she had a choice in this. It wasn't *Jeopardy*, "I'll take Cancer for a thousand, Alex."

She knew one thing: she had to get back to being Donna. She had changed from just a few weeks ago, but whoever she was now, she wanted to feel at least a skosh normal.

Once alert enough, Donna was back to business, even if it was from a hospital bed. She had lost a couple of days, not something she enjoyed, even when she was "walking into the white light or whatever it is they say happens to you when you die," as she told her nurse, Stephanie, who laughed a lot at Donna's crusty sarcasm.

What Donna hated most was that, once the word was out, she felt people were treating her as a dead-man-walking. But Donna being Donna, instead of getting angry about it, opted to use it to her advantage and wheedle as much sympathy as she could to get what she wanted for Cam and Andie's wedding, which would be her last job, to create something beyond their wildest dreams.

"You only die once," she muttered as she waited for a phone call, propped up with a few pillows in her hospital bed.

It was Donna's goal now to be remembered for this wedding as much as Cam and Andie were. It was going to be her show-stopping masterpiece. Spectacular. Talked about. An event.

Donna realized she hadn't heard from Caroline since the news broke. The Hunes had sent flowers. But since Mrs. Hune no longer had a secret to keep, which had to be a burden lifted, Donna thought she would at least call.

Neither did Mr. Hune for that matter.

Donna guessed they felt they weren't really close enough to her, which at its core they weren't. Or that they would be intruding on a private situation that turned out quite public. And it wasn't like there weren't people in and out. Donna's mother, Geena, was there, doting over her; Cam almost never left her side except when Andie was there to take over. Three-and-a-half days of constant attention. Yuck. Donna was thankful but still, yuck.

And the entire time Cam and Andie were in the hospital room together, allowing Donna's mom to go home and get some rest, there was a silent conversation occurring between them. It was like the energy Donna felt when they were laying with her. Only louder.

They kept slipping out of the room whenever someone else was visiting, avoiding the sobs and questions about how this could happen to a person like Donna as if cancer selected only special people to obliterate.

Donna spied them pow-wowing in the hallway, heads nodding, hands gesturing. Her fear was that they were plotting a way to tell her they were bringing in another wedding coordinator. Donna had done so much and they were so close, and even though she was laid up and out of it for a few days, things were still nearly, and surprisingly, on schedule. There was little for someone else to do, but damn it, that little bit was still Donna's to finish and she wanted to take care of the job without interference. She might be sick but, so far except for this crappy setback, not that sick.

But that never came up. Neither mentioned it, which had Donna wondering what else they were ducking out to deal with. There was certainly a lot on their plate at the moment, but Donna couldn't help but feel it concerned her.

Although everything in this hospital room, or just outside it, concerned Donna. Laying in this uncomfortable bed was making her paranoid on top of everything else. Donna was simply hoping she hadn't ruined what was supposed to be one of the greatest moments in their lives. The days leading up to a wedding, while busy, stressful, and often bordering on the insane, were also effervescent and delicious.

It all depended on how the couple, especially the bride, dealt with the details. She wanted nothing more than for her friends to be happy remembering these moments and enjoy the run-up to the wedding.

Finding out Donna was dying certainly put a damper on that.

Finally released and back home, Donna jumped on the wedding detail work express.

Andie checked in a couple of times a day, more to see how she was feeling than to talk details, which she was sure Donna was taking care of. Donna asked Andie specifically not to mention cancer or that she was sick. In return, Andie made Donna promise that if she was feeling bad, she would not try and hide it. But something had changed between them and while not a surprise, Donna wished it hadn't. Donna could hear it in Andie's voice.

Andie was kid-gloving her now instead of fighting the world alongside of her. Donna was now a wounded warrior in Andie's eyes and Donna felt she was being treated as such. She would have loved to call Andie on it, but this had already gotten weird.

As much as Donna reiterated that she didn't want to dwell on being sick, that she didn't want it to be part of the conversation, she was sure now it was the first thing people thought about when they saw her. Andie and Cam included.

Time was limited for Donna, not for them. Her two best friends were going to remember her forever. They were going to love this day so much. Donna resolved that not only were they going to name their first daughter after her, they would name every baby they had "Donna". Even the boys.

"There's a problem with the dress," Donna heard the distress in Andie's voice.

"LeAnne didn't call me," Donna responded, already texting the owner of the bridal shop where the dress was bought and fitted.

"And Sarah can't be a bridesmaid," Andie continued, almost breathlessly so.

"When did this happen?"

"She called me this morning. I don't want to get into the reasons, and honestly, she's a cousin and I only asked her because she's a relative. I can always get another bridesmaid...like you," she said.

"No, no, don't try pulling me in. I love you, Andie, but I have a job to do, and I cannot do it in a salmon-colored dress. No offense."

"None taken. But think about it, think about it," she pleaded, "as a back-up, if I get stuck. Please."

"As a back-up if you get stuck? We have two weeks. You'll think of someone. Stay calm."

"Aren't you calm enough for the both of us?" Andie laughed.

"I always am. I always will be. This wedding is going to go off without a hitch," Donna assured her.

"I needed to hear you say that," Andie responded. "Now, please meet me at the dress shop."

It was Donna's turn to laugh. "Like I got something better to do? I'll see you there in a half an hour."

Jumping in the shower, Donna quickly washed and towel-dried her hair. She didn't have time for anything fancy so once it was dry enough, she tied it back. Throwing on clothes, she wasn't as concerned about how she appeared as a month earlier. Who was she dressing for?

Even if "the guy" were to bump into her tomorrow, Donna wouldn't think Mr. Right would like the answer when he asked her what she was doing with the rest of her life. Having cancer had taken a lot of the stress out of driving as well. She couldn't get worked up about it as she did before.

Donna wished she had the time to chronicle all the things that feel different now that she knew her time was limited. Sort of a before-and-after cancer journal. There were things that just didn't feel as stressful as they used to, which made her slightly insane because she realized how much of life she freaked out over, and it had no real validity in the scheme of things. Worrying over nonsense, things Donna knew were bullshit, was such a complete waste of energy and time and reason. If someone wore a smile that was the best accessory anyone could dress in.

Why wasn't I this wise before? See what death does? It makes you smart, Donna mused, a smile wide on her lips.

Arriving at Perfect Touch Bridal Shop, Donna stepped in, spotting Andie talking with LeAnne, the flamboyantly wonderful owner. They were holding hands, talking closely, while another young bride-to-be was going through gowns with two of the assistants, Jacey, and one who was so new Donna didn't know her name. As she walked in they turned, Jacey giving Donna a smile. She waved as she moved toward Andie and LeAnne.

"What's the problem with the dress?"

"Don't be mad at me," Andie offered as a lead.

"About...?"

"I want you to try on a dress---" she offered next.

"I told you, you will find another bridesmaid," Donna interjected, cutting her off.

"Please. Try on a dress. For me. I'm the bride. I have seniority in this case," Andie giggled, disarming Donna slightly.

"You think so?"

Andie nodded firmly.

LeAnne bowed to Andie as she whispered, "Humor the lass, the wedding is in less than two weeks."

Donna sighed. She had a suspicion Andie was going to try and pull this. Having Donna in her wedding was something Andie talked to Donna about early on and she nixed that idea for obvious reasons.

Coordinating a wedding is never easy under the best of circumstances on the day of. People get crazy. You have to remain the voice of calm. The person everyone looks to when whatever little hell that can break loose does. Donna didn't think she could do that when she was strolling up an aisle, smiling at people with a bouquet of lilacs locked in her fist.

Fine, Donna thought, *I'll try on a dress. But this fight is not over. I'm just not having it here. I'm outnumbered and I know once I talk to Cameron, I can convince him to let me have my way. My dying should trump Andie's bride-ness.*

As horrible as that sounded.

LeAnne opened the dressing room door, escorting Donna in. There was a box on the chair. Sarah's dress. Being one of Andie's out-of-town cousins, Donna had never actually met Sarah, only Facetiming with her twice. The only thing Donna really remembered about her was that she was the out-of-town cousin who wasn't lying about her dress size.

Popping open the box, Donna flipped the lid to find a wedding dress. Pulling it out, it resembled Andie's dress, which Donna loved, but there were alterations.

Great, wrong dress! And why didn't she tell me about the changes to her gown?

Donna was more than aware that there had been a few other things occupying everyone's head, but still, she thought Andie loved the dress she helped design. Donna admitted, looking at this dress, that she actually liked this cut a little more, and the Venetian straps were certainly more attractive, in her opinion than the simple spaghetti straps Andie originally picked.

"Andie," Donna called out from inside the dressing room, "wrong dress. This one is your wedding gown."

When no answer came back through the dressing room door, Donna stepped out.

Cameron appeared out of seemingly nowhere and stood next to Andie. Confused, Donna took a step back as if she couldn't see them well, trying to make sense of what he was doing there. Donna shook her head as she gazed at him oddly, unsure.

The hair on the back of her neck stood up as she corner-eyed him.

"What are you doing here?" Donna uttered, suspicious.

Cameron let loose with a big smile, a weapon of superiority when he had pulled something nefarious and either gotten away with it or believed he would. He used it as a kid and he was still using it to this day.

"I came to see the dress," he said.

"The dress? I have the wrong one, and you're not seeing Andie in her wedding gown until the day of the wedding and you're certainly not seeing me in a bridesmaid dress, thank you very much. I told Andie she should look for someone else, and clearly, she brought you here with the hopes of changing my mind. But it just saves me the time talking to you later. Talk to your bride-to-be and explain that a wedding planner doesn't have time the day of the wedding to be walking up the aisle and standing at the altar holding a bouquet. I have too many details to be attending to while all of that is going on."

"First," Andie said, her smile suddenly matching Cameron's, which made Donna freak out even more, "you don't have the wrong dress."

Again, Donna looked at the dress and then back to Andie and Cameron, both wearing big, goofy smiles.

"Do you like the dress?" Cameron asked. "Andie designed it."

"I know she did," Donna responded, still unsure what exactly was going on.

"For you," Cam added firmly.

Donna stood silently, her brow furrowed. For me? What the hell does that mean? Do they think I want to be buried in a wedding dress? Especially Andie's? Is this the right time to tell them I intend to be cremated?

"What am I going to do with a wedding dress?" Donna snapped. "Be buried in it?"

Cameron stepped toward her. He took a glance back at Andie whose smile grew even bigger. Fishing into his jacket pocket, Cameron slipped down to one knee. Opening the box, he displayed a ring. A diamond which glistened in the overhead lights.

"Donna, we've been best friends since we were kids. And now I'm asking you if you would do me the honor of marrying me." His eyes involuntarily rimmed with tears as he spoke.

Donna could not comprehend what was going on.

Marry him? He's marrying Andie. In twelve days.

"But you're marrying...you can't..." Donna stammered. "Get up. Get up. Get up! What are you doing?"

"He's asking you to marry him," Andie stated, stepping up behind Cameron, her hands resting on his shoulders.

With everyone looking at Donna, her head shook. Whatever was happening, she didn't like it.

"But..." was all she could sputter out.

Cameron rose to his feet, the ring still in his hand as Andie stepped to his side.

"Donna, Andie, and I talked about it. A lot. Over the last few days. She and I are in complete agreement. Getting married has been your dream since before you and I met, and that's a hell of a long time ago. If we can give you that the one gift, then we want to do it," he said, his voice catching on his words.

Though Donna's head was spinning and her knees wanted to buckle, it crystalized in her head what they were talking about in the hospital hallway while she was stuck in that bed, entertaining all the sorrow one could possibly bear. They were planning this.

Dear God, these two shining souls decided to put their needs second and give me what they both know I have secretly—and not so secretly—desired since I was a kid. Donna felt like she had been broadsided by a rogue wave and now the undertow was dragging her out to sea. The sea she was drowning in was a sea of love.

"I can't! I can't do this to you. Either of you," Donna declared, focusing on Andie, looking deep into her eyes, which were swollen with tears. "Your wedding is right in front of you. Thank you. Thank you both for this, I love you, but I can't!"

"This was my idea," Andie said. "I want this for you. I don't know how to say it other than to say I will have the rest of my life with Cameron. But you've known him and you've loved him since you were little. Maybe not romantically, but you've loved him for longer than most people ever get the chance to love anybody." Choking on the words, she added, fighting the emotions swirling through her body, "Your time is limited. I know getting married and having a dream wedding is something you've wanted since you were a little girl. Let us give it to you. Let yourself have that day. We want to do that. *Please* let us!"

Donna felt like she was being hugged so hard that she was being smothered. She was not a person who accepted gifts well. And she absolutely hated surprises. She was utterly helpless at the power of their overwhelming generosity. What they were suggesting was so vast and huge, giving up their wedding for her, to give Donna a gift she would never get on her own.

But as much as Donna loved the gesture and the sacrifice, her words laid bare what she was feeling. She could not do this to them. Cameron was in love with Andie, and she was in love with him. How could Donna marry Cameron, taking Andie's rightful spot next to him at the altar?

It was too great a sacrifice, and she could not take away this day, this event, this magical moment in their lives.

"Please don't make me say yes. I am happy just to see you two get married and know I put it together for you," Donna sobbed through an ugly cry, her head shaking, tears dripping off her cheeks.

"Come on, let us do this. We want to give you something you've always wanted," Andie stepped up, taking Donna's hand. "This is your moment, say yes, please. Marry Cameron, please. What comes next, we can't control. But this we can."

Andie took the ring from Cameron and slid it onto Donna's finger.

Cameron hugged Donna, holding her tightly as she sobbed uncontrollably against his chest. Andie moved behind Donna and held her as well, the two of them squeezing her between them as they held onto each other.

"You're doing this for me," Cam stated softly.

"And you're doing it for me," Andie added. "There's no saying no to this. We didn't come to this decision lightly and if you turn us down, it will crush us both. We love you that much."

Donna didn't speak for what felt like an hour. She couldn't. Between the tears and the awesome, overwhelming emotions crashing through her, she didn't know what to say even if she could. What words were "thank you" magnified to infinity, by the brightness of every star in the heavens?

Donna's mouth opened but no words emerged, just an anguished sob. She didn't know what to do. Feeling them holding her, she felt that energy again. An energy she could not fight.

"Can I marry you both?" Donna cried out, between sobbing breaths.

Both of them laughed, their tears continuing to fall onto Donna.

Nearly staggering, Donna sat on a nearby chair. It took almost twenty minutes for all of them to stop crying and contain themselves, though Donna's head was still reeling at not only their selflessness, but at the fact that somehow, against her will, they had convinced her it would be worse turning them down.

It still didn't feel right but it did feel treasured, a gift Donna couldn't completely comprehend.

LeAnne appeared at the door from the showroom and smiled, holding a bottle of champagne, having obviously been in on this secret.

"You all can have a drink, can't you? I mean, nobody's pregnant?"

Cam and Donna's tear-rimmed eyes darted to Andie, whose own eyes widened like she'd been caught in a lie.

"I'm not! No, no, no...I can drink!" she exclaimed, causing everyone to laugh.

After pouring flutes of champagne, LeAnne turned to Donna with a big smile.

"Why don't we get that dress on so we can get it altered?" she asked, "We don't have a lot of time."

Standing, Donna wobbled, and she'd love to blame the champagne but it was sheer emotion keeping her unsteady. She took the dress and shuffled off to a dressing room. This was the worst for her; being blindsided, and not in a way she could get mad about.

The dress was beautiful and had already been altered to specifications that Andie clearly made note of when she and Donna talked about Donna's dream wedding dress one afternoon.

Slipping out of her clothes, Donna again found herself short of breath. This was a wedding dress. And she would be wearing it. Marrying a man she loved, while his actual fiancée stood next to her as her maid of honor, smiling assuredly and crying simultaneously.

Climbing into the gown, Donna slipped her arms through the sleeves, adjusting her body as the dress fell around her. Wow! In all the years she had been planning weddings, she'd never put on a wedding dress; as a little girl, she wore her father's long-sleeved white shirts backward and pretended to be a bride. LeAnne knew Donna, and Andie was keenly in-tuned to her as well. They had given her exactly what she would have selected for herself.

Taking a deep breath before stepping out of the dressing room, Donna again felt apprehension. How could she do this to Andie? But when Andie's smile beamed with joy at the sight of Donna, and she quickly moved behind her to zip up the back of the dress, Donna relaxed. She spied Cameron watching in a mirror in the other room. He smiled and nodded, his eyes still glistening with tears.

Donna wondered if she would die from sheer elation before the cancer could take her.

Once the dress was zipped, Andie walked around to get a good look at Donna. Donna stood tall and breathed in, feeling a bit of a fraud. And while she didn't have Andie's statuesque body, Donna had curves that allowed the dress to take shape. Although she had never had a dress made by LeAnne, she mused that LeAnne had seen her enough times through the years to be remarkably accurate in her shape.

"You'll be a beautiful bride, Donna," Andie grinned, clapping her hands together as she rushed to hug her again.

Donna clung to Andie, whispering "thank you," over and over again.

The words thank you would never be enough. But for right now, they would have to do. But the real blessing of it all was that Andie was ecstatic she was able to do it for

Donna. This woman had given Donna the greatest gift she could ever ask for. Donna was going to be a bride.

TWENTY-NINE

D onna inherited a lot of wonderful pieces from Andie's wedding, which was perfectly fine with her; centerpieces and flower arrangements, the DJ, and some of the catering. Each one was a blessed asset and Donna had her hand in every one of them. There was no time at this late date to cancel and rather than not use them, Andie told Donna as maid of honor, she was donating them to her for the wedding.

The most massive headache would be the guest list. Not her own, but rather Cam and Andie's. The ceremony Cam and Donna would have would be very, very small. But for Andie and her parents, canceling two weeks out would be a huge undertaking. They would have to contact the dozens of people coming in for the wedding and announce that the ceremony was off. Donna was sure there were already gifts stacked at Andie's place, and at the Hunes', which would have to be returned as well.

And all because the groom was busy marrying another woman that day and Andie was her maid-of-honor. Oh, to be in on some of those conversations...

Donna hadn't spoken to either Mr. or Mrs. Hune, to thank them for this sacrifice they were making. Cam advised her to steer clear. Even though they understood on an emotional level, he told Donna, they were "butt sore" over Cam and Andie calling off their wedding after all the expense and work. Donna couldn't blame them. The fur that must have flown when Andie and Cam broke the news, although that was probably only a minor cyclone compared to the reason they were putting their nuptials on ice.

Even Donna's impending death couldn't put a salve on the fact that Cam was still getting married, but not to the woman whose parents had paid for everything. Donna was surprised any of them were left standing after what she was sure was the most difficult conversation of Andie or Cam's life thus far.

Yet every time Donna saw Cam, he was exuberant. Grabbing lunch a week before the wedding near his work, Cam plopped into the chair across from Donna and shook his head.

"What a shitty day!"

"How can it be bad? You're marrying me," Donna quipped, wanting to make him smile, which he did.

"Well, yeah, there's that. And I'm still engaged to another woman, as well. I guess that's pretty cool."

"You're doing far better than most guys," Donna chuckled, happy to lighten her friend's mood.

Cam's smile faded again.

"How are you feeling?" he asked, more to change the subject than concern, knowing with everything out in the open, Donna would have told him anyway.

"Fine, I guess. I mean I don't feel anything truly horrible. I don't know how this is supposed to make me feel," Donna responded, reading his face. "You going to tell me what's going on?"

Cam shook his head swiftly, planting a fake smile on his lips.

"It's all good," he answered quickly. "Just...stuff between me and my boss."

"Work...or wedding?"

This caused him to break out in a big smile.

"Mr. Hune is suffering from pain in the ass-itis. Nothing I can't handle, but..." Cam's voice trailed off, one of those things he did when he didn't want someone to know something. "It's just been difficult being around him. As I'm sure you can figure."

Considering everything that was going on, Donna didn't push too hard. Her need to know was tempered by giving Cameron his right to his space. What he was doing for his best friend, this incredible gift he was bestowing on her, was monumental and rare. Donna owed it to him not to pry. Since she was sure Andie already knew what was going on at work between Cam and her father, Donna knew Cam would come to her when he was ready to talk. And Donna would be ready to listen...and agree that Mr. Hune was being a jerk.

After lunch, they kissed each other on the cheek as they said goodbye out front.

"Where's your car?" he asked.

Pointing to the parking lot behind the building, Donna returned the question.

"I'm...right down the block," he answered, pointing. "You heading straight home?"

This question struck Donna as odd. If she were Andie, it might be a legit question but to Donna, it seemed off.

"Yeah. Got some things to do, you know, wedding stuff."

Cam nodded and gave Donna another quick peck on the cheek before they parted ways. Donna walked toward the parking lot behind the restaurant as Cam headed down the block. As Donna strode toward her car, she couldn't shake this quirky feeling.

Once she tipped the valet and got in her car, it was really bugging her. There was no way on earth Cam would park Betty Blue on any street in this city. Not even a remote chance. Half the time he wouldn't even allow a valet to park the car, much less park it where someone could easily side-swipe it or crunch it while attempting to parallel park in front of or behind it. He only worked a few blocks away, and on a sunny day like today, he would have walked.

As Donna pulled out onto the street, she didn't turn toward home. She turned in the direction Cameron pointed. Three blocks down, she found him walking.

Pulling up next to him, she rolled down the window. He stopped in his tracks, unable to hide the expression of being caught.

"You're walking? Didn't you say your car was down the block?" she quizzed.

"I meant it was back at work," he smiled as if that was going to distract Donna, "Why would I drive on a beautiful day like today?"

"Then why did you tell me your car was right down the block instead of saying you walked?"

"Because you'd insist on driving me back," Cameron stated, leaning down to look at her through the open window, hoping the closer he got the more innocent it would all seem.

"You're not telling me the truth," Donna stated, her eyes locking on his.

Cam's shoulders stiffened.

"What's going on? Tell me!" Donna begged.

Cameron stood up, cutting off her view of his face for a few seconds. He then squatted again, his head down, not giving her his eyes.

"I sold Betty."

"Your car?!? What?!? Why?!"

Looking up, an injured smile washed over his lips.

"Look, uhm, the Hunes are really, really pissed off about what Andie and I decided to do. Mr. Hune lost it when Andie first told them. And Mrs. Hune stood by him. Which surprised Andie since Mrs. Hune's never been the biggest fan of mine. I think she's pissed he had to uninvite everyone and Mr. Hune feels like he's been played. He said while our hearts are in the right place, we didn't take into account the sacrifices of everyone else. People who got plane tickets, people who sent gifts, all the money he shelled out. They are refusing to let us use anything from Andie's wedding unless we reimburse them for the cost."

"I've got some money...I'd be happy to...what am I saying? He's right. You and Andie should be getting married next week, not you and I. I should never have agreed to this. It was selfish of me. I appreciate what you and Andie are sacrificing, but this is wrong. I shouldn't be stepping in like this---"

"Stop, stop, stop!" Cameron demanded, emotions climbing to the surface. "This was Andie's decision. I could never have made it. I couldn't have asked this of her. Even for you, my best friend. But she could. Because it's the one thing we can do for you. So, I need you to buy in with me and be as excited as we are. I am ecstatic to marry you! Andie wants me to marry you! We know we're doing the right thing because it is the right thing! And one day all these people who have their drawers knotted up their ass will understand it's the right thing."

Cameron reached in through the window, touching her hand.

"I'm going to lose you. The one constant in my life since I was a kid. This is crushing me. I try not to think about it because it hurts so much. I love you. No, not in the way I love Andie, but I've loved you longer. And one day I will marry Andie, and you have learned exactly why I am so in love with her—because she's so giving, and loving, and ridiculously special that I don't think I deserve her."

"You do. And she deserves you," Donna answered.

Cameron shrugged, shaking his head. "She's amazing. She told you the truth. Me marrying you, it was her idea. And I agreed. She and I made this decision together. We can't stop what's coming down the road but we can change a little piece of what's right in front of us. You and I are getting married next week. Period. Only mistake Andie and I made was thinking her parents would be more understanding and get why we are doing what we are doing. But..."

Cam glanced up at Donna. He was not crying but tears wet his lashes. He nodded.

"It's the only thing I have of any value," Cam stated, sorrow inching into his words.

Donna fell back in the seat, her head falling back.

"Your heart is of far more value."

Cam chuckled softly. "I imagine if I could have sold that to Mr. Hune he would have taken me up on it. But I probably wouldn't have gotten as much as I did for the car. He gave me top dollar," Cam added, trying to put a positive spin on having sacrificed his prized Camaro.

"Dying is so damn complicated..." Donna huffed out, her mind unable to land on anything long enough to make a constructive suggestion and feeling like this was her fault.

"So is marriage," Cameron chuckled. "But that's life, Donna. And you're still living life. Please don't blame yourself. You're going to be leaving me. I don't know what that's going to be like. I don't know my life without you."

"Maybe that's why Andie came into your life when she did. Ever think of that?"

"Maybe," he nodded, "But whatever it takes to make the time you have left filled with cool memories and maybe knock a few things off your bucket list, we are going to do it."

Cameron squeezed her hand. Donna didn't want to cry but she couldn't help it. How did she ever deserve someone so wonderful in her life? And Andie, with what she was sacrificing and being put through. Having these two wonderful people filling her life with this much greatness for whatever time there was left, Donna simply didn't deserve to be blessed this deeply.

All she could think was that it was never about the things you have, but about the people who love you. She had heard that all her life; it was on cards, memes, posters, people spout it off to each other in silly self-examination. And for the most part, it bounced off her steely exterior because she never had perspective on it.

Until there was a perspective on it.

Dying pretty much gives you a crash course in perspective.

But truly, love and friends, people that hold you dear and make you laugh, give your life meaning, they are the real gift. Don't count blessings; count those you love and who love you.

"I'm sorry," is all Donna could say.

"Not your fault," he answered quickly, standing, "I gotta get back to work. Don't want to give Andie's dad another reason to bitch at me."

He squeezed her hand one more time before disappearing from the car window. She watched him walk down the block. The confidence in his stride never faltered. Cam knew he was doing the right thing and it showed in how he carried himself, as painful as this had to be for him to sacrifice the one material thing he held onto in his life.

And he did it for her.

Donna wasn't good at taking things; even small gifts often made her uncomfortable.

But this...how do you accept the sacrifices of two people that were so grand they didn't qualify as gestures, they were sweeping motions? Not just waves rushing onto a shore, but big waves crashing. These sacrifices were life-altering.

But unfortunately, not death-altering. Which was why Donna felt so humbled and grateful.

Before I go, she thought, *I need to give it all back.*

THIRTY

With the wedding two weeks away, Andie had attached herself to Donna's hip, angering her father even more by taking a leave of absence.

"Are you sure this is such a good idea?" Donna quizzed, almost afraid of her answer.

"Please," Andie responded, waving her hand dismissively. "He was already mad. And I'm mad at him, so we're even. And what's he going to do? Fire me?"

Since they were working on an even slimmer budget than originally planned, everything was tailored around the cash on hand. But Andie was more than up for the challenge and admitted she found this more fun than running around blowing money simply because her father had signed a blank check.

"This might make me a better shopper," Andie admitted. "That would please Cameron to no end. He winces every time we go to the mall, which is not his favorite place on a good day. So, the important things make the cut, the rest...bye-bye."

Donna always preferred a set budget. Most weddings were not carte blanche, and you had to work within perimeters to get the best deal on the best things and know what was essential and what was not. Donna prided herself on being a professional at it.

Money can do a lot of things but it can't make a wedding a day that will never be forgotten.

Many of the vendors were perturbed that Donna canceled the orders a couple of weeks out, but most let her and the Hunes out of the contracts. Donna was not above playing the dying card to guilt them into it.

"Come on, Sal, cut me a break," Donna said to the chef who had created this gourmet menu for Andie's wedding. "You won't have me to push around much longer."

Sal didn't know whether to gasp or laugh. But he did let Donna break the contract.

Liz, who Donna always used for flowers, offered to donate flowers for the wedding but told Donna she would not send flowers for a funeral because she would never accept that Donna was dying.

"Me either," Donna responded with a slim laugh.

"What's it feel like?" Liz asked hesitantly, as she sat across from Donna and Andie in her small office at her flower shop, "Knowing?"

"Like being blindfolded and you're running near the edge of a cliff because you're scared. You don't know where you're going or when you're going to fall. But you know the cliff is there and each step could mean falling," Donna opined.

Liz nodded, absorbing each word. Donna could see Liz's imagination running with that scenario, knowing you're going to fall to your death but not knowing when and running faster because of fear.

"Time is not your friend anymore," Liz added.

"It never was, I just didn't know it."

When the word spread through the vendors that Donna was getting married—and more pointedly, the reason behind it—many bucked up, offering Andie and Donna discounts or gratis.

Donna loved that Eddie Truman, a self-proclaimed descendant of Harry Truman, who was her liquor vendor for every function she planned over the last four years, called and told her all the liquor, top shelf, was on him. And if his beer guy, Gus, didn't do the same, to call him and let him know and he'd "put a foot up Gus's ass."

You have to love the way people in St. Louis express themselves.

Although the freebies made the money spread further, Donna was not exactly sure how much Mr. Hune paid for Betty Blue. Andie kept telling her not to worry about money, that she had money of her own and would cover whatever else was necessary.

"You know," Donna said to Andie, "I would expect what's happening from Cam. We've been friends since we were little and I know he's one of the most generous, loving, wonderful people in the entire world, but you...Andie, what you've given up, what you're doing for me, what you're giving me, it's beyond remarkable. I mean that."

Andie smiled, lounging back in the chair across Donna's small dining room table. "I don't think it's remarkable. I don't. Then again, it seemed so natural when we found out what was going on. I didn't even have to talk to Cam about it, we both knew."

"I felt that," Donna admitted, "when I was in the bed and you two were holding me."

"You did?"

"I didn't know exactly what but I felt you two communicating without speaking. Do you know what that says about you and Cam?"

"Well, I'd like to think it's good."

That made Donna smile.

Andie again waved her hand in the air as if swatting away doubt. "What kind of person would I be if I didn't allow you to have your biggest dreams before...you know? I mean, I can't give you time but I can give you this. And Cameron loves you. Before I met you and honestly even after we met for a little bit, I felt like you were competition."

"I never was," Donna blurted out, surprised she felt that.

"Yeah, you were. Not in an entanglement sort of way, Donna, but more like, could Cam love me the way he loves you? I know it's different, what he and I have as compared to what you two have, but the way he talked about you before we met, the way he acts when he's around you. It's noticeable and it's different and it's kind of daunting. Or it was until I got to understand it by being around you. I didn't know if I would get that from him. If I deserved it. I mean you had all this history. I had never met a man who had a woman for a best friend. Or even wanted one for that matter. And I thought it was really great that he did. Different. Better than most guys. But then it scared me. Because there is a competition."

"You think?" Donna asked.

"Women are stupid like that. And I'm guilty of it."

"Cam loves me," Donna admitted, "but he loves you."

Andie smiled with a laugh.

"We sound like middle school girls," she cackled. "You know, I've had a lot of girlfriends in my life, but I've never had someone like you. Someone who only wanted her other friend to be happy and when you found out he was, you threw open your arms to me and I became family to you."

"That's how I feel. You're like a sister," Donna stated, actually getting it as her words came out of her mouth.

Andie's smile grew but then very suddenly, her eyes filled with tears. "I never had a sister. And you're going to leave me."

Donna nodded, feeling the tears coming on as well. "Yes, I am. I'm sorry."

Andie came around the table quickly and grabbed hold of Donna. They hugged tightly, both crying. They *were* middle school girls. Middle school girls, best friends forever, facing tragedy. Time was essential.

Donna pulled away, reaching out and drying her tears first.

"We have a lot to do and only two weeks to do it," Donna reminded her. "We can cry later. Okay?"

"Deal," Andie responded.

THIRTY-ONE

P ain. Acute and intense. Down in Donna's lower abdomen.

Please God, no, not now. Four more days I'm exchanging vows with my best friend. Take me after that. I don't care. Not now, let me do this one thing. Please. She held her stomach, sitting with her head between her legs, her teeth gritted.

Pushing herself off the bed, Donna used the wall to nearly drag herself to her small kitchen. Water. There was no way she could eat, not with whatever this was.

Damn it, please! I have to make it through this wedding. Andie and Cam have done so much to give me this day. I'm not going to disappoint them.

Donna found the sofa and let her body fall onto it. Lying there, staring at the ceiling, she wondered, *Should I call the doctor? An ambulance? Will this go away? I cannot, will not, be admitted to the hospital. They will keep me and I swear, after all the sacrifice, I am walking up that aisle this Saturday. I am cutting the cake. I am having a first dance. There isn't time for anything else in my life so I am getting these things. I don't care what it takes. I am not getting married in a bed. I am putting on that goddamn dress!*

Donna made herself laugh at all the plans she had for herself. Evidently, life, and more certainly death, had other thoughts. Maybe this wedding, even more than Andie and Cam's, was causing her stress and that was what she was feeling. Stress couldn't be good for cancer. Donna always believed stress was one of the causes of cancer, and if that was true, it was the circle of death: stress causing cancer, causing more stress, causing more cancer. Donna smiled wryly as she thought, *Apparently, I'm killing myself...*

And then she laughed harder. *Why do I let myself go to these places?*

Donna didn't know when she was going to die. She only knew it felt soon enough to touch. But she wouldn't let herself believe it would be this week; this was just cancer's warning shots flying across her bow. Damn it! She vowed to not let this scare her and it was most definitely not going to beat her, not right now. Cancer may be tough but when Donna wanted something, she could be a junkyard dog with a bone.

Sorry, can't slow down until Sunday, she mused as she forced herself to sit up, *I've got a wedding to go to. And it's mine.*

By sunrise, Donna felt slightly better. The pain had subsided to a degree she could tolerate with the pain pills and she didn't have to wince or grit her teeth when she moved. It was still there but dulled. She was hoping no one would call and check on her, or her mother wouldn't just drop by, which she had become prone to. Donna wanted to be alone to make sure this wasn't something that was going to stick around and ruin her plans.

Come on, God, I don't have a lot of time and not a lot of happiness on the agenda. Throw me this canard. She opened her curtains to let more sunlight into the apartment, hoping that would change things.

By eleven, the phone hadn't rung and Donna was finally able to take a deep breath. For her, that had become the bellwether of being well. If she could breathe deeply everything was a go. She took the initiative and called Andie to check in.

But even Andie's "hello" sounded stressed.

"I stopped by work to handle a few emails, and people were all talking in hushed tones, which tells me something is coming down," Andie stated.

"This have anything to do with Cam?" Donna reluctantly asked, hoping against hope it didn't.

"He called my father an 'unfeeling bastard' when my dad drove Betty Blue to work this morning," Andie said. "That was a couple hours ago and it's gone downhill from there. I actually thought my dad was going to fire him this morning and Cam's sitting in his office, steaming."

"Oh, God..."

"When he saw my dad pull into the garage, I thought Cam might punch him," Andie whispered. "And I kinda wanted him to. He doesn't need to rub it in Cam's face. Especially when Cam is doing something epic."

"Agreed."

"Can you hold on a second?" Andie asked, quickly putting Donna on hold. Donna heard nothing for almost a minute before Andie picked up again.

"Sorry," Andie sighed, returning to the call.

"What's going on?"

"My dad. He stopped by my office to tell me he's going to lunch at Leta B's if that's okay with me and Cam. He doesn't want to step on anyone's toes," she sighed again, only this time with more exasperation.

"Oh, God..." Donna mumbled again.

"Yeah, it's that kind of day," Andie sniffed. "See what feeling guilty and coming in to take care of a few things for my father gets me?"

After hanging up, Donna quickly showered and grabbed her purse and keys. She wanted to get out of the house while she felt well enough to do so. Whatever was stabbing her in her lower stomach was still there and she wanted to use the discomfort from that digging pain as motivation for going into battle.

Donna drove over to Leta B's and pushed through the front door. Coming from the sunlight into the dark wooded bar, she had to let her eyes adjust. Mr. Hune was not in the bar area, so she stepped quickly to the restaurant on the other side, giving the bartender, Janie, one of the few people she was taller than, a quick hug.

Mr. Hune was eating alone, his back to the room. Odd. Men usually face into the room so they can see who is entering. Sort of an Old West mentality.

I guess he really does want to be alone, Donna thought. Too damn bad.

Slipping into the chair across from him before he could deny her permission, Henry was in mid-bite of his pork tenderloin sandwich.

Donna's hand hit the table hard and she slid a personal check over to him.

"I'm not sure what you paid for Cam's car, but I'm buying it back. I would imagine since you had him bent over a barrel, it's not more than I'm offering you."

Mr. Hune paused and wiped the corners of his mouth before turning the check over. He looked up at Donna, trying to control his ire. It was clear he came here to get away from this.

"Generous. But not for sale."

"Sure it is," Donna responded, equally in no mood for this game. "And you're going to sell it to me because it's my dying wish."

"I thought this wedding was your dying wish?"

"Wishes change. And the wedding, that's a gift from Andie and Cam. Because they know it's always been my dream to get married. And I love them for it," Donna answered, sitting back in the chair, staring directly into Mr. Hune's eyes. "You don't seem to have any conception of the daughter you raised or the man she's marrying. They are two spectacular, wonderful, selfless people. Why are you punishing them for that?"

"I'm not. I'm just not paying for a wedding where my daughter is not the one getting married. You should be able to understand that."

"Fair enough. Then sell me the car."

"Look, Donna, this is nothing against you. And I'm really, really sorry for what's happening with you. But you have to understand--"

Her fist slammed down on the table, sending silverware jumping. She gritted her teeth. She had always liked Mr. Hune and had a respect for him she felt was reciprocated. But she was too close to the end—not of her rope, but the absolute end—to put up with bullshit.

"Stop talking. Don't explain. I get it. But you are selling me that car. And you are going to find a way to support your daughter and her future husband in what they are doing for me. Not financially, I get that, and you shouldn't have to. But emotionally, let them know they are doing something pretty damn terrific," Donna stated solidly, no tears, no venom.

"I am dying. To be completely honest, I think I'm dying quickly. I don't care if you care, I don't care if you feel bad about it or good about it. Don't. Care. But I do care that, other than your daughter, the one thing that Cameron has taken care of is that car, and he was willing to sacrifice that for me to have a wedding."

She went silent for only a second, not allowing Mr. Hune to grasp hold of a rational reason to fight her on this.

"And I am getting it back for him. Or I will spend every day I have left making your life miserable one way or another. I'm that serious about it. So, we can do this the easy way or the hard way. And yes, sooner or later, and it feels like sooner, I'll be dead and you won't have to put up with me anymore. But do you want to take the chance that it'll be later because I'm apt to live just out of spite toward you? I can haunt you, alive and maybe even dead, and make you look like an ass to the entire community. I will. That's the hard way. And I hope you don't choose it. I really hope you don't because I would like to enjoy the time I have left with the people I love. But that's up to you."

Donna pointed to her check.

"Put it in your pocket and take it to the bank," she told him, "Sign the pink slip over to me, and tell Cam and Andie nothing."

Donna pushed herself away from the table and stood.

"I'll come by your office at the end of the day. Once Cam is gone. We'll finish our deal. Enjoy the rest of your sandwich. And don't be a dick to your future son-in-law anymore. There's no reason, he loves your daughter and will treat her better than anyone in the world ever could. Even you."

Leaving him with that Donna turned and walked out, passing Leta, the owner of the restaurant as she was coming in. Seeing Donna, she wrapped her arms around her, having heard the news.

"I'm sending over trays of appetizers for your reception," she stated, pulling a wisp of hair off her forehead with her elbow as she held Donna's face, used to multitasking.

"You don't have to do that," Donna told her.

"You've brought me business, let me do something for you. I want you to have a great wedding!"

Leta smiled sincerely. Donna couldn't help but smile back.

"I want that too," Donna responded, taking Leta's hand and walking back to the bar side of her business. "And I want to pay for Mr. Hune's lunch."

Leta smiled. "Do you want to do it anonymously?"

"Are you kidding?" Donna smiled back. "I want him to know exactly who paid for it."

Leta let go with her signature cackling laugh that nearly shook the building.

At five minutes to six, once Donna saw Cameron leave for the evening, she walked into Mr. Hune's building and clipped down to his office. She would like to say she knew he'd be waiting for her, but she had been camped out in the parking lot for the last hour and a half just making sure Henry didn't leave. She liked to think that when she wanted something she got it, and considering she was dying, she was most certainly playing that card. But Mr. Hune had already proven to be a wavering advocate and a slippery opponent. Trust and time were both in short supply.

Walking into his office without knocking, at least Donna took a bit of glee from the surprise on Mr. Hune's face when she was standing across the desk from him.

"What? Did you think I wouldn't be here? I handed you a check for thirty thousand dollars. I'm often an idiot, but not that big of one."

"How do you know I didn't cash it?" he quizzed, sitting back in his big chair that looked wonderfully comfortable.

"Because I think you want to make a point again before you do that."

"Do you really think that little of me?"

"No. I'm just trying to stay one step ahead."

He nodded.

"Thank you for lunch. Leta made sure I knew you paid for it."

Donna nodded back.

"So, do we have a deal?" Donna asked, not wanting to draw this out and give him time to rethink what she believed he was going to do.

"If you can tell me something," Henry said.

Puzzled, Donna nodded.

"What did you say to my wife?"

Donna froze for a second. First not understanding and then realizing. She shook her head. "I didn't say anything." The seriousness in Henry's eyes told her he knew.

"I told her that having someone who obviously loved her was worth the effort to love back," Donna stated.

He held his gaze on Donna in silence. The quiet stayed long enough for Donna to wonder whether he had digested her words and was now trying to gauge how long she was actually going to live. She didn't look like she was dying—whatever that was supposed to look like—but she didn't look all that wonderful either; the lines around her eyes were deeper, the pallor of her skin having yellowed to a degree that Donna was using a heavier base to cover it up when she went out.

Reaching into his desk, Mr. Hune took out the pink slip and the state documents. He dramatically flipped them over and quickly scribbled his signature on them. Pushing them across the desk at Donna, he said nothing.

Not waiting, Donna snapped them off the desk and gave him a whisper of a smile.

"Thank you."

Walking out of his office quickly, she heard, "Donna."

Well, the papers are signed, so he can't renege, she thought, before turning. Taking a deep breath ready for another skirmish, Donna stepped back into his office.

"You forgot something."

He pointed to a check on the edge of his desk, facing her.

It was the car keys and a personal check. For eight thousand dollars. Donna's confusion showed on her face.

"I got the car for twenty-two," he said. "I'm not going to make a profit on this."

A thousand and one remarks crackled through Donna's mind like rolling thunder but she declined to snark out a single one of them. She understood. He was trying to say he was sorry in the best way he could without actually saying it. And while she would have loved to hear it from him, Donna decided to take what she could get. So, she nodded, locking eyes with him. He didn't speak, picking up the car keys and holding them out to her.

As she took them, Henry debated how to say goodbye. This very likely would be a "goodbye goodbye", not a "see you later". Donna could see in his eyes that he was at a loss for what to say.

"Take care of yourself, Mr. Hune. It was a pleasure meeting you. Maybe I'll see you in the next life," Donna smirked.

Henry opened his mouth to respond but had nothing. A smile widened on his face.

"Touché," he responded, his mood growing more serious. "I'm sorry. Truly. You don't deserve this."

Donna shrugged. "And yet, here I am."

"Cameron is lucky to have you as a friend. I think part of the reason he's such a good man and has been so good to my daughter, is because of you."

Smiling almost sadly, Donna nodded. "Thank you. You're a good man too, Mr. Hune. I don't care what your daughter and Cameron say about you," she added with a grin.

As Henry broke out in a bellowing laugh, and Donna stepped toward the door, she doubted she would ever see him again. Or his wife for that matter. But she had what she came for, so she opted to call it a victory. There had been so few, that she knew she should take the ones she got. But she couldn't help herself. She stopped.

"Seriously...Cameron will marry your daughter soon. Not sure if that makes you happy but they will make insanely good parents. As I said to you before, I don't think you grasp the depth of goodness in the daughter you raised."

"I do," he said.

"And she wouldn't be that person if she didn't have someone to model that on," Donna said honestly, before walking out.

Henry didn't move. He didn't come out of his office to watch her leave. Falling back against his chair, he sat silently. Rubbing his eyes, he sniffled once before dropping his head and covering his face with his hands and wept for Donna.

THIRTY-TWO

The pain continued in dark waves that splintered through Donna's body, but she was determined that no one would know when it felt like someone was sticking a hot knife through her intestines. Thankfully, so far, it had subsided each time and she was managing the pain, even though at moments it hurt so bad she fought not to sob.

The buzz around the wedding was too thick between Cam, Andie, and Geena, who couldn't help but remind Donna daily that she always thought she would end up marrying Cam. Saturday was just over the horizon. Donna was going to be a bride. Her lifelong dream, as provincial as it was for a woman who had prided herself on being anything but.

A gift. From the most wonderful people she knew.

And Donna hoped her wedding gift to Cam would blow his mind.

Andie and Donna rolled through the last-minute details and Cam and Donna met with her minister friend, Joe Elvis. Joe and Donna had known each other for about six years; she had utilized him in at least a dozen weddings when neither the bride nor groom had a minister or priest who was close to them, or a parish priest or minister their parents insisted should marry them.

Having been a professional dancer and actor, Joe was very theatrical and funny. He offered Cameron and Donna free dance lessons so they "don't just stand there and sway" on their first dance. With time being as crunched as it was, they couldn't do it, but he still grabbed an hour after they met to teach Cameron a few moves so Donna would "twirl around the dance floor like a bride should," he insisted.

Joe knew the situation. Donna felt funny calling her impending death a "situation" but for lack of a better term, that was what it was. A situation that was going to kill her. Donna was becoming more at ease with the death sentence that cancer had given her, more accepting that there was a period at the end of the sentence.

Strangely enough, this wedding had helped with that. She felt like she was climbing to the peak of at least one of her mountains before she passed. It had given her something to focus on instead of holding a daily pity party, complete with balloons and a piñata for her to beat with a stick.

"Don't get me wrong, I have anxiety over death. And actually, it's not even the dying that scares me, it's what comes next. I am a woman who has always thrived on absolutes. And there isn't much consensus about the after-life. Since people have found out I'm dying, I'm hit with all sorts of weird comments about God, seeing my father again, being locked in a box forever, planes of consciousness, planes of existence, all sorts of new-agey, religious and spiritual remarks about the after-life. Or the lack thereof.

In all honesty, I don't know what I believe. If there is a God, I'm not sure I'm the type that's going to be sitting on a cloud near him. I wish I could say I was. But I don't know if I've been that good to people if I've been 'enough' for God. I just don't know. But if he's listening, I do hope he takes into consideration that I've tried. Does God give points for that?" Donna rambled on one evening while talking to her mother.

But she did know she wouldn't be here, on earth, with her friends and her mother. For Donna, at this point, that was the harsh reality. The inevitability. And she was getting married, so as long as death didn't occur before then, she was adjusting as best she could to the concept.

"I still think you should have more bridesmaids than just me," Andie stated out of nowhere as she and Donna were sitting in chairs getting mani-pedis.

"I don't want anyone other than you," Donna insisted.

"It just popped into my head, so I said it," she laughed.

"You're more than enough," Donna commented.

Andie flipped her side eyes.

"Now you're sounding like Cam," she said. "He didn't want any groomsmen for our wedding. Kept telling me he had too many guy friends to pick just six, but I think he just didn't want to be bothered with all that. Me, I could have had two dozen bridesmaids, I mean with the relatives my parents were demanding I have in the wedding, including, as you know, cousins I see once in a blue moon. That's the difference between Cam and me, he has literally thousands of people that love him, yet he's perfectly content flying solo or with a single co-pilot. For me, you're the first real friend I've made in years."

"Thank you," Donna inserted.

"You're welcome," Andie laughed like the tinkling of crystal flutes chiming off of one another.

"I've never had friends either," Donna opined. "Not really. I mean other than Cameron. I'm nice to everyone until they give me a reason not to be, but I don't think that many people even know I exist outside of me being a wedding planner. It's kind of a regret now that I'm thinking about it. I should have tried harder with people."

"I think there are a lot of people that love you," Andie stated. "Sometimes we don't know the impression we make on people, you know?"

Shrugging, Donna shook her head.

"At this point, I'd like to say I don't worry about it. But I do. I'd like you to be more right about it than me. Other than you, who has become almost as close to me as Cam over these last few months, I'll be surprised if anyone shows up at this wedding."

Andie studied her without a word, making Donna uncomfortable. She could see her mind working but she said nothing. Panicking, Donna barked out, "How long do you think you are going to wait after I'm gone to marry Cam?"

Donna's question even stopped the women from doing their pedicures. Andie's eyes widened, her lips parting but no sound coming out. That was until she laughed at her horror.

"I'm sorry," Donna said. "That didn't come out right. I was going to say you shouldn't wait long. He loves you so much."

Andie reached over and took Donna's hand, their fingers interlocking, being careful not to smudge their nails.

"I can't think of our life without you anymore. But I don't know. Cam and I haven't discussed it and I don't think we will for quite a while. I don't know what kind of wedding I want now. I mean without you there to make it happen. Though they haven't said it, I know my parents still want that. But now...I don't know. Like you, I'm taking it day by day."

That made Donna smile and she wanted to hug Andie but knew it would really rankle the ladies doing their toes.

"I could see you two running away and getting married."

"I can too," Andie nodded. "Then we will come back, tell my folks, let them be sore a while, and get on with our lives."

"Invite them."

Again, Andie looked at Donna.

"You need them there. Have your dad give you away. Let your mom see you get married. Your folks love you," Donna told her.

"After my dad forced Cam to sell him his car, I don't know," Andie retorted.

"Momentary anger. And I can say this from my Yoda-like knowledge that has come with being this sick, forget about it. Seriously. Forgive and move on."

"You think that's possible when every time Cam comes over to my parents', his car is going to be in their garage?"

"It won't be. I have Betty Blue."

Andie's eyes widened more than Donna had ever seen them, even when she found out how sick Donna was.

"I bought it from your dad. I'm going to give it to Cam as a wedding gift."

"Donna...that's expensive!"

Donna laughed heartily.

"What am I going to do with money where I'm going?"

Andie didn't have a response to that one, wiping her tears with the sleeve of her blouse.

"I just want one day where I don't cry," Andie huffed out between breaths.

"Guess that's not today."

Andie laughed.

"Guess not."

"This is what they call getting your affairs in order," Donna told her. "And I've made peace with your dad for forcing Cam to sell his car to pay for this wedding. Your father was good to me. So was your mom. Don't punish them, Andie. There's no reason. And regrets are just stupid."

"I love you," Andie stated, her lips tight, fighting every urge to cry harder.

Donna lifted Andie's hand to her lips and kissed it. Andie knew Donna loved her too. And any woman who would sacrifice her wedding and her groom, even for a limited time, was someone you couldn't help but be in love with. Donna thought her pal Cameron was the best person in the world. Truth was, the best person in the world was his bride-to-be. His real bride-to-be.

And what was more profound, Andie found another exceptional human to fall in love with. How rare was that? Talk about divine intervention. Of all the people in the world for Donna's best friend to fall in love with, it was the one person who might actually be more incredible than he was.

Donna was going to die having met two of the most generous, special, remarkable people on this planet. She only wished she could live so that, if she had children, she could point to Cam and Andie and tell them to emulate them, not her. But they would have their own one day and hopefully, those kids would understand just how great their parents were. It may take a few years; most kids didn't get it until they were adults.

One of Donna's few regrets was that she wouldn't be here to tell these kids that their parents were the best. Donna went home that night and did something she hadn't done in years. Wrote a letter. To people she would never know. Andie and Cam's future kids. Maybe they wouldn't care, maybe her cursive handwriting would be nothing more than hieroglyphics to them. But it was necessary for Donna to tell them how lucky they were. These children weren't even thoughts yet, but she knew the life they would have because she knew the sacrifices their parents would make for them. And Donna understood just how blessed they were.

THIRTY-THREE

*D*amn, *I look good in this dress!*
Which was a positive, considering how bad she felt. She had thrown up that morning; she wished she could tell everyone it was from butterflies over her wedding later that day, but there was blood in it. If she weren't getting married in a few hours, she would have called the doctor or checked herself into the hospital. Good thing Dr. Muliski was coming to the wedding.

Donna had never been a woman who liked a lot of makeup. But being a bride and looking like death warmed over, no pun intended, she opted to ladle it on. Her mom helped. She'd been applying a thick coat of foundation since turning forty-five. Geena could sense Donna was not feeling well at all, but she didn't make a peep about it. Although, there was worry in her eyes, which made Donna feel guilty as she stood behind her, placing her Nana's cameo around her neck and clasping it. Donna wished she could make all this worry go away but the fact was, there was only one thing that would do that and Donna didn't want to think about that today.

After Geena finished, Donna kissed her on the cheek.

"You know I love you. I know I haven't always shown it, and I know I can be a real pain sometimes but, Mom, I do, I really love you. Thank you for being here for me."

Geena nodded. "Where else am I going to be on my daughter's wedding day?" Geena snapped off as she grabbed the makeup and dashed from the room just as her tears fell. Donna laughed. "I'm getting good at that!" she called to her mother. "Making people cry!" It wasn't her intention, but Donna knew her mother was elated and devastated in one big jumbled mess of feelings. And Donna knew Geena knew she loved her, but still, Donna needed to say it to her. She needed her mother to hear it.

Andie called Donna right after she was bent over the toilet again, throwing up whatever was left in her stomach. Donna feigned the most chipper voice she could muster, hoping whatever was lacking she would chalk up to nerves.

Andie had found out that the previous night Donna called and left a message for her parents, inviting them to the wedding. Donna didn't hear back.

"Can we handle two more people at the buffet line?" Andie asked.

"We'll manage," Donna laughed.

"I promise, I'll try and keep my mother down to two glasses of champagne."

"You don't have a problem with this?" Donna asked.

There was a pause and then Andie answered, "No. I'm glad you did it."

Donna wanted this to be a great day, filled with love and joy. Whatever problems Donna had with people, whatever problems they had with Donna or each other, for one day they could bury them deep and just have fun. Donna's favorite DJ, Fat Marco, was going to spin until midnight. Donna wanted people dancing, drinking, eating, and laughing. Everything else could wait until tomorrow.

To calm whatever was going on in her stomach, Donna took a swig of Maalox, hoping that would at least get her through the ceremony without projectile vomiting bloody barf all over Cam.

That would certainly be something the small crowd would remember.

Unless cancer killed her today, Donna vowed to make it through the day with a huge smile on her face. And she couldn't wait to surprise Cam with his third girlfriend, Betty Blue. Donna had her mom hide it behind the chapel where the wedding was being held.

Geena and Donna climbed into the car, Donna in the fancy-schmancy wedding dress too big to stuff into the front seat so she plopped herself down in the back while her mother in her mother-of-the-bride ensemble, her hair done, her nails all shiny and red, climbed in behind the wheel. They laughed.

"We are both hot messes," Donna chuckled.

"Just like it should be," Geena answered.

"You know I love you, too," Geena said to her, something she had been saying a lot recently. "You are one of the few joys I've had in life."

The words struck Donna as odd, but she realized her mother never had much, and having only one child, one daughter, there was so much poured into Donna that for her mother, it was a vast river of love, even at their worst. And there had been worse. But at this moment, Donna couldn't remember what the hell was so bad.

"Yes, I do," Donna answered as she laid back in the seat of her Chrysler sedan, making sure she didn't wreck her hair that her great hairstylist, Wendy, had done for her that morning.

"And if I could take what's going on inside of you and put it in me, I would."

"Let's not go there today, Mom. I know you love me, always have. And you know I love you. And I get to walk down the aisle at my wedding with you. There's no better tonic for me right now than that."

Donna could see her smile in the rearview mirror and smiled back.

"It's all good," Donna assured her mother.

Arriving at the chapel, a little place in South City across from Bader Park—but certainly big enough for the small crowd they invited—Donna sat up in the backseat. There were a lot of cars parked everywhere. She sighed. Damn, parking is going to be hard!

But, thinking smartly, Geena pulled the car behind the chapel into the one empty spot, not far from where she'd stashed Betty Blue, covered with a tan tarp so Cam wouldn't see her until the surprise was revealed.

"What's going on down here today?"

"Who knows? There's always some festival or concert or something going on in this city," her mother responded, putting the car in park and stepping out. Geena opened the back door and helped Donna to her feet. Straightening out her dress and making sure her hair and makeup were perfect, Geena took her arm with a smile.

"This is going to be fun!" Geena exclaimed.

"That's the spirit," Donna giggled, happy she was on board with her hopes for the day.

But as they walked into the back door of the chapel, it was empty. Donna blinked. "I thought that at least...some people would show up," she said softly to her mother as Geena tightened her grip.

"A little change of plans, honey," Geena said as she guided her daughter down the aisle of the sparsely decorated chapel towards the arched wood doors leading out to the front. Pushing open the door, Donna again was astounded, not immediately grasping what she was seeing.

Confused, Donna looked at her mother. "There were a few last-minute additions to the guest list," Geena uttered with a smarty-pants smirk pressed onto her lips as Donna gazed out at not fifty people, but a mob of hundreds. When they saw Donna standing on the steps of the chapel, a rousing cheer erupted.

Donna saw people from the past—so many of her vendors, high school friends, people she knew in college but never kept in contact with, and couples whose weddings she pulled together, many now with kids, some with their parents in tow.

Then Donna saw Andie talking with her parents. Andie turned to her with a huge grin and threw up her arms, laughing at Donna's surprise. Absolutely radiant in her bridesmaid dress, Andie pushed through everyone and climbed the steps to where Donna stood, leaning on her mother, and took her hand.

"I know you hate surprises at weddings, but we had to make some last-minute accommodations. The little place we picked couldn't hold everyone who wanted to be here for you, and could we have asked for a more beautiful day?" Andie whispered in Donna's ear

"How did...who put this...we can't afford this..." Donna muttered.

"Au contraire. Everyone donated food, or flowers...pretty much everything. Anything I asked for people gave. Look at these people, Donna. They wanted to give you this. They are here for you. These are lives you've touched. You may not have realized it at the time but you did something special for everyone here and they want to honor you. They wanted to give you this gift as much as Cam and I do."

"My makeup," Donna cried, unable to stop it from turning into a sob as she turned to her mother and buried her face into Geena's shoulder, overwhelmed. Geena held her daughter tightly, Donna's shoulders shuddering with each sob.

"You listen to me," Geena uttered softly. "Pull yourself together. You're getting married today. And people want to celebrate you. I want to celebrate you." Geena separated from her daughter, looking into Donna's tear-glimmered eyes. "This is your day. Let's make it the best," Geena added as she took a tissue from her pocket and cleaned her daughter's face softly.

As Geena hooked her arm into her daughter's, Andie moved to the other side of Donna and did the same to support her. As they descended the chapel steps to the sidewalk, almost as if planned, everyone stepped back on either side, making a path across the street, all the way up the hill to where Donna could make out Cam in a white tux, waiting under the branches of a large oak tree.

"I love you," Donna stated, looking at Andie.

"You know, you can marry me," she giggled.

"Don't think I didn't think of it," Donna giggled back, dabbing at her tears. From at top of the small hill, Donna's favorite local musician, saxophonist Johnny Feuer, began to play This Is the Day as Donna continued through the passageway of friends and loved ones, greeting each and every person, meeting children of couples whose weddings Donna created, vendors, friends, people from Donna's past that she didn't recognize but was grateful they took the day to be there with her.

As she passed Mr. and Mrs. Hune, they both hugged Donna.

"You are a remarkable woman," Mr. Hune said. "Thank you for inviting us."

Mrs. Hune didn't speak. She just touched Donna's stomach, a tear in her eye. Donna wiped it off Caroline's cheek before leaning in and whispering, "Effort." Caroline smiled and squeezed Donna's hand before Donna continued through the tunnel of people, all there for her.

It took over an hour for Donna to make her way through the people, taking selfies with dozens of friends, drying more than a few tears, her own as well as others, reminding any person filled with sadness that this was a good day, a blessed day, a wonderful day. She kept glancing at Cam, raising her finger to indicate that she might be slow but she would get there, eliciting laughter from the guests who were more than patient with her.

Johnny Feuer joined his band behind Joe Elvis, the minister. They played music, which had more than a few people dancing or swaying as Donna greeted them, adding to the merriment of the day. Donna laughed as she saw Joe dancing with a few of her vendors, twirling them around to the music, as the sun shone down brightly, making her almost feel giddy and light. And almost forgetting about the awful churning in her stomach.

Walking through the line of guests was not how Donna saw her wedding. It was far, far better. Even Donna, the queen of weddings, couldn't have envisioned this. She knew she was one lucky woman.

Donna leaned over to Andie and said, "I don't have to go to heaven. I'm here."

She finally arrived next to Cam. He had his jacket off as he leaned against a tree.

"About time. I was just about to go get a couple beers," he remarked.

"Should have thought to bring a cooler," Donna shrugged. "You know I like to talk."

As they stepped up in front of Joe Elvis, Andie kissed Cam on the lips. They shared a few whispered words and then Andie moved to Donna and took her face in her hands.

"Take care of my man," she said with a wink, before kissing her.

"I promise to return him as good as new."

She hugged Donna, holding her for a long moment. What neither of them expected was the applause, which started small and blossomed through the people who were now crowding close for the ceremony. They knew what sacrifices were being made. They could feel the love.

Andie and Donna both turned, startled by the response. Realizing, Donna gestured to Andie and then bowed to her, letting everyone know what this remarkable woman had done for her.

The crowd cheered her as Andie fought a losing battle against her emotions, tears sliding down her cheeks. She nodded to everyone in thanks before stepping back to fix the train of Donna's gown and then taking her place next to Donna. She wiped her tears and took Donna's hand, holding it more for her own trepidation than Donna's, as Geena kissed her daughter and then Cam before stepping back.

Joe Elvis greeted everyone, his voice booming through the crowd with the help of an amp and wireless mic. He thanked the large gathering for being there and said an opening prayer; a prayer for love, a prayer for healing, a prayer for the future. Donna wanted to say she was in the moment, but she was too overwhelmed at the array of people surrounding her that Joe Elvis invited forward, asking them to surround Cam, Andie, and Donna, in a "circle of life and love."

When it came time, Donna held onto Andie's hand tightly as she recited her vows to Cameron. He choked up, his voice breaking as he said his back to her. They exchanged simple bands. When Joe announced they were man and wife, Donna couldn't help but look back at Andie as she whispered, "I'm sorry."

Andie simply shook her head, wiping a tear. She wished it were her in the wedding dress, holding Cameron's hands, the ring on her finger. Donna could see it, the sacrifice she made was never more real.

And Donna knew it should be Andie.

It would be.

But they'd given her the gift.

Cameron leaned over and kissed her softly on the lips, as he had many times before. Donna was married. To her best friend. For however long she had left on the planet.

Donna turned to Andie and gave her another grateful look. Donna could tell how complex and difficult this was for her, much more than Andie expected. Andie pointed and Donna nodded, both of them knowing the surprise. Donna held Cameron's hand as Andie slipped away and dashed off through the crowd, disappearing before Cameron knew she was gone.

Grasping Donna's hand, Cameron moved them through the mass of bodies, people grabbing them, hugging them, wishing them well. Even Mr. and Mrs. Hune stopped Cameron and hugged him warmly, which he clearly appreciated.

Donna held his hand again, pulling him with her as they continued through the crowd, the reception now being held in the old warehouse near the chapel. They headed down to the street and were about to cross when Betty Blue, top down, raced up with a big red bow on the hood.

Cameron looked confused for a moment as Andie, who was behind the wheel, gave him a big smile.

"You two need a ride to the reception?" she asked.

"Your father's letting us use the car?"

"It's your car," Andie responded, pointing at Donna.

As Cam's head spun in Donna's direction, she giggled.

"I made him an offer and dared him to refuse it. It's my wedding gift to you."

Cam's eyes narrowed as if he were trying to decipher what language she was speaking. He couldn't wrap his mind around what Donna just said.

"You bought this for me?" he uttered.

Donna simply smiled. "You don't like it? I'm sure Mr. Hune will take it back."

Suddenly, Cameron swung open the passenger door and shoved Donna in, causing Andie to scream as he dashed around to the driver's side and scooted her over, crushing the two women into one seat, both of them mashed up against each other, laughing, Donna's dress flouncing around like it had a life of its own.

Revving the engine, Cameron grinned broadly as he slammed the door and threw Betty Blue into drive. He spun it up the block and back, all the while honking, guests cheering and howling with laughter as he squealed the tires with each sliding turn that scared the bejesus out of Andie and Donna as they fell over each other, crowing with laughter.

"Best. Gift. Ever," Cameron stated as he slid the car around again, entertaining everyone watching. He then looked over at Andie and Donna and added, "Except for marrying you. And someday marrying you."

"Good save," Donna said. "Not great but good."

Andie high-fived Donna.

Cameron made one more screeching turn and then waved at the guests, screaming, "Follow us to the reception!"

The warehouse was done up in pale lavender, Donna's favorite color. Donna knew it was Andie; well, at least she knew it wasn't Cam. Donna assuredly mentioned it to her about a hundred times as they were looking at colors for her wedding, forbidding her from choosing it.

The place quickly filled with bodies, and Donna awed at the length of the buffet line, with over a dozen restaurants and caterers that she had done business with in the past carrying in their signature dishes. It was an open bar with top-shelf liquor, all donated by people she had been working with for years.

Donna wished she wasn't feeling so horrible because this was a reception unlike any other she had ever put together. God only knew what this would cost if it was added up. It made Donna's head spin even thinking about it.

She moved from table to table, hugging more people, some she hadn't seen in ages, some she didn't recognize at all. Many spent the moment they had together telling her something nice she did for them, something she helped them out with, a favor she performed that went unmentioned.

Donna couldn't believe she'd been this nice to people. To her, what they were praising her for, was just part of life, just what you did; treating people kindly, taking care of things, handling a situation, not something special.

But gifts weren't given, they were received.

She didn't think most people recognized that the little things they did often meant the most. She had created big weddings, huge receptions, galas and had been involved with a few fundraising balls. But it was the details people remember; the kindness you show them when they feel they had been taken care of without fuss.

I guess it's better to be eulogized when I'm alive, Donna mused. It confirmed that her life and her choices hadn't been wasted. She didn't know if anyone not going through what she was going through could appreciate that to the extent she did. But it didn't matter, she knew how grateful she was and it radiated off of her like a beam of sunlight.

The boisterous crowd meandered through the food line, where there was more than enough for everyone and plenty for people to take home. She saw caterers and restaurant owners gushing over each other's delicacies, laughing and chumming through the line.

That day, everyone was everyone else's friend. Plates were piled high, food spilling over as guests carried them back to their crowded tables. Everyone wanted to taste everything; their eyes, which were wide at the amount of food they'd been able to stack on their plate, were definitely bigger than most of their stomachs because Donna had seen a few of them devour some quantities of food that would put a hippo to shame.

Say what you will about Donna's hometown, people here love to eat and drink, and they know how to have an unbridled good time.

And it put Donna in the best of spirits.

After the meal, Andie stood, gently tapping her champagne flute with a spoon, a hush moving through the decorated warehouse almost in waves from front to back.

"First off, I want to thank everyone for coming. And for everything that everyone did to make this day as incredible as it's turned out," an indebted grin on her face. "It means a lot to me, and I know it means the world to Cam and Donna."

The crowd applauded which made Donna giggle.

"Now, I know most of you know what's going on so I won't say anything more about it, other than I've known Cameron for over two years now and I've known Donna for about a year. And everyone knows I love Cameron because he's got the biggest heart of any man I've ever met. Donna would attest to that. She's been witness to it since she was a little girl.

But I adore Donna, and she's become my best friend. We have spent so much time together over the last year, hanging out, working together on, not one but two, weddings," Andie said, her brow raising in Donna's direction, "and I've seen who this woman is. And I don't think this enormous space would be as packed as it is if all of you didn't know how wonderful she is."

Donna kept repeating in her head that she didn't want to cry again, and by all reasonable standards, she shouldn't have a tear left to shed. But she did, and as hard as she tried, she felt them building again.

"Donna, this room loves you. It loves Cameron. We are here for you, to celebrate you and your life, to give you something that will be remembered by all of us here for the rest of our lives. You always wanted your wedding to be something people talk about...well, I think we may have accomplished that. This will be on everyone's lips for years to come.

But that doesn't matter as much as you knowing...you feeling...the love in this room, the gratitude for what you've done for others. From all of us to you. Weddings are about celebrating the love of two people, but today, this wedding is also about celebrating the love this entire room has for you. And to let you know we have your back, we are here for you, we adore you."

Wiping a tear, Andie raised her glass.

"So, everyone, please, raise a glass to Cameron...but most especially to Donna, who we love so much. Our lives are forever blessed because we have you in them."

The cheer in the room was deafening, literally shaking the floor, as everyone put their glasses to their lips. Donna wrapped her arms around Andie as Cameron stood, giving Andie a kiss and taking the mic.

"My turn," he said, smiling his big grin at the guests. "I'm going to make mine short and sweet. I've been lucky enough in my life to have the love of two great women. Three if you count my mom. I am so happy today to marry one of them, to give her a day that she's dreamt about since she was a kid, with the other woman I love at my side. How cool is that? I know there's nothing conventional about this, Andie and I didn't make this decision lightly," Cameron continued, his eyes glancing in the direction of Mr. And Mrs. Hune. "We made this decision with our hearts. Right or wrong, I have to trust my heart. And more than I trust mine, I trust Andie's. Marrying Donna, the other woman I love, is the right thing, the best thing, and I am honored to call her my wife. I love you, Donna. I think everyone here does so I'm in fine company. Thank you for being my wife."

The crowd applauded, even Donna until she realized she was expected to say something as well.

"You want to say anything?"

"Not really," she playfully responded, covering the microphone so people couldn't hear what she was saying. "Everything is so perfect, I don't want to ruin it."

"Then just tell them all thank you. I think they'd like that," Cam answered.

Relenting, Cameron slipped the mic into Donna's shaky hand. Slowly, she stood, taking Cameron's arm for support. Between the pain in her body and abject fear of speaking to this many people, even though they all had been part of her life, toppling over wasn't out of the question.

"Uhm..." Donna began, her throat dry. "They say that when you're speaking in front of a large group of people, to calm your nerves, you should pretend they're naked. Well, I want to say you all look fabulous!"

A rolling laugh echoed off the walls of the warehouse.

"Thank you. Everyone. For creating this incredibly amazing day for me. For being here. For your kind words. For your love. And your tears. I've...cried a lot over the last few months. I've felt a lot of emotions. Some of them pretty dark, pretty sad. I'm scared, and not afraid to say that out loud. But I've also been blessed like never before. I have a perspective on things and I cherish each moment, looking for the good, the positive, and the strong. Because they all matter more than anything else. I look around this room and recognize that my life is good, even while I'm dying."

That elicited a laugh.

"Actually, especially while I'm dying."

The guests applauded, and Donna took the crowd in before speaking again.

"Be good to each other. Be good to yourselves. Love. Love very, very hard. And know that you are loved because that will change your behavior for the better. I love you all. I am so blessed. So blessed. Thank you, Cameron, for marrying me. You are my best friend. And thank you, Andie, for the gift of Cameron and what you sacrificed so I could have this day. You are one of the greatest, most selfless people I've ever known, and I love you. I have but one request for the both of you, and I'm putting you on the spot here...name your first daughter after me. Let her live a great life for me. I would love that."

Andie nodded, fighting tears.

Donna's eyes stayed on her.

"I love you," Donna stated without any irony or coyness.

Turning to Cameron whose eyes were floating in his tears she smiled.

"And I love you."

Finally, Donna turned back to the room and beamed.

"And I love all of you. Now enough with the damn tears, let's get some music on and dance!"

The place erupted with a frenzied craziness Donna had never felt. Music blasted through the speakers and everyone, almost as if on cue, rushed the dance floor, needing the physical release from the raw emotions that had filled the day. Cameron and Andie helped Donna down to the dance floor and the three of them danced like crazy, each movement a chore, her body screaming for relief. But she was not about to stop. If she died tomorrow, that would be okay but today, no matter how much her body was begging her, she was not walking away from the incredible love that surrounded her.

She danced with everyone around her, Cameron, Andie, and a few others actually holding her up for part of it, until she simply couldn't stand on her own two feet any longer.

Cameron grabbed Donna up in his arms, holding her so her feet weren't touching the floor and they slow danced. Looking into his eyes, Donna could see his love for her. They had said everything, and at this moment, all Donna wanted was to be in the arms of her best friend, letting his love radiate through her.

Pulling free, she shuffled over to Andie who was dancing with her parents.

"May I borrow her?" Donna asked.

Taking Andie's hand, her arm going around her waist to help Donna, she walked her over to Cameron.

"Finish this dance for me?" Donna asked her as she put them together.

As they coupled, Donna took her Nana's cameo and slipped behind Andie, placing it around her neck.

"What are you doing?" Andie gasped, realizing what Donna was putting on her.

"I gave Cam a wedding gift. I wanted you to have this. One day you'll give it to little Donna," she said, clasping it behind Andie and letting it fall. Andie clutched the cameo in her hand as Donna kissed her cheek and then kissed Cameron one more time.

They watched Donna saunter achingly through everyone, people somehow recognizing that her body was giving up. One by one, friends took her hand, helping her along, passing her from person to person, each step more difficult than the last, but with each a smile, each a touch, each a thank you. Donna's heart was more grateful with each person she came face to face with. She was escorted to the door by people who truly loved her.

Turning, Donna took in everyone. Every smile. Every tear. Every look of love. Every look of fear. They were all hers.

She smiled and waved.

They recognized this would be the last time they would ever see Donna. And Donna them.

She couldn't make out faces but she could feel exactly what it was each of them wanted her to know.

Looking back toward Andie in Cameron's arms, she saw her still holding the cameo tightly, and Donna couldn't help but smile. They were so perfect for each other. It amazed Donna when two people who were so right for each other actually found one another, as if the entire universe stood still for that simple moment, allowing them to realize the greatness of what their lives would be and the enormity of what their love would grow into.

Throwing them a kiss, Donna turned to Geena, who held the door for her. Then she kissed her mother on the cheek and walked out.

Stepping out into the night air, the coolness helped. Geena had arranged for a car to be on standby if she needed to leave; it was parked a few steps away and, as the driver saw Donna exit, he rushed to her, aiding her as she climbed into the back of the car.

Closing the door, Donna lay down, her arm over her face, her wedding ring sparkling from the moonlight coming through the window. It was the first time all day she let the intensity of the pain in her body overtake her.

She cried from the pain. Smiling with joy at the same time.

My God, my life is blessed, Donna thought.

EPILOGUE

Simple white dress. No shoes. Men in white linen. Gorgeous exotic flowers all around. Donna's Nana's cameo around Andie's neck. Just like Donna planned.

Mr. Hune walked Andie to the edge of the surf where Cameron waited barefoot, the bottom of his white linen pants soaked by the ocean. Together, with their feet in the water, they said their vows, with only the Hunes, Cam's mother, and Geena surrounding them.

Donna was there. Watching from someplace else. Someplace wonderful.

With the money Donna had left in her savings, she paid for their wedding on the beach.

Oh, there was a caveat: Donna was a wedding planner and she knew what she envisioned for them, so she left explicit instructions of exactly how Andie and Cameron should get married. She wanted them to have a wedding they would remember, and she knew after the wedding they gave her, the simpler it was the more memorable it would be.

Donna died three weeks after her wedding. She didn't think she actually recovered from the joy of that day. It was as if her body knew this was the greatest day of her life and knew it was time. She had a couple of rough days afterward, she saw the doctor and she prepared her for what was to come. Donna grew weaker. She bled. She cried. She laughed. She spent every day with people she loved and all they did was talk about was that wedding.

Not bad, huh?

Six months had passed since Donna's funeral; a small, very private affair. Who would want to compete with the wedding her friends blessed her with? Cameron and Andie flew with their parents and Donna's mother to Barbados. It was the most gorgeous wedding she'd ever planned. Ocean, sunset, gentle waves, a beautiful bride, a handsome groom. And love. Lots of love.

Donna knew their future. Where she was now, she could see everything. Backward and forwards. Cameron and Andie were going to have a beautiful life together. And yes, there would be a little Donna. She would be their third child after two boys, who, fearing they'd never have a girl, named, Donte and Donnato. And every day, Andie would tell Cameron that the wild, little girl with the sharp tongue and big laugh reminded her of Donna in almost every way.

"If that little girl didn't come out of my body, I would swear she was Donna's," Andie would repeat to people until they were tired of hearing it.

Life could be complicated, and hard. Dying, and living with dying, was actually very easy. Painful and regretful in pieces, sure, but you also no longer had anything to lose by loving more than you ever thought possible, by laughing harder, and filling your life with joy; things you don't always do when you believe your sunset is far, far off.

But because Donna wanted you to love her too, she was going to tell a secret from this side; something to make whatever journey you have ahead, for however long, truly memorable.

Love. Seek joy. Serve.

Pretty simple. Yet hard to actually accomplish. If you can, if you can find a way to make those three gems shine in your life, you will find that your life—like Donna's—is treasured both while you're living it and long after in people's hearts.

Andie and Cameron released a white balloon in the air and watched it twirl. On it was printed Donna's name underneath a photo of Donna in her wedding dress. Donna didn't plan that, but from where she was, she loved them for it.

Love. Seek joy. Serve.

If you do, you'll find yourself with deep, inimitable friendships like those of Cameron and Andie. And you'll be astonished just what gifts you might get for your wedding.

More About The Author

B art Baker has written five novels, including Honeymoon With Harry, A Second Honeymoon With Harry, What Remains, The Virgin Daiquiri and After Ozz. All are available at most on-line stores and brick-and-mortar retailers. The movie rights to his novel, Honeymoon With Harry were purchased by New Line Cinema and is considered one of the best-unproduced projects in Hollywood. Beginning his writing journey in the theater, Bart has eight plays produced around the world, including Relay, the movie rights selling to Warner Bros. Moving into film and television, Bart worked steadily and has 19 produced film and TV credits, working for most networks and studios.

At Bart's website bartvbaker.com, you can sign up for information on upcoming projects, including the final Harry book, The Last Honeymoon With Harry, coming in November. And follow Bart on social media: Instagram @thefirstbartbaker, Twitter @firstbartbaker, and Facebook. Leave a review of The Wedding Gift on any and all review sites. Letting others know about a book is a gift to the author and to other readers.

www.ingramcontent.com/pod-product-compliance
Lightning Source LLC
Chambersburg PA
CBHW051636260626
47170CB00004B/1193